City of Sand

A novel by

Robert Kroese

WESTMARCH
PUBLISHING

For Dad.

....

With thanks to:
- My editor at Westmarch Publishing, Richard Ellis Preston, Jr., for his numerous helpful suggestions for improving this book;
- The Kickstarter supporters who made this book possible: Neva Cheatwood, Taki Soma, Dan McCann, Kristi Michels, Tommy Stanley, Sean Simpson, Christopher Turner, Josh Creed, Brian Hekman and Eric Sybesma;
- Kristin Crocker, who assured me after reading an early version of the first half of this book that it was not, in fact, complete shit;
- My volunteer proofreaders, Chantal Ouellette, Mark Fitzgerald, and Wes Kenney;
- And my mom, for fueling this book with curry and lasagna.

CHAPTER ONE

Benjamin Stone awoke in a haze, unsure of where he was. At fifty-eight, habits had congealed to the extent that waking up in a strange place required a few moments of adjustment. Something was different: the mattress was too firm, the sheets too rough, and sunlight was pouring through ill-fitting curtains to his left. A motel room, he thought. But where?

Then it hit him: Sunnyview. Jessica. Oh God, Jessica.

He had driven all day yesterday, starting out from Portland at just after nine in the morning and getting in to Sunnyview just before sundown. As he sat up, he felt the tightness in his left shoulder from holding the wheel, and he sat on the edge of the bed massaging the tendons with his right hand. Yesterday his only thought had been getting here as fast as he could, but now he felt inertia taking hold. He was a stranger in this town now. He had no authority here. What did he hope to accomplish?

Find Jessica, he thought. But what if she doesn't want to be found?

He got out of bed, showered, got dressed and brushed his teeth. Felt marginally better, but his mind was still fuzzy. Gotta get some coffee, he thought. Clear my head.

He went to the motel office and made sure the staff weren't expecting him to check out today—he had been so exhausted last night that he wasn't sure he had thought to pay for more than one night. Evidently he had paid for a full week, though. Was that evidence of optimism or pessimism? Hard to say.

He walked across the parking lot to a Starbucks, got a large coffee, and made his way to the dusty old Buick he'd driven from Portland. He folded the visor down against the rising sun and rolled his head from left to right, squeezing the shoulder tendons with his right hand again. A crack of vertebrae, and some of the tension drained away, but his head hurt and the glare of the sun wasn't helping. Even with the visor down, it seemed unnaturally bright. Benjamin's glasses were the kind that darkened in sunlight, but the geniuses who had invented them apparently had never figured out how to get them to work inside a car. Someone had told him once that the glasses were activated by ultraviolet rays, which couldn't penetrate glass. It seemed like a pretty big oversight to Benjamin. Somebody needs to invent glasses that will darken in bright light, period. That's a multimillion dollar idea right there, he thought. Maybe I'll swing by one of those venture capital places downtown while I'm here and pick up a big fat check. He'd heard of people getting rich in Sunnyview on far worse ideas. But Benjamin would never get rich here. He didn't speak the language. He didn't know what a "vertical market" was or how to "monetize" anything. The last time he had been in Sunnyview, "low hanging fruit" was something you'd find on his father's apricot trees.

Benjamin started the Buick and drove toward downtown. The scenery had changed completely since he had been here last, but he was able to follow the same route to the police station that he'd have taken fifty years earlier. It was almost eerie, the way modern-day Sunnyview had supplanted the sleepy farming town of his youth, like one image superimposed on another. Office buildings and parking lots had taken the place of vacant lots and mom-and-pop stores, gravel roads had been paved, main arteries had grown from two to four or even six lanes, but the basic structure of the town remained much the same. The shimmering glass and steel structures certainly were impressive, and Benjamin figured that to the extent that the residents thought about it, they thought of modern Sunnyview as an improvement. Benjamin wasn't so sure, but then he was probably just old-fashioned.

The police station was in the same place it had always been, but the tiny concrete-and-stucco building he remembered had been replaced by a massive block of blue glass identified by a sign as the Sunnyview Administrative Center. Benjamin parked the Buick and went inside, following signs to the Sunnyview Police office. Approaching a receptionist behind a glass window, he said, "Benjamin Stone. Here to see Peter Lentz."

"What's this regarding?" asked the woman, a heavyset Hispanic.

"My daughter," said Benjamin, the words almost sticking in his throat. "Jessica Stone. Missing persons."

The woman nodded and picked up a phone. She spoke for a moment in hushed tones, and then set the phone down. "Detective Lentz will be with you shortly."

Benjamin mumbled a thank you and walked away from the reception desk. The walls of the lobby were covered in framed black and white pictures of Sunnyview from fifty years earlier. Benjamin couldn't help smiling as he studied them. This was the Sunnyview he remembered: a sleepy town surrounded by orchards and dairy farms. He had grown up on one of those farms, not far from here. His father sold the land shortly after Benjamin left home in 1960, and the trees had been torn out to make room for several hundred nondescript stucco houses. His father moved to Tucson, Arizona after the sale, and died of a heart attack three years later. Benjamin hadn't been back to Sunnyview since the sale; he had never seen what had become of his father's orchard. He would have liked to have seen it—but the way it was, not what it had become.

"Mr. Stone," said a voice behind him. Benjamin turned to see a wiry man wearing gray slacks and a white-button down shirt. His sleeves were rolled up nearly to his elbows and a blood-red tie hung loosely around his neck. In his left hand he held a small spiral notebook and a mechanical pencil. He held out his right hand and Benjamin shook it.

"I'm Detective Lentz," he said.

"Benjamin Stone," said Benjamin. Lentz had small hands but his grip was firm. His face was youthful, but his thin hair was wiry and gray, and dark circles had begun to appear under his eyes.

"Come with me, Mr. Stone," said Lentz. He led Benjamin past the reception desk down a hall past a row of cubicles where khaki-clad civil servants stared at beige monitors and tapped away at beige keyboards. On the walls were "inspirational" posters featuring snowboarders and majestic mountain ranges with captions like PERSEVERANCE and IMAGINATION. Benjamin had been retired from the force for ten years now, but he had a hard time believing that police work had come to this. This place resembled his idea of a greeting card factory more than a police station.

Lentz opened the door to a conference room and gestured for Benjamin to enter. Benjamin took a seat and Lentz closed the door and sat down across from him.

"Thank you for coming down," said Lentz, and Benjamin couldn't help but smile. It had been Benjamin's idea to drive down from Portland, but Lentz was establishing his authority over the investigation. Fine, thought Benjamin. It's what any good detective would do.

"Have you learned anything more since we talked on Monday?" asked Benjamin.

"Nothing substantial," said Lentz. "Did you just get into town?"

Benjamin nodded. "Last night."

"You drove?"

"Yeah. Left yesterday morning."

"Portland, right? Long drive. You must really care about Jessica."

Benjamin frowned. Awkward segue, he thought. It was Lentz's first misstep. "She's my daughter, Detective Lentz," said Benjamin. "What would you do?"

Lentz nodded hurriedly, seeming to realize his mistake. "When did you last talk to Jessica, Mr. Stone?"

"Nearly eight years ago. As I told you on Monday, I last talked to her the day after Thanksgiving, 1992."

"In person?"

"On the phone," said Benjamin. "As I told you on Monday." He answered without inflection, terse but polite. He was willing to cede to Lentz's authority, but he wasn't about to play the *We don't know exactly what happened but we haven't ruled anything out* game.

"And the last time you saw her in person—"

"Spring of 1988, as I also told you. I assume it's all there in your notes."

"Mr. Stone," said Lentz. "I realize that you're a retired police detective yourself, and that a lot of these questions are going to seem—"

"Insulting?" asked Benjamin, without any change in inflection. "Repetitive? Pointless? All of the above, Detective Lentz. I wasn't a great father. Jessica and I fought a lot. We haven't talked for eight years, and that last conversation didn't end well. It's quite possible that she hates me. But she's still my daughter, and I still love her. I didn't have anything to do with her disappearance, and I want nothing more than to find her and make sure she's okay. Can we move on to doing something that might actually bring that scenario about?"

"Where are you staying while you're in Sunnyview, Mr. Stone?"

"Some dump called the Sandman Inn," said Benjamin.

"I know the place," replied Lentz. "You could do worse. How long are you planning on staying?"

"Until we find Jessica," said Benjamin.

Lentz nodded. If he had a problem with Benjamin's use of the word *we*, he was smart enough not to mention it. "What's your room number? I'll call you if we find anything."

"Where does the investigation stand at this point?" Benjamin asked.

"Well, Jessica has been missing for a week. I don't have to tell you that in a case like this—"

"You've talked to her roommate? Friends? Boyfriend?" Benjamin didn't know if she even had a boyfriend, but boyfriends were always likely culprits in missing persons cases.

"We've talked to everybody we could find who knew Jessica well."

"*We* meaning you personally, or you sent a couple of uniforms down to ask a few questions?"

"Mr. Stone, I can't—"

"Look, Detective Lentz," said Benjamin, allowing a hint of anger to creep into his voice. "I get that you have limited resources, and that you have a policy against discussing the details of open cases. But I intend to find my daughter, with or without your help. If something happens to my daughter and I find out that you've been sitting on information that could help me find her, I'm going to devote whatever time I have left on this planet to making your life very uncomfortable."

Lentz stared hard at Benjamin. "Is that a threat, Mr. Stone?"

Benjamin stared back. "Not at all, Mr. Lentz. But I like this town. I think I might move here. Maybe buy the house next to yours. I've always wanted to learn to play the electric guitar. They say you can master anything with ten thousand hours of practice."

Lentz smiled. "Your concern for you daughter is touching." His smile faded. "Honestly, Mr. Stone, we don't have much to go on."

"Who was the last person to see her?"

"As far as we know, her roommate."

"Valerie Rocha," said Benjamin.

"Yeah," said Lentz, raising his eyebrow. "You seem to know quite a bit, for someone who hasn't had contact with Jessica for eight years."

"Not really," replied Benjamin. "I had a friend with the Portland PD cross-reference DMV records."

Lentz nodded. "According to Valerie, Jessica left for work around seven-thirty on the morning of the eighth. She never got there."

"What do you know about this Valerie Rocha?"

"Average nobody. College friend of Jessica's."

"Did Jessica have a boyfriend?"

Lentz paused, seeming uncertain how much information to give Benjamin. "There was a guy she dated up until a couple of weeks ago. She broke up with him."

"Sounds like a good prospect."

"Yeah, I talked to him. He seemed genuinely upset about Jessica's disappearance. And he's a bit of a sad sack, you know? I could see him sulking and listening to a lot of Joy Division after a breakup, but I don't think he's got it in him to kill someone."

"This boyfriend got a name?"

"Yep," replied Lentz, meeting Benjamin's gaze.

Benjamin took the hint. "Friends? Coworkers?"

"I talked to a few of her friends, but that was a dead end. Also talked to her boss, Cameron Payne. You've heard of him?"

Benjamin shook his head.

"He's been in the news lately," said Lentz. "He's the guy behind XKredits.com."

"Behind what?"

"Startup company. The latest next big thing. Some kind of Internet-based money, I guess? There are so many of these little companies starting up that I can't keep them all straight. My brother-in-law won't shut up about XKredits, though. I guess they've got an IPO coming up. Initial Public Offering. That's when they let the public buy stock in the company."

10

"Yeah," said Benjamin. He wasn't up on all the latest Silicon Valley jargon, but he knew what an IPO was. "Last I heard," Benjamin said, "Jessica was working for Glazier Semiconductor," said Benjamin. Glazier Semiconductor was one of the largest employers in the Silicon Valley. Benjamin was old enough to remember when it was just a couple of guys working out of an abandoned auto body shop east of town.

Lentz nodded, paging through his notes. "Up until December, yeah. She just started working for Cameron Payne a few weeks ago."

"You suspect this Payne guy?" asked Benjamin.

Lentz shook his head. "We have no suspects."

"No suspects and no leads, is that about right?"

"Afraid so," said Lentz. "If you give me your room number, I'll call you if anything changes."

"I'd appreciate it," said Benjamin. "But let me give you my cell phone number. Hang on, I've got it on me somewhere." He fumbled through his pockets for the card on which the Cingular Wireless salesman had written the number. He'd just bought the thing yesterday. He'd never had a cell phone before, but figured he might need one if he was going to be in Sunnyview for a while. He'd splurged for a tiny Nokia that the Cingular guy had told him was top-of-the-line.

Finally Benjamin located the card and slid it across the table to Lentz. Lentz jotted it down in his notebook and slapped it shut. "Alright, Mr. Stone. I think we're finished here. If we have any breakthroughs, I'll give you a call."

They shook hands and Detective Lentz escorted him from the building.

CHAPTER TWO

Benjamin had Jessica's address and phone number, thanks to his friend in the Portland Police Department. He tried calling in the hopes that her roommate, Valerie Rocha, would pick up, but there was no answer. He left a message on their machine and then stood for a moment outside the Sunnyview Administrative Center, assessing his options. At last he decided the best use of his time would be to look into Jessica's boss, Cameron Payne. He walked across the parking lot to the public library, which he had noticed on his drive in.

He spent the next two hours browsing newspapers, magazines, and websites looking for information on Cameron Payne and XKredits.com. There was plenty of coverage, particularly in the *San Jose Mercury News* and various techie magazines. A long bio in *Wired* detailed Payne's upbringing in southern California and his founding of XKredits.com while he was a senior at Stanford.

For all the hoopla, it didn't sound like XKredits.com was a very big outfit. They operated out of a rented office in downtown Sunnyview, and Benjamin got the feeling from his research that the company probably only employed a few dozen people. On a whim, he dialed the number listed on the "contact" page of the website, and a cheery female voice answered.

"XKredits.com, the future of currency," said the woman. "How may I direct your call?"

"I'd like to speak with Cameron Payne," said Benjamin.

"Certainly," said the woman. "Can I tell Cameron what this is regarding?"

"It's about my daughter," said Benjamin. "Jessica Stone."

A pause. Then, "Can I get your name, sir?"

"Benjamin Stone."

"Thank you. Please hold."

A librarian glared at Benjamin, who hadn't noticed the "PLEASE GO OUTSIDE TO USE CELL PHONES" sign taped to the front of her desk. There didn't seem to be anyone else in the library, but that evidently made his breach of decorum no less severe. Benjamin gesticulated in what he hoped was an appropriately supplicatory manner and made his way to the foyer.

When the woman came back on the line, Benjamin wasn't surprised to hear her say, "Sir, I'm afraid Cameron's in a meeting right now," but then she added, "Can I have him call you back after lunch, say one p.m.?"

"Sure," said Benjamin. "That would be fine." The mention of lunch made his stomach growl. It was after eleven, and he hadn't had anything yet but coffee and ibuprofen. "Do you need my number?"

"Is it the one you called from?"

"Yes."

"Then I've got it. I'll have Cameron give you a call at one."

"Fine," said Benjamin, and ended the call. He left the building and walked toward his car. He had seen a Carl's Jr. sign on the way over; it was as good a place as any to get some lunch. But he hadn't even opened the door to his car when his cell phone rang.

"Benjamin Stone," he said.

"Mr. Stone," said the male voice on the other end, "this is Cameron Payne. My secretary said you wanted to talk to me. Have you had lunch yet?"

"No," said Benjamin. "I was about to head over to Carl's Jr."

Payne laughed. "I think we can do better than that. Do you know downtown Sunnyview?"

"I knew it fifty years ago," said Benjamin. "Shall we meet for ice cream at Fenneman's Corner Store on Second and Palm?"

Payne laughed again. "Don't know the place," he said. "But there's a restaurant not far from there called Blue Agave. On Second, between Palm and Walnut. It doesn't look like much, but their burgers beat Carl's Jr. any day of the week. I can meet you there at noon."

"Works for me," said Benjamin. "I'll see you then."

Benjamin hung up and took a moment to get his bearings. The Sunnyview Administrative Center was on a long, winding road west of downtown called Orchard Parkway. Looking down the road to the north, Benjamin could just make out a street sign reading "Guadalupe." To the south was Coburn Street. "Guadalupe" didn't ring any bells, but Miles Coburn had been a prominent local dairy farmer when Benjamin was a kid. There was no sign of Coburn's Dairy now; it was all nail salons, copy centers, and other establishments catering to the upscale clientele of Sunnyview's suburbs. But if that massive old oak on the corner was the same one Benjamin used to park his bike under and eat ice cream cones from Fenneman's, then downtown was only about half a mile to the east. He could easily walk there by noon.

Slipping his car keys back in his pocket, Benjamin waited for a break in the parade of SUVs and minivans down Orchard Parkway and jogged diagonally across toward the oak tree. It was definitely the same tree; it was a little bigger, and the nearly leafless limbs were more ridden with bunches of mistletoe than he'd remembered, but there was no mistaking the gnarled shape of that massive trunk. The dirt track that he'd remembered from his youth was gone, overwhelmed by sidewalks and patches of sprinkler-watered grass. Coburn Street seemed to run parallel to the old track, though, so Benjamin began walking down the street to the east.

After a few blocks, Coburn dead-ended into Bayner Avenue. Benjamin turned left and then right on Walnut, which would take him the rest of the way downtown. He was in a residential part of town now; big stucco houses with tiny lawns lined the street. All of these houses had been built in the years since Benjamin left, and most of them looked like they were less than twenty years old. After another few blocks, Benjamin found himself in an older part of the town; a few of the buildings he even recognized, although most of them now housed businesses that were foreign to him. The Sunnyview Drugstore was now a Blockbuster, and Jack's Farm Service was an organic grocery store.

Downtown Sunnyview was surprisingly unchanged for the most part; it seemed that some effort had been expended to retain (or recreate?) the folksy charm of the downtown area. The feed store was now a tanning salon, and Schulman's Hardware was now a Starbucks, but if Benjamin squinted a little, he could almost imagine he was in the downtown of his youth. Only the BMWs and Acuras clogging the brick streets and the throngs of khaki-clad twenty-somethings on the sidewalks spoiled the illusion. Fifty years ago these streets would have been nearly empty except for the occasional farmer heading into town for feed or supplies, and housewives visiting the butcher shop or a family-owned grocery store.

Benjamin passed what used to be Fenneman's Corner Store—now a Kinko's—and turned left on Second Street toward Palm. The sign for Blue Agave was so unobtrusive that he would have walked right past it if a young man standing outside hadn't reached out and put his hand on Benjamin's shoulder.

Benjamin started, pulling back out of the man's reach. The man smiled, slipping a cell phone into his pocket. "Sorry, didn't mean to startle you," the man said. "I'm Cameron Payne. I'm guessing you're Benjamin Stone."

So this was the millionaire genius founder of XKredits.com, thought Benjamin. There was nothing to differentiate him from any of the other young men he'd seen walking the sidewalks of downtown Sunnyview. The *Wired* bio put Payne at twenty-four, but the rings under his eyes and thinning hair made him look older. He wore khaki pants, a black t-shirt, and a lightweight gray zip-up sweatshirt. His skin was pale from spending too much time indoors, and his sparse, jet-black hair was just long enough to stick out from his head in a way that made Benjamin want to spit in his hands and smooth it down. Presumably that would be a violation of social etiquette even in the notoriously relaxed Silicon Valley.

Benjamin held out his hand. "How did you...?" he began.

Payne smiled, shaking Benjamin's hand. "You sort of stand out," he said, jerking his chin to point at the passing pedestrians.

"I suppose I do," acknowledged Benjamin.

"Come on, let's go inside."

Payne led Benjamin into the restaurant, holding two fingers up for the hostess, who nodded and hurried away. Less than a minute later, she returned, grabbed two menus, and led them to a table by the window. Benjamin noted that a dozen people who had arrived before them still waited in the foyer. Payne didn't look like much, but they definitely knew him at this place.

Benjamin ordered the Monterey Burger on Payne's recommendation, and then Payne got down to business. "I assume you're here because of Jessica's disappearance," he said. "I'm not sure how I can help, but I'll do whatever I can."

"I appreciate that," said Benjamin.

"You've talked to the police?"

Benjamin nodded. "This morning. No leads. They've interviewed you, I take it?"

"Yes," said Payne. "A Detective Lentz. I understand you're a cop yourself."

"Retired," said Benjamin. "You've been researching me?"

Payne smiled. "Jessica told me. She speaks highly of you."

Benjamin looked into Payne's eyes, trying to gauge whether he was being facetious, but there was no sign of malice there. Either Payne was an excellent liar, or Jessica really had said good things about him. He found that hard to believe, unless it had been part of a façade to endear herself to her new employer. Happy new employee, no personal baggage. It actually surprised Benjamin to hear that Jessica had spoken in depth to Payne at all, about him or anything else. As far as Benjamin knew, she was just a low-level web designer, and she'd been with the company for less than three months. She'd dropped out of San Jose State to take an entry level marketing position with Glazier Semiconductor, and then less than two years later she'd quit and gone to work for XKredits.com. He couldn't imagine why someone like Cameron Payne would spend much time talking to her—unless he was interested in more than her professional expertise. He hated himself for thinking it, but Jessica had always been prettier than she was smart.

"Are you close?" asked Benjamin.

"We work closely together," said Payne. "She's a valuable member of the team." Benjamin's dubiousness must have showed on his face, because Payne added, "We just work together, Mr. Stone. There is no romantic involvement. Anyway, she has a boyfriend. Guy named Chris Sandford."

"I understand they broke up a couple weeks before Jessica disappeared."

"Did they? Well, as I say, our relationship was purely professional. I wouldn't know the details of Jessica's personal life."

"So you don't know this Chris Sandford?"

"I met him once. Jessica took him to one of our company parties. I think she was trying to get me to hire him. He didn't particularly impress me. Just out of school, no real skills or motivation. He didn't have the sort of spark that Jessica has."

"What does Jessica do for you exactly?"

"Her job title is 'web designer,'" said Payne. "But it was clear early on that she had a lot more to offer the company. We were talking about moving her into a position with more responsibility when she...."

"What kind of position? What do you mean when you say she had more to offer the company?"

Payne shrugged. "It's not something I can easily put into words. I mean, look at me. You almost walked right past me on the street. Even people who knew me in college are surprised at how successful I've been. I wasn't the smartest guy in my classes, and I certainly didn't have the best grades. There's nothing about me that obviously sets me apart from any of the rest of these guys." He waved his hand to indicate the khaki-clad horde surrounding them. "But I'm worth a hundred times everybody else in this restaurant combined."

"So what's your point?" asked Benjamin. "That Jessica has some sort of hidden talent?"

"Not exactly hidden," Payne replied. "It's apparent to anyone who looks beneath the surface." He took a bite of his salmon burger.

It was all Benjamin could do not to visibly wince at Payne's remark. Was Benjamin's low regard for his own daughter's ability so evident? And more to the point, was Payne right? Had Benjamin been mistaken in his assessment? Maybe there was more to Jessica than Benjamin realized. Either that or she had changed a lot since he had last talked to her.

"You said she was a web designer," said Benjamin. "What does that mean? She made your website?" Benjamin found it hard to believe that Jessica had mastered something so technical. But then, her generation seemed to have a knack for this stuff. The Internet was something of a mystery to Benjamin.

"She built a lot of it, yes," replied Payne, still chewing. "She's very good with graphic manipulation and layout. But she clearly has other talents as well."

"You keep saying that," said Benjamin. "And while I don't doubt it's true, you aren't being very specific."

"Well," started Payne, "the problem is that it's difficult to explain if you don't know what XKredits.com is all about. How familiar are you with our company?"

"I did a little research at the library," said Benjamin. "XKredits are some kind of digital currency?"

Payne nodded. "That's the long term plan. We call them the future of currency. What we do is, we partner with online retailers to accept XKredits as a form of payment. You can earn XKredits by shopping at one of our partner sites, and then spend them at another partner site."

"I have a credit card that gives me frequent flyer miles when I buy something," said Benjamin. "Is it like that?"

"Same basic idea," said Payne. "But our goal is to be much more pervasive than that. In three years we plan to have a thousand online retailers as partners. Our system also allows for micro-payments. Are you familiar with that idea?"

Benjamin shook his head.

"One of the problems with the web is that it's very difficult to charge for content. Do you have any hobbies, Benjamin?"

"Fly fishing," said Benjamin. He'd only tried it twice, but it was easier than saying "no." He got the feeling that Payne had delivered this speech a few hundred times, and that it didn't particularly matter what Benjamin said.

"Great," said Payne. "Let's say you write a how-to article about fly fishing. And like most writers, you want to get paid. So you sell your article to a fly fishing website. The question is, how do the people running the fly fishing website recoup the cost of paying you for the article? They can try charging a subscription fee, but most websites that have tried that haven't done very well. People expect content on the Internet to be free."

"Advertising," offered Benjamin.

"That's a possibility, but online ads don't pay very well. What you really need is a way to charge people a very small amount of money for reading your article—large enough that if they have a few thousand readers, they can recoup their costs, but small enough that the typical reader won't think twice about paying it. Maybe a few cents, or even a fraction of a cent."

"Makes sense," said Benjamin.

"We call them micropayments," said Payne. "The problem is that the typical way to make an online purchase is with a credit card, but the transaction costs are prohibitive. In other words, it would cost the credit card company fifty cents to charge you a nickel. And the average fly fisherman probably doesn't want to give his credit card information to some random fly fishing website—nor does he want to spend five minutes doing it just to read one article. What is needed is a simple way for a website to show a visitor a pop-up message, 'Do you want to pay a nickel to read this article?' The visitor clicks yes, and boom, they're learning Benjamin Stone's patented fly fishing techniques. Except instead of paying a nickel, you'll pay some number of XKredits."

"XKredits that they earned by buying stuff from your partner sites," said Benjamin.

"Exactly!" cried Payne.

"And you have this all in place now?" asked Benjamin.

"We've got twenty-six partners already," said Payne, "and a lot more in the pipeline."

"But the micropayment thing, that's working?"

Payne nodded excitedly. "It's in beta right now."

Benjamin nodded as if he understood what this meant. The truth was, he wasn't particularly interested in XKredits, and to the extent that he understood what Cameron Payne was saying, he didn't find it reassuring. As far as he could tell, XKredits was a company that didn't produce anything, sell anything, or, when it came right down to it, *do* much of anything at all. He supposed there were hundreds of companies like it in Silicon Valley; maybe that was just how the new "Internet economy" worked. But it seemed like a lot of smoke and mirrors to Benjamin. And Payne still hadn't answered his most pressing question.

"So how does Jessica fit into all this?" asked Benjamin.

Payne nodded, as if anticipating the question. "Jessica has been instrumental in getting several of our partners on board."

"I thought you said she's a web designer."

Payne sighed. "You have to understand, Benjamin, XKredits.com is a small company. And we're what you would call a matrix organization. Do you know what that means?"

Benjamin simply stared at Payne. The young man's condescending manner was starting to grate on him.

"It means we don't operate under a strict corporate hierarchy," Payne continued. "Our team members are free to contribute in any way they see fit. So if someone like Jessica has a good idea, she can run with it. We encourage our people to think outside the box. Jessica saw some opportunities to reach out to new partners, and we value that sort of orthogonal thinking."

Benjamin nodded, mostly to keep Payne from spouting any more bullshit corporate jargon. He wondered if anyone was impressed with Payne's corporate-speak. Somebody must be, if Payne was telling the truth about the partner companies "on board" and "in the pipeline." And somebody was paying the salaries of Payne and his employees. On the other hand, maybe XKredits' partners were more nebulous companies that didn't produce anything tangible. Glittering buildings filled with pimply faced kids drinking Frappucinos and thinking outside the box. Orthogonal, my ass.

Payne's cell phone rang, and he looked at the display. "Gotta take this," he said. "My lawyer calling about the IPO. Very nice to meet you, Benjamin. Call my office if you have any more questions." Before Benjamin could reply, Payne handed him a business card, threw a hundred dollar bill on the table, flipped open his phone, and walked away.

"Asshole," muttered Benjamin to himself. He finished his burger and walked outside, just in time to see a bright red BMW 3 Series with the license plate XKREDIT pull out. However nebulous XKredits' business model was, somebody was paying for Payne's lunches and toys. Somebody with real money. And once XKredits.com went public, there would be a lot more real money coming in. Investors were climbing over each other to get in on the ground floor of companies like XKredits.com. Despite his skepticism, Benjamin found himself wondering if he should call his broker. If he moved even a thousand dollars from his IRA into XKredits.com and it took off the way some of these other little startups were, he'd make out very well. And it might be a good way to get a little more involved in Jessica's life—assuming she was still alive, and could be found.

He made his way back toward the Buick. The sun was high in the azure sky, and Benjamin blinked in the bright light. His glasses had darkened, but the angle of the sun was such that the rays sneaked through the crack between his brow and the lenses, reawakening his dormant headache. He rarely saw this much of the sun in Portland.

As he crossed the alley next to Kinko's, he nearly ran into a long-haired man wearing a dirty brown overcoat. In fact, everything about the man was dirty: his hair, his hands, his pants—his feet were so dirty that Benjamin didn't realize at first the man was wearing no shoes.

"...blind?" the man muttered. His tone was more confused than accusatory.

"Sorry," said Benjamin. "The sun..."

"Blinded by the glare," the man said, and laughed as if he had made a joke. He looked expectantly at Benjamin, his mouth hanging open slightly. His pupils darted back and forth.

"Yes, that's right," replied Benjamin, with a forced laugh, trying his best to maintain eye contact. "Blinded by the glare."

"The glare!" exclaimed the man again. With that, he turned away and continued across the alley, mumbling incoherently to himself.

Benjamin shook his head, brushing at his sleeve where the man's filthy hand had left a mark. As disconcerting as the encounter had been, Benjamin also found it somewhat reassuring that Sunnyview had at least one crazy homeless person in addition to the khaki-clad throngs. It made it feel more like a real city and less like some bizarre hive of drones toiling away at incomprehensible tasks in the service of insubstantial projects.

Benjamin found a number for Chris Sandford in a phone book in a booth outside the restaurant, and gave it a call with his cell phone. To his surprise, a man answered after only two rings.

"Hello?" said the voice.

"Chris Sandford?"

"Yeah. Are you a reporter?"

"No, I—"

"A cop?"

"My name is Benjamin Stone. I'm Jessica's father."

"Oh," said the voice. "What do you want?"

"I'm trying to find my daughter. I was hoping to ask you a few questions."

"I don't know where Jessica is. She broke up with me three weeks ago."

"I know. You might still have some information that will be useful in finding her."

"I already told the police everything."

"I'm sure you did. I'm making sure the police didn't miss anything. Are you home right now?"

"Yeah."

"Would it be okay for me to come over for a few minutes?"

"I guess."

Benjamin got the address and drove to Sandford's apartment, a run-down building on the west side of town. After several knocks, a young blond man came to the door. He was lean and tall; Benjamin supposed he was good looking in a lanky sort of way. Was that what had attracted Jessica to him? It certainly wasn't his personality. Lentz had described Jessica's boyfriend as a "sad sack," and Benjamin would be hard-pressed to think of a better description.

Sandford invited Benjamin into his dimly lit and unkempt apartment, and they sat on lumpy furniture in Sandford's small living room. Over the next hour, Benjamin questioned Sandford regarding everything he knew about Jessica, but learned very little. It was clear that Sandford still believed himself to be in love with Jessica, but it was a sort of love that made Benjamin think of the way a damp dishcloth sticks to a countertop. It was a vague, desperate kind of love that was more about Sandford's own inadequacy than anything to do specifically with Jessica. Benjamin still couldn't understand what Jessica had ever seen in Chris Sandford, but he certainly respected her decision to dump him.

According to Sandford, Jessica had broken up with him two weeks before she disappeared, and he hadn't seen her since she'd left him blubbering in a booth at Chevy's. Contrary to what Cameron Payne told him, Sandford seemed to believe that their breakup had something to do with her relationship with Payne.

"He used to call her late at night," Sandford told him. "She'd sneak off to talk to him."

"About what?" asked Benjamin.

"I don't know. She wouldn't tell me."

23

"How often did this happen?"

"Maybe a few times a week."

"You think they were romantically involved?"

"I don't know. She said they weren't, but why else would he call her at eleven o'clock at night? She was a web designer. That's not the kind of job where you get late night calls from your boss."

"I understand that you met Cameron Payne at a party. Did he make advances toward Jessica?"

"Not that I saw."

"Did she seem interested in him?"

"Everybody's interested in Cameron Payne."

"I mean romantically."

Sandford shrugged.

"Did either of them ever do anything to make you think they were romantically involved?"

"Besides the phone calls?"

"Yes."

"I guess not."

"Was the tone of the calls intimate?"

"Intimate?"

"Romantic. Did it seem like she was giddy to hear from him?"

"I wouldn't say giddy."

"What would you say?"

"I don't know. Secretive. Like they were planning something."

"Like what?"

"I don't know."

Benjamin tried for another ten minutes, but that was the extent of the useful information provided by Chris Sandford. Either he was extremely proficient at hiding information, or he was simply too self-absorbed and depressed to see much outside of his own lonely existence. Benjamin could see why Detective Lentz didn't think Sandford was a promising suspect.

Benjamin thanked Sandford for his help and left. Walking out of the apartment building, he was for once relieved to find himself assaulted by the California sunshine. Chris Sandford's apartment was like a shrine to hopelessness, and some of it clung to Benjamin even after he left. He imagined it boiling away in the relentless glare.

He returned to the library to continue his research on XKredits, but found little of interest. Most of the articles seemed more interested in Cameron Payne as a person than in XKredits itself, and those that covered the company did little more than rehash Payne's marketing spiel. The most recent issue of a magazine called *Red Herring* had an article headlined "Can Cameron Payne change the future of money?", but offered little in the way of a definitive answer. It described Payne's plans as "ambitious" and even "audacious," and noted that there were two possibilities for XKredits.com: either it would succeed on a massive scale or it would collapse under the weight of its ambitions. There was no chance of a moderate success, according to the author. If XKredits didn't become a sort of *de facto* standard for micropayments on the web, it was going to fold. And its investors would either become very wealthy or lose everything.

The initial public offering was set for this Tuesday, less than a week away. That would mean a huge influx of cash for Cameron Payne's operation. Would it be enough for XKredits to achieve market dominance? In the words of the *Red Herring* writer, it was "anybody's guess."

"Jesus Christ," Benjamin muttered. The standards for tech journalism were evidently somewhat lower than for detective work. Benjamin could only imagine the shit storm that would have ensued if he'd ever used the phrase "it's anybody's guess" to answer a reporter's question about a murder investigation. On the other hand, wasn't that essentially what Detective Lentz had told him? No suspects, no leads.

What happened to my daughter, Detective Lentz?

Well, Mr. Stone, it's anybody's guess.

Benjamin's stomach growled and he looked at his watch. It was nearly six pm.

He got up and drove the Buick to a place called Andalé Burrito. Sitting alone in a booth eating a chicken burrito and sipping a Diet Coke, he found himself wondering how things had gone so wrong with Jessica. The two of them had always butted heads, and things had only gotten worse after Katherine died. Or maybe their relationship had deteriorated even before that; Benjamin couldn't pinpoint the moment he lost her. He hadn't had much time or energy to give Jessica during Katherine's seemingly endless chemo treatments, and then there had been the gray haze of her hospice stay, during which Benjamin wore a plastic smile and drank himself to sleep at night. He had gotten the drinking under control eventually—about six weeks after the funeral—but by then Jessica had left for college. He'd tried to reconnect with her, give her some guidance, but it came across as an attempt to control her. He didn't think that art classes were a good investment. Evidently he was wrong. It had been her facility with graphic design that had landed Jessica her first real job, at Glazier Semiconductor, and got her in on the ground floor of XKredits.com. And if XKredits.com took off the way Cameron Payne expected, she'd do very well indeed. He'd read that XKredits.com, like most Silicon Valley startups, enticed employees with generous stock options—options that would suddenly become very valuable once the company went public.

Benjamin finished his burrito and drove back to the Sandman Inn. He tried calling Valerie Rocha again, but still there was no answer. He left another message.

Benjamin sat on the bed and rubbed his temples with his fingertips. He'd taken several more ibuprofen, but his head still hurt and he felt extraordinarily tired. Not wanting to wake up at four am, he managed to keep his eyes open long enough to watch the first half of *Chinatown* on cable. The Chinese gardener was explaining to Jake Gittes why maintaining the lawn around the pond in Mulwray's backyard was so much work. "Salt water," the gardener was saying. "Bad for the glass."

CHAPTER THREE

Benjamin awoke with a start, the dream still fresh in his mind. He had been in his father's apricot orchard, running toward home. It was spring, because the trees were in bloom. Apricot trees weren't much to look at for most of the year, but for a few weeks in spring they were glorious.

There may have been more to the dream, but that's all that stuck with him: the light filtering through the apricot blossoms, now peeking from behind the dingy motel curtains. The chirping of birds transmuted into the ringing a cell phone. The clock on the nightstand said 10:19. How could that be? How long had he slept? Twelve hours? It seemed impossible.

Benjamin reached groggily for the cell phone and flipped open the face plate. "Hello," he rasped.

"Mr. Stone?"

"Yeah."

"Mr. Stone, this is Detective Lentz." A pause. "From the Sunnyview Police. We met yesterday?"

"Yes. Yes, of course. Hello, Detective."

"Mr. Stone, we found her. We found Jessica."

Benjamin's heart sank. He'd been on the other side of this sort of call too many times to have any illusions about what came next.

"I'm sorry, Mr. Stone. She's dead."

"Yeah," Benjamin said. Part of him had known it all along.

"Mr. Stone?"

"Yeah, I heard you," said Benjamin. "Where is she?"

"Mr. Stone, it would be better if you wait for us to—"

"God damn it, Lentz. Where is she?"

A pause. "You know where Fourth Street dead ends at Sand Hill Creek?"

"I know the place."

"Meet me at the cul-de-sac in twenty minutes."

Benjamin grunted assent and put down the phone. He got out of bed, used the bathroom, brushed his teeth, got dressed. Just keep moving, he told himself. One foot in front of the other. Autopilot. You can go to pieces later.

The cul-de-sac was lined with police cars and emergency vehicles. Benjamin parked the Buick several houses down and made his way toward the hubbub. This part of Fourth Street had been a dirt road cutting between two orchards when Benjamin was a kid, but now it was a paved street lined with houses. It was clearly a low-income part of town; the houses were small and close together, with stucco walls and aluminum-framed windows. Several residents stood in their driveways watching the scene in the cul-de-sac unfold; they watched Benjamin suspiciously as he passed, speaking to each other in Spanish.

As Benjamin approached the cul-de-sac, he noticed Detective Lentz leaning against a champagne-colored Ford Taurus, sipping out of a Styrofoam coffee cup and nodding his head as a uniformed officer spoke to him. As Benjamin approached, Lentz dismissed the man and turned to face Benjamin.

"Mr. Stone," said Lentz, holding out his hand. "I'm so sorry." It was a practiced delivery, one that mimicked actual human sympathy almost perfectly. He admired Lentz's professionalism while simultaneously wanting to tell him to go fuck himself.

"Where is she?" Benjamin's voice was stilted, almost robotic.

"Are you okay, Stone?" asked Lentz.

Benjamin glared at him.

"Look, I get it," said Lentz. "She's your daughter. Obviously you're not okay. What I'm asking is, are we going to have a problem? Can you hold it together? Because if you make a scene, it's my ass, got it?"

"I'm fine," said Benjamin coldly. "Where is she?"

Lentz shook his head. "Some kids found her body in the creek," he said, jerking his thumb over his shoulder. "Back that way." A pathway behind one of the stucco houses had been cordoned off with police tape wrapped around mailboxes and ash trees.

Benjamin moved as if to walk the direction Lentz had pointed, but Lentz put his hand firmly on Benjamin's shoulder.

"Where the hell do you think you're going?" Lentz asked.

"To see my daughter," said Benjamin.

"The hell you are," said Lentz. "You're going to wait right here for the uniforms to carry her up here on a stretcher. Then, *if* you can hold yourself together, I *may* let you have a look at her, as a professional courtesy."

Benjamin stared at Lentz open-mouthed, hardly believing what he was hearing. "Listen to me, you son of a bitch—" he started.

"No, *you* listen to *me*," Lentz snapped, jabbing his finger at Benjamin. Lentz was smaller and leaner than Benjamin, but he had youth—not to mention about two dozen local police officers, several of whom were watching with interest as the confrontation unfolded—on his side. "I saw the look you gave me when I told you how sorry was about Jessica. That was the 'fuck you and your professional condolences' look. Well, if you don't want to be the grieving father here, then I'm not going to treat you that way. Grieving fathers get to identify their daughters' bodies at the morgue. Is that what you want?"

Benjamin shook his head, still somewhat taken aback by the change that had come over Lentz.

"Okay, then you're here as a professional courtesy. Got it? And that means that you wait here for the uniforms with the stretcher to arrive. I'm not going to have you trampling all over my crime scene."

Benjamin nodded. "All right," he said, swallowing his anger. Lentz was right: he couldn't have it both ways. He was either a grieving father or he was a cop from out of town expressing a professional interest. Either way, there was no way Lentz was letting him near the actual crime scene, but as a fellow cop Benjamin wouldn't have to watch from a distance as Jessica was loaded into an ambulance to be transported to the morgue.

A few seconds later he saw several cops making their way up the path toward the cul-de-sac, and he instinctively knew what was coming. He forced himself to breathe normally, relaxing his shoulders and letting his eyes unfocus a little. It was the reflexive detachment he'd learned to invoke after witnessing a few dozen grisly murder scenes in Portland.

The men with the stretcher followed shortly after. Lentz and Benjamin walked to the ambulance that sat with its doors open like a mobile sarcophagus waiting to swallow his daughter's body. Lentz held up his hand and the two officers stopped a few feet from the ambulance. He glanced at Benjamin, and Benjamin gave him a slight nod. Lentz pulled back the plastic sheet covering the body.

Her skin was pale and bluish, and her ordinarily lush brown hair was damp and plastered against her forehead and cheek. There was a deep, jagged cut on her forehead, but it wasn't swollen or bloody, making Benjamin think it was post-mortem. Her neck seemed twisted at an unnatural angle. Benjamin would have liked to inspect her body more closely, but he knew he was pushing it as it was. Lentz pulled the sheet back over Jessica's face and nodded to the officers, who loaded the stretcher into the ambulance. There was a brief exchange between the cops and the ambulance driver, after which the ambulance pulled away, followed by two police cars.

"You got a preliminary cause of death?" asked Benjamin.

"Neck's broken," said Lentz. "The M.E. will confirm."

"Foul play?"

"You tell me."

"She was in the creek?"

Lentz nodded. "Looks like she's been there a few days."

"Strange place to dump a body. The creek is what, fifty yards from the house at the end of the cul-de-sac?"

"Maybe they wanted it to look like a drowning."

"Unless that creek is a lot deeper than I remember," said Benjamin, "you'd have to work pretty hard to drown in it. I'm surprised there's even any water in it."

"Heavy snowfall in the Coastal Range this past winter," said Lentz. "The creek is as deep as it's been in fifty years. Can you think of any reason Jessica would be in this area?"

Benjamin shot Lentz a quizzical glance. "You're asking me?"

"Didn't you used to live around here?"

"Sure," said Benjamin, a little surprised. "Sand Hill Creek was the southern boundary of my dad's orchard. Our house was about a half mile that way." He pointed in the direction of the police tape. "But so what?"

Lentz shrugged. "Like you say, strange place to dump a body. I'm thinking it was a crime of opportunity."

Benjamin snorted. "What, Jessica was fishing in the creek when she ran into the wrong element?"

"Either that or someone killed her and then transported her body to the creek, where it was certain to be found eventually. Take your pick."

Benjamin shook his head. Neither possibility made much sense. "Is this the only way to get to that part of the creek?" The real estate had changed a lot since Benjamin had last been here; he had no idea what lay behind those houses.

"This is the closest road," said Lentz. "But the housing development continues on the other side of the creek. There are any number of routes that the killer could have taken to the creek, but most of them involve sneaking through somebody's backyard. Or slogging a ways through the creek bed."

"Difficult if you're carrying a body."

"Exactly."

"Are you releasing anything to the media?" Benjamin asked. Jessica's disappearance had made the national news, as disappearances of young, attractive white women often did.

"We're planning a press conference at three this afternoon. Gotta feed the beast."

"I'm surprised there are no cameras here now."

"We managed to keep the discovery quiet for now," said Lentz. "But they'll find out soon enough. We'll try to get ahead of it with the press conference."

Benjamin nodded. He knew the drill. Try to stay a step ahead of the press, control the flow of information.

"They'll cover it on all the local stations," said Lentz. "But I wouldn't watch it if I were you. We'll release all the basics, but you won't learn anything. It'll be the usual media circus." He paused a moment and then added, "You're lucky they don't know you're in town. It would add a whole new dimension to the story."

"Try to keep it to yourself if you can," said Benjamin.

"They won't find out about you from me," said Lentz. "I did give your name to the coroner's office, though. They had no next of kin listed."

Benjamin nodded and shook Lentz's hand. "Thanks, Detective Lentz."

"You're welcome, Mr. Stone."

Benjamin turned and walked back to the Buick. He started the car, drove down the street and made a couple of turns at random, finding himself in a virtually identical part of the housing development. He pulled over and took a look around. The only significant difference between this cul-de-sac and the last was that this street had no police cars, ambulances, or gawking residents. It was enough.

Benjamin rested his head against the steering wheel and sobbed.

CHAPTER FOUR

If the Sunnyview authorities worked on the same timeframe as Portland, it would take them seventy-two hours to release Jessica's body. That meant seventy-two hours for Benjamin to spend in Sunnyview with nothing to do but wonder how his daughter had ended up face-down in a creek.

As he had been standing there looking at the face of his dead daughter, something else had come back to him from the dream: when he was standing in the orchard, he had reached into his pocket and found an apricot pit. A stone, they used to call them. Hard and substantial, and holding within it the potential for an entire tree. Sitting alone in a booth at Carl's Jr., he reached into his pocket, half expecting to find the apricot pit, but the only thing in his pocket was Cameron Payne's business card.

"XKredits," he read aloud. "The future of currency."

The flimsy card with its airy slogan seemed ridiculous and insubstantial in comparison to the apricot pit. But the apricot pit was the one that wasn't real, being only a remnant of a half-remembered dream of a reality that no longer existed. XKredits were the future, and the Sunnyview of venture capital, IPOs and intellectual property was the present.

But Stone's thoughts drifted back to Cameron Payne's BMW with the XKredit license plate. Someone had paid for that car— someone with real money earned by creating something with actual value. How Cameron Payne had convinced someone like that to fund his castles in the sky was something of a mystery to Benjamin, and he had a hunch that if he could solve that mystery, he might gain some insight into what had happened to Jessica.

After lunch he headed back to the library, where he did some research into XKredits' funding. Their major backer was a company called Farscope Capital. The principal owner of Farscope was William Glazier, the elderly founder of Glazier Semiconductor. Jessica had worked for Glazier Semiconductor before her stint at XKredits. And that wasn't the only connection: Benjamin's father had sold their orchard to Glazier in 1960. He wondered if William Glazier would remember him. Benjamin had been only eighteen years old when he'd met Glazier, and Glazier had to be in his mid-eighties by now.

Benjamin found a contact number for Farscope Capital and pulled his cell phone from his pocket, earning a glare from the librarian. He held up his hands in supplication and walked outside. The odds of William Glazier remembering him—or returning his call even if he did remember—were slim, but Benjamin figured it couldn't hurt to try. He left a message with Farscope's secretary—who was polite but non-committal, and left the library to go for a walk downtown.

He was standing on the corner of First and Main, trying to picture the downtown Sunnyview of his youth, when his phone rang. The voice was raspy and quiet, but clear.

"Benjamin?" the voice said.

"Yes," Benjamin replied. "This is Benjamin Stone."

"You're Andrew Stone's son?"

"Yes, sir."

There was a sound like tree branches rustling in a fall breeze. After a moment Benjamin realized William Glazier was laughing. "What can I do for you, Benjamin? I'm afraid I can't give you your orchard back."

"No, sir," said Benjamin, aware that he was speaking like a child addressing an elder—or the way children used to address their elders, anyway. He didn't seem to be able to help it. "I was wondering if I could ask you a few questions about Cameron Payne and XKredits."

The line was silent for a moment. "You fishing for investment advice, Benjamin?" said Glazier curtly.

"No, sir," said Benjamin again. "My daughter works… worked for them. She…" Benjamin's voice cracked, and he paused to take a breath.

"My God," said Glazier, more quietly. "That girl, Jessica Stone. The one that's been on the news. She's your daughter, isn't she?"

"Yes, sir," said Benjamin. "She was. They found her body this morning." Lentz had told him there was going to be a press conference this afternoon, so he figured there was no harm in telling Glazier she was dead.

"I'm very sorry for your loss," Glazier said. "But why do you want to know about XKredits?"

"I wasn't very close to my daughter," said Benjamin. "I was just hoping to learn a little more about her life."

"I see," said Glazier. "What are you doing for dinner tonight, Benjamin?"

"I have no plans."

"Well, I'm not planning anything fancy, but how would you like to come up to the house for dinner?"

"That would be very hospitable of you, sir," said Benjamin.

"Fine," said Glazier. "1010 Skylark Lane. Be here at six."

"Sounds good," said Benjamin. "Thank you, sir."

Benjamin hung up and looked at his watch. It was two thirty. Lentz had said the press conference was at three. He'd also said not to watch, but he couldn't seriously think Benjamin would miss it.

He drove the Buick back to the motel and found the local NBC affiliate station on the crappy old TV in his room. The press conference started shortly after three, and Lentz was right: Benjamin didn't learn anything. Lentz spoke for about thirty seconds, and then took three questions. He didn't mention the cause of death, and he was noncommittal about the possibility of foul play. As far as the media were concerned, Jessica may have just stumbled into Sand Hill Creek and drowned. After the press conference, the station cut to an interview with Cameron Payne, who somehow managed to use the occasion as an opportunity to plug the XKredits IPO.

After easing a bit the previous night, Benjamin's headache had returned in full force. He downed three more ibuprofen tablets and lay down in bed. He hadn't intended to sleep, but woke with a start at 5:45. He jumped out of bed, used the bathroom, and grabbed his keys. Mercifully his headache had ebbed to a dull throb.

William Glazier's house was in the Hidden Oaks subdivision, on the opposite side of town from the low-income housing development where Jessica's body had been found. As Benjamin made his way down Skylark Lane, he marveled at the disparity between Hidden Oaks and the Sand Hill Creek neighborhood. The two areas were roughly equidistant from downtown, and fifty years earlier they had both been primarily agricultural. As Sunnyview developed and became a hub of information technology (and land became too valuable to be used for such mundane purposes as farming), one might have expected the Sand Hill Creek area to become an enclave for the new rich and Hidden Oaks to become the working class ghetto, but the opposite had occurred. Whereas the houses in the Sand Hill Creek area were small, crowded stucco structures with scraggly Bermuda grass lawns, Hidden Oaks had been taken over by sprawling "McMansions" with painstakingly manicured lawns and gated entryways. Broad sidewalks featured an assortment of joggers, dog walkers and bicyclists in brightly colored Lycra, Gore-Tex and rayon. The residents were all white, and an unlikely proportion of them were young or blond, and many were both. The only brown-skinned people Benjamin saw were raking bark near a white pickup with MAVERICK LANDSCAPING scrawled on the side.

The lawns got larger and the houses more opulent as Benjamin continued down Skylark Lane, and at the very end of the street was William Glazier's house. It was older and less ostentatious than the other houses in the area, but it had a certain stately charm. Glazier probably had the place built back when real estate was affordable and Hidden Oaks was synonymous with "the middle of nowhere." The rest of the neighborhood seemed to have grown up around his estate.

Benjamin pulled up to the gate and pressed the call button on the intercom. A moment later the gate swung open and he continued in toward the house. He had to laugh as he pulled up behind a later model Buick parked in front of the garage. Evidently Glazier's distaste for ostentation extended to his choice in automobiles.

He was met at the door by an attractive Latina who seemed to be in her mid-thirties. "Come in," she said with a shy smile. "Mr. Glazier is waiting for you on the patio."

She led Benjamin through the tastefully but sparsely decorated house to the back patio, where an elderly man sat stooped in a wrought iron patio chair in front of a small table. He stared out across the spacious yard, seemingly transfixed by the light of the afternoon sun filtering through the redwoods planted at aesthetically pleasing intervals just inside the tall fence that hemmed in the yard. Redwoods were popular trees in this area, particularly for borders, because they looked impressive and grew fast, but they weren't a native species. There were no redwoods in the Sunnyview of Benjamin's youth. In fact, there had been few trees of any sort outside of orchards, now that he thought about it. The natural landscape had tended toward more drought-resistant plants, given the fact that it rarely rained in this region from May to October. It was only the large-scale importing of water from the Sierras that made the lush lawns and landscaping of Hidden Oaks' palatial homes possible. In Portland, trees grew anywhere there were a few square feet of vacant ground. In Sunnyview, trees grew where the gardeners had planted them. Benjamin found the thought vaguely disquieting; it was just one more way in which modern-day Sunnyview seemed artificial, even insubstantial.

William Glazier took no notice of Benjamin until he and the housekeeper were standing only a scant few paces away, and even then he didn't stir until the housekeeper cleared her throat.

"Thank you, Lucia," Glazier said, and the woman slipped away like a shadow. He smiled at Benjamin. "Have a seat, please."

Benjamin sat down across from Glazier, and a moment later Lucia reappeared, deposited a platter of roasted chicken and vegetables on the table, and vanished again without a sound. Benjamin mumbled a thank you as she disappeared into the house.

"Very sorry to hear about your daughter," said Glazier, stabbing a chicken thigh with his fork and moving it to his plate. "Please, help yourself."

"Thank you, sir," said Benjamin.

"I'm not sure what I can tell you about Cameron Payne's operation," said Glazier. "I'm just an investor."

"You must be pretty familiar with the company, though," said Benjamin, "to put up that kind of money." *Wired* estimated that Farscope Capital had invested twenty million dollars.

Glazier shrugged. "We invest in a lot of companies."

"Yes," replied Benjamin, "I did a bit of research. But Farscope has a pretty conservative portfolio. You haven't put a lot of money in these dot com companies."

"That isn't true," said Glazier with a frown. "We just put $800,000 into SurfDaddy.com."

"Yes," said Benjamin, "but Surf Daddy has been around for twenty years. They're well known in the Bay Area as a manufacturer of surfing accessories. SurfDaddy.com is just an online extension of an established business that manufactures actual products."

A smile crept across Glazier's face. "You *have* been doing research, *haven't* you, Benjamin?" he said. "You know, you sound like your father. Did you know that when I bought your father's orchard, I originally offered twenty percent more than the price we eventually settled on? I was going to pay him in Glazier Semiconductor Stock. You know what he said? He said, 'Keep your stock. I want something *real*.'"

Benjamin nodded. That sounded like his father alright. "*Real* meaning *cash*," he said.

"Exactly," said Glazier. "The irony being that there are few things less substantial than cash. It's a paper note that is backed up by nothing more than the good intentions of a government that is five trillion dollars in debt. The U.S. dollar has lost ninety-five percent of its value in the past fifty years. Meanwhile, Glazier Semiconductor stock has risen six hundred percent."

"Dad did okay," said Benjamin.

"Absolutely," said Glazier. "He provided for his family. That's the most important thing. Like a lot of people who grew up during the Depression, he was risk averse, and that served him well, given his goals. But as the senior member of a venture capital firm, I can't afford to take no risks."

"Well, I'm no expert," said Benjamin, "but if you're looking for risk, XKredits.com seems like a good bet."

Glazier laughed out loud. "You may be right," he said. "Maybe I'm just sick of seeing these snot-nosed kids drive by my house in their goddamned BMWs blasting their rap-metal shit. Did you know that Yahoo! is worth more than Glazier Semiconductor these days? It's insane. Our components are used in machines in forty-six countries. Do you even understand what Yahoo! does? They call it an Internet portal. A portal is a *door*, for Christ's sake. A fucking door is worth a hundred and forty *billion* dollars?" Glazier was trying to maintain his light-hearted manner, but Benjamin saw the fork shaking in his hand.

Benjamin nodded, taking a bite of carrot. The food was delicious. He made a note to thank the housekeeper. Lucia?

He and Glazier ate in silence for some time. When it seemed that Glazier had calmed a bit, Benjamin asked him what made him pick XKredits.com, of all the Internet startups in Silicon Valley.

Glazier gave him a strange look. "But surely you know, Benjamin. I thought that's why you're here."

Benjamin was confused. "I'm sorry, Mr. Glazier," he said. "I don't understand what you mean."

"Jessica was the one who suggested I look into XKredits," said Glazier.

Benjamin nearly choked on his food. His daughter was the last person on Earth he'd recommend seeking out for investment advice. Glazier must have picked up on his skepticism.

"I didn't invest purely on her recommendation, of course," Glazier said. "I talked to Cameron Payne, reviewed their business plan, and ran a lot of numbers before I decided to commit any of Farscope's funds. But it was Jessica who first brought the company to my attention. She used to work for me, as I'm sure you know."

Benjamin nodded uncertainly, not sure how to proceed. None of this sounded right to him. When he'd spoken to Glazier on the phone, he'd gotten the impression that he only knew Jessica from the news reports of her disappearance. But now he was saying she had given him investment advice? Jessica Stone giving William Glazier investment advice. That was a million kinds of wrong.

"Did you know Jessica well?" asked Benjamin at last.

"Honestly, no," said Glazier. "As I mentioned, I didn't even make the connection that she was your daughter. But when she came to my office to talk about XKredits.com, I had to admire her resourcefulness. Not many people would have the balls to make that sort of overture—if you'll pardon the expression."

"She just walked into your office and told you that it would be a good idea to give XKredits twenty million dollars?"

Glazier chuckled. "The details of my investment aren't public, so I'm not going to verify the dollar amount. But yes, that's more-

or-less how it went. She was very professional about it. She'd done her research."

Benjamin had to exert significant mental effort to reconcile what Glazier was telling him about Jessica with his memories of her. Had he really been so blind to his daughter's potential? Worse, had Benjamin been the one holding her back? Was it only after she had gotten out from under his thumb that she'd been able to become the savvy, assertive person that Cameron Payne and William Glazier described? If that was true, then the success she'd achieved was only in spite of him.

"I'm sorry," said Benjamin. "I'm just having a hard time seeing how this works. An ex-employee walks in off the street and gives William Glazier a hot investment tip?"

Glazier frowned. "You don't think much of your daughter, do you?" he asked.

Benjamin didn't respond.

"It's often difficult for parents to see the potential in their own children," said Glazier. "I myself never had children, so I won't theorize as to why that is. But if nothing else, you must have known how beautiful Jessica was."

"You're saying you gave money to XKredits.com because my daughter is pretty?" Benjamin asked. The idea of William Glazier noticing his daughter's looks struck him as a bit creepy.

"I'm saying it got her noticed. I didn't know her name, but I remembered seeing her in the office. Half of life is just getting noticed, you know. For all the gender inequality bullshit you hear about, attractive young women have a big advantage in business, if they're confident enough to use it. Of course, you have to follow up with some substance, and Jessica did. She put together a solid case for why I should invest in XKredits.com. My research confirmed XKredits' potential."

"What did Jessica get out of this?" Benjamin asked. "She was just a low-level XKredits employee. Why would she go to bat for Cameron Payne?"

Glazier shrugged. "You'd have to ask Cameron. Presumably he offered her some options. Actually, not to pry in your personal affairs, but if you're Jessica's next of kin, you may own a pretty good stake in XKredits. Or you will, once the legalities get sorted out."

Benjamin nodded dumbly. The thought of him inheriting assets from Jessica—possibly significant assets—was so bizarre that he had to file it away for later processing.

Glazier must have sensed his discomfort. "Strange how reality shifts right underneath your feet, isn't it?" he asked. "Sometimes it happens suddenly, and other times the change is so gradual that you don't realize it's happening until one day you look around and you don't recognize your own city."

"Sunnyview feels like a completely different place to me," said Benjamin. "And I guess most of the change has been good—it's busier, wealthier, more diverse—but somehow it feels less real to me. I feel like I'm walking around a Hollywood set. Does that make any sense?"

"Welcome to the twenty-first century," said Glazier. "Nothing has seemed real to me since the Moon landing. You know, it occurs to me that you may be interested in attending Glazier Semiconductor's fiftieth anniversary celebration tomorrow night. They're going to be doing a big presentation about the history of the company and Sunnyview, and if I'm not mistaken, Jessica helped put the presentation together."

"I'm not sure I'm in the right frame of mind for a party," said Benjamin.

"Understandable," said Glazier. "I'm sure we can arrange for you to see the presentation another time. Supposedly they are putting it up on our website after tomorrow. In any case, I'll add your name to the guest list in case you change your mind. Six p.m. at the social hall downtown."

"I appreciate it," said Benjamin. "I'm sure the presentation will be fascinating. I remember when you and Dominick Spiegel were just starting out in that old body shop west of town. A lot has changed since then, with Glazier Semiconductor and Sunnyview."

"Indeed it has," agreed Glazier.

The remainder of the dinner was spent reminiscing about the Sunnyview of Benjamin's childhood. Benjamin didn't feel comfortable probing any more deeply into Glazier's relationship with his daughter, and doubted he would provide any more information of value in any case. There was an old adage that a lawyer should never ask a witness a question he doesn't know the answer to, and the adage often applied to cops as well. It was impossible to tell how much of what Glazier had told him was true, and Benjamin felt no desire to climb out onto an epistemic edifice of Glazier's construction. What he needed was a foundation of verifiable facts, and he wasn't going to get that from William Glazier.

After dinner, Benjamin excused himself, and found himself being escorted back through the house by the housekeeper, Lucia. "Gracias," he said as she opened the front door for him. Benjamin's Spanish vocabulary was limited to about a dozen words, but he tried to conduct basic pleasantries with Mexican immigrants in their native language, as a show of respect. Or maybe it was just Benjamin's white guilt expressing itself. In any case, Lucia seemed amused, if not impressed. "I hope dinner was okay," she said. "Mr. Glazier didn't give me much warning you were coming."

"It was excellent," said Benjamin. "Muy bueno."

"Don't hurt yourself," Lucia said, with a wry smile.

"I'm sorry," Benjamin said. "I don't speak much Spanish."

"No kidding," said Lucia, in mock surprise. "I thought you just got off the bus from Tijuana."

"By way of Portland, yeah," he said, grinning back at her. "Actually, I grew up here, and I always felt a little bad I never learned the language. Most of my father's... the people who worked on my father's farm spoke Spanish."

"Well, it's not too late to learn," she said. "usted es un hombre joven todavía."

It took Benjamin a moment, but he caught the meaning: *you're still a young man.* In fact, he was at least twenty years older than Lucia, but he wasn't about to correct her. "Gracias," he said.

"De nada," she replied. "Goodnight, Mr. Stone."

"Goodnight." Benjamin let the door close behind him and he walked to his car. He felt a fluttering in his chest that he hadn't felt since long before Katherine died.

CHAPTER FIVE

In the dream, it was spring. Dazzling white and pink blossoms covered the trees that extended in endless rows. The view was the same any direction he looked; with the sun directly overhead, it was impossible to tell which direction was north. Benjamin wandered aimlessly through the trees for some time, but it felt like he was walking on a treadmill. He would occasionally stop, trying to get his bearings, but the way the trees were planted, it felt like anywhere Benjamin stood, he was at the epicenter of the orchard. He had no frame of reference, no way of knowing from whence he had come or where he was going.

Then he noticed the boy. At first, just a dark flicker of movement, twenty or so trees away. It could have been a coyote or jackrabbit. But somehow he knew it wasn't.

Benjamin ran. The boy had come from somewhere, and he was going somewhere. If Benjamin could follow him, he might have a chance to escape the endless maze of trees.

The boy was fast, but Benjamin was faster. The boy frequently changed directions, and Benjamin occasionally lost sight of him and had to stop until he caught sight of him again. Sometimes the boy seemed to reappear in impossible places, as if he'd blinked out of existence behind one tree and re-materialized behind another. Even so, Benjamin was slowly gaining on him. It was hard to tell what he looked like—he was young, maybe eight or nine, with straight, jet black hair and swarthy skin. And he ran like a deer.

The boy showed no signs of tiring, and Benjamin was soon sweating and out of breath. It had been a long time since he had run like this. If the boy didn't stop soon, Benjamin was going to lose him.

Benjamin's calves began to ache, his eyes stung, and his heart felt like it was going to explode, but still the boy ran, and still there was no sign of any variation in the endless sea of trees. Somehow Benjamin knew that if he lost the boy, he'd be stranded amongst the trees forever, a hopeless wanderer in an endless arboreal landscape. Anything—even collapsing from a heart attack—seemed preferable to that. So Benjamin ran.

And then, suddenly but almost imperceptibly, something changed. The ground had dipped, and there was a break in the trees. Benjamin stopped, dizzily grabbing hold of a trunk to steady himself while he scanned the trees for the boy. Between gasps of air, he noticed something else new—the unnatural still of the orchard was broken by a constant, barely audible sound—the sound of flowing water.

Letting go of the tree, Benjamin took several steps forward, finding himself in a long, irregular break in the orchard. He saw now that the incline grew more pronounced ahead, until it gave way to a near-vertical drop of several inches, terminating in a nearly-flat creek bed. Maybe six inches of water rushed along the bottom, gurgling and sputtering as it went.

As Benjamin staggered toward the creek, he wiped his brow with his shirt sleeve, trying to find the dark-haired boy. But he was nowhere to be found. How could he have gotten away? Had he fallen into the creek? There was so little water in the creek, it would be nearly impossible to drown, but he could conceivably have fallen and hit his head on a rock.

As if in response to his thoughts, something seemed to flutter in the water, and Benjamin ran to the edge of the creek to get a better look. It was hard to tell with the way the sunlight glittered on the creek's surface, but Benjamin thought he saw a vaguely human shape under the water.

Benjamin took a step forward, his shoe splashing into the water and sinking into the sandy muck at the bottom. Losing his balance, he pitched forward, landing on his hands and knees on the creek bed. Cold water swirled and bubbled around him, and his hands sank into the sand. If he tried to extract one hand, the other would sink deeper, and soon he was hopelessly mired. His shoes were completely enveloped and his knees were stuck as well. He was helpless to prevent himself from being pulled into the cold water.

Still panting for breath, it wouldn't take him long at all to drown. He took one final breath as he disappeared under the surface. So this is how you die in six inches of water, he thought.

Benjamin awoke with a gasp, disoriented and surprised to find himself in the motel room. Sunlight was streaming through the cracks in the curtains, and everything seemed the same as it was yesterday when he awoke. For one hopeful moment, before memories settled into their proper places in his mind, he imagined that everything that had happened the previous day—the call from Detective Lentz, seeing his daughter's body being moved into an ambulance, the press conference, the dinner with William Glazier—was all some horrible dream. But no, his daughter was really dead. It was the orchard that wasn't real, not anymore. The trees had long ago been torn out to make way for stucco boxes crammed full of Sunnyview's underclass.

Benjamin got up, used the bathroom, showered, and got dressed. His headache was mostly gone, but he felt exhausted even though he had—according to the clock—slept almost ten hours. The dream of the orchard was fading, but he felt a tightness in his muscles as if he really had been running. In the shower he had found himself trying to wash imaginary mud off his hands.

When he turned off the shower, he heard his phone ringing. He swiped a towel across his face and ran to pick up the phone. The display showed that it was Jessica's number calling. He suppressed the kneejerk feeling of hopefulness that momentarily welled up inside him. Jessica is dead, he told himself. She isn't calling you. She never even called you when she was alive.

"Benjamin Stone," said Benjamin.

"Hey, are you the guy who called me?" asked a woman's voice.

"Yes," said Benjamin. "Are you Valerie?"

"Yeah. You're really Jessica's dad? Not a reporter?"

"I'm Jessica's father, yes. I was hoping to ask you some questions about Jessica."

"Ok," said Valerie. "What do you want to know?"

"Can we meet in person?" asked Benjamin.

Long pause. "I guess. Right now?"

"Sure, if that works for you."

"Ok. Blake's Coffee, downtown. Corner of Third and Alta Vista. I've got a break coming up. I can be there in twenty minutes."

"That works," said Benjamin. "How will I know you?"

"People say I'm elfish," said Valerie. "So look for someone elfish."

"Ok," said Benjamin, uncertainly.

"If that's not enough, I have pink hair and three nose piercings."

"Got it," said Benjamin. "I'll be there as soon as I can."

"See you."

Benjamin finished drying off and got dressed as quickly as he could. He found Blake's Coffee without difficulty and went inside. It didn't take him long to locate Valerie Rocha: a diminutive, pink-haired woman with multiple facial piercings sat alone at a table in the corner.

"Valerie?" asked Benjamin, approaching the table.

"Yeah," said the girl, who was wearing headphones and holding an iPod. She didn't look older than seventeen, but Lentz had told him she had been a college friend of Jessica's, so she had to be in her early twenties at least.

"Let me get some coffee," said Benjamin. He was still feeling foggy, and his headache was creeping back. Valerie nodded and went back to tapping buttons on her iPod.

Benjamin ordered a large coffee and returned to the table, taking a seat across from Valerie. He sipped his coffee while he waited for her to acknowledge him. Finally she looked up.

"So, I guess Jessica died?" she said. She was still wearing her headphones.

"Yes," replied Benjamin. "They found her body yesterday."

"Jeez," said Valerie. "I'm sorry. That sucks."

"Thank you," said Benjamin. It was, oddly, the most sincere-sounding expression of condolences he'd heard. Valerie didn't seem particularly broken up, though. Her slightly glum expression could be explained by annoyance at her need to find a new roommate. "How long did you live with Jessica?"

"Like six months," said Valerie. "But we knew each other a little before that in college. Was she murdered?"

"I think she was," said Benjamin. "Do you know anyone who might have wanted to hurt her?"

Valerie shook her head. "No way," she said.

"What about her boyfriend?"

"She didn't have one."

"I'm thinking of Chris Sandford."

"They broke up."

"She broke up with him, right?"

"Yeah."

"Was he upset about it?"

"Upset? Sure, Jessica was like… I mean, she was out of his league, you know? But Chris wouldn't hurt anyone. He was a vegetarian."

"So was Hitler."

"Yeah, you got me there, inspector," Valerie said sardonically. "Chris Sandford killed like six million Jews. But I'm pretty sure he didn't hurt Jessica."

"Why not?"

"Honestly, he just isn't that motivated. The guys works at In'N'Out Burger."

"You said he was a vegetarian."

"Yeah. Complicated fucking guy."

"Did Jessica talk much about her job?"

"Are you a cop?" Valerie asked. "Jessica said her dad was a cop."

"Yeah?" said Benjamin. "What else did she say about me?"

"She said you were kind of an asshole."

Benjamin couldn't help but smile. Finally, something that sounded like the truth. "Do you think I'm an asshole?" he asked.

Valerie shrugged. "I just met you. I once dated a guy for two years before I realized he was an asshole. Are you trying to find out who killed Jessica?"

"Yes," said Benjamin, trading honesty for honesty.

"Aren't the regular cops supposed to do that? I already talked to some guy named Lint."

"Detective Lentz," said Benjamin. "And I hope they do. I'm here in case they don't."

"So what do you want to know? Where she worked?"

"I know she worked for XKredits.com, and before that she worked for Glazier Semiconductor. Do you know what she did for those companies?"

"Web stuff," said Valerie. "Jessica was good with graphics. And sometimes she wrote content for their websites. You know, like marketing stuff."

"Did she ever talk about doing anything else for those companies?"

"Like what?"

"I mean, did it seem like she had other responsibilities, besides just working on the websites?"

"Not really. She did a lot of research for Glazier, but it was all for their website."

"Research on what?"

"They were doing some kind of retrospective thing on their website, to celebrate their fiftieth anniversary. Jessica was just supposed to be putting the site together, but she ended up having to spend a lot of time going through their historical archives for pictures and stuff. Jessica did this cool time progression thing with Flash that shows how Glazier Semiconductor changed from 1950 until now. She showed it to me once."

Benjamin nodded. It did seem that Jessica had developed some talents he wasn't aware of. He doubted she was killed because of an online slide show she'd made, though. "Did she ever have any arguments with people at work?"

"I don't know," said Valerie. "I guess. Doesn't everybody? My boss is a complete douchebag, but I don't think he'd, like, kill me or anything. She worked really long hours at Glazier, but I don't think they were forcing her to or anything. She just really liked her job."

"Why did she leave?"

"It was a temporary project. They didn't need her anymore when the retrospective site was finished."

"And she went to work for XKredits right after the contract ended?"

"Pretty much. Web design people are in demand these days. Jessica kept trying to get me to take some classes in Photoshop or whatever, but I don't think I have the kind of natural talent she has. Had. Sorry."

"It's okay," said Benjamin. "Did she seem to like her job at XKredits?"

"Yeah," said Valerie. "Although… I don't know, it was weird. Their office is pretty small, so they let people work from home a lot. So Jessica would be working on her laptop in the apartment, and sometimes she'd get a call from her boss."

"Cameron Payne?"

"I guess so. Anyway, she'd be talking about boring work stuff, like graphic resolutions or something, and then all of a sudden it would get kind of hushed and secretive."

"What did they talk about?"

"Well, that's the thing. It was all boring stuff, except sometimes she'd start talking real quiet, and sometimes she'd go outside. I don't think all their conversations were about website stuff."

"Do you think something was going on between Payne and Jessica?"

Valerie shrugged. "Like, romantically? I doubt it. Payne is single, right? Why would they keep it a secret? Anyway, I didn't get the impression they were hooking up."

"So what do you think they were talking about?"

"When she got quiet? How would I know? That was the point, right? She didn't want me to hear."

"I'm asking you to make a conjecture," said Benjamin. "What sort of thing might Jessica and Cameron Payne be talking about in secret?"

Valerie gave him a puzzled look. "That doesn't sound like a cop question."

"I'm not a cop."

"Well, I have no idea."

"Not a romantic tryst," said Benjamin. "So, what? A surprise party? A plot to take over the world?"

"Neither," said Valerie. "But more like the second one."

"World domination?"

"Nothing on that scale. But, like, conspiratorial."

"Something illegal?"

"Maybe."

"Would you say the mood was more excited, like they were getting away with something? Or more anxious, like they were worried they were going to get caught?"

"I couldn't hear them!"

"I understand that," said Benjamin. "But the human mind is extremely adept at picking up the emotional subtext of a conversation, even when most of the conversation can't be heard. Don't think about it too hard. Just give me a kneejerk reaction. Anxious or excited?"

"Anxious. No, excited."

"The first answer is usually the more reliable response."

Valerie thought for a moment. "I think it started excited, and then got more anxious toward the end."

"The end."

"When Jessica disappeared."

"How long did this go on?"

Valerie shrugged. "A month? Maybe six weeks?"

"Did you tell Detective Lentz about this?"

"More or less," said Valerie. "I told him about Jessica going outside to talk to Cameron Payne sometimes. Lentz wasn't this thorough."

Benjamin nodded. This wasn't the first time he'd heard that. Most investigators didn't realize how much the average witness knew without even knowing they knew it. "The funny thing about people talking in hushed tones like that is that it makes you pay even more attention to what they're saying," Benjamin said.

"Yeah," Valerie said. "But I didn't hear anything."

"Nothing?" asked Benjamin. "Not a phrase here or there? Or even a single word?"

Valerie thought for a moment. "I got the feeling they were talking about money sometimes. I remember Jessica saying, 'is it going to be enough?'"

"Good," said Benjamin. "Anything else?"

"I don't think so," Valerie said. "Well, there was something she said that was a little weird."

"What?"

"I mean, it's not what she said that was weird, so much as the way she said it. Like you said, how your ears perk up when somebody starts talking all quiet. Normally I would have thought she was just talking about some web thing having to do with colors or browser settings or something…"

"But it stuck with you, because of the way she said it."

"Right. Like it was some kind of big secret or something."

"What did she say?"

"Just a word. It kept coming up. After a while I was listening for it, you know? A lot of times it was the only word I could make out."

"Valerie, what was the word?"

"Glare," said Valerie. "Like I said, it's probably just a web design thing, but the way it kept coming up when she was..." Valerie trailed off, realizing that Benjamin was staring at her. "What?" asked Valerie, suddenly nervous. "Does it mean something to you?"

"Did you say anything about this to Detective Lentz?" Benjamin asked.

Valerie shook her head. "No, I just thought of it now. Should I have said something?"

"No," said Benjamin. "It wouldn't mean anything to him."

"Does it mean something to you?"

"No," said Benjamin. "Not yet."

CHAPTER SIX

It couldn't be a coincidence. Could it?

Benjamin found himself wandering around downtown aimlessly, and realized that he was hoping to run into the strange homeless man he had encountered the previous day—the man who had muttered about being "blinded by the glare." Did it mean something? Or was Benjamin finding connections where there were none, out of desperation to make sense of what had happened to Jessica?

He didn't find the homeless man, and once again his head hurt from being assaulted by the California sunshine. Finally he broke down and bought a baseball cap from the Walgreens downtown, which helped somewhat. He popped a couple more ibuprofen and had a tuna sandwich and a Diet Coke at a café, then returned to his car. Once ensconced in the warm Buick, he realized how exhausted he was. For all the sleep he had been getting, he felt like he'd been up most of the night. Feeling the need to rest his eyes for a moment, he leaned back in the seat—and awoke hot and sticky with sweat.

The Buick's clock said 4:25. He started the car, rolled down the windows and cranked up the air conditioning. What was wrong with him? He had no sensation of time passing at all, and he felt groggy and unrefreshed. He felt like someone else was borrowing his body and running up the mileage without his permission.

Once the chill of the air conditioning had cleared his head a bit, he drove back to the motel, stopping along the way at Starbucks for another large coffee. At the motel he stripped off his damp clothes, took a shower and brushed his teeth. Once he had gotten dressed in clean clothes and downed half the coffee, he felt more alert, but now a low-grade anxiety had seized him, and the caffeine was not helping.

For the first time since he'd arrived in Sunnyview, Benjamin felt truly alone. More than alone, he felt unmoored. The problem, he decided, was that Sunnyview was simultaneously familiar and foreign, like a stranger who is the spitting image of someone you once knew. The familiar served only as a reminder of how much had changed, how much was lost. His daughter was gone, and the conversations he'd had with Cameron Payne, William Glazier and Valerie Rocha made him think he'd never truly known Jessica in the first place. Their portraits of Jessica conflicted with each other, and none of them matched his memories. And in the end, thought Benjamin, what am I but the sum of my memories?

What he really needed was some normal interaction with people, a confirmation that life went on outside the solipsistic trap he was building for himself. Benjamin hadn't planned on attending Glazier Semiconductor Fiftieth Anniversary party, but now he began to think it might be just what he needed. Meet some people, have a few drinks, reconcile the Sunnyview of the past to the Sunnyview of the present. And maybe, in the process, learn something about the daughter he didn't know as well as he had thought he had. In fact, now that he thought about it, he'd made a rookie mistake in his investigation of Jessica's disappearance: he'd spend most of his time asking about her friends and employers, assuming that he had little to learn about Jessica herself. Maybe if he made an effort to understand her better, he'd have more luck figuring out how she'd ended up face down in a creek. It was too late to be a better father to her, but he might still be able to bring her killer to justice.

He wasn't sure what the appropriate attire at such a gathering would be; Silicon Valley was famously informal, but Glazier Semiconductor was one of the oldest companies in town, and presumably one of the most conservative. Benjamin hadn't bothered to pack a suit, but he threw on a jacket and tie. As long as the party wasn't a formal affair, he wouldn't look terribly out of place.

As it turned out, he was overdressed. William Glazier was the only person in the place wearing a suit and tie. Everyone else looked like they had just come from work or were on their way to a church picnic. The event was held in the Sunnyview social hall, which had all the glamor—as well as the acoustics—of a high school gymnasium. The venue's primary virtue seemed to be its size; Benjamin estimated that there were close to a thousand people in attendance. Most of these were presumably Glazier Semiconductor employees, but even so, this had to be a very small fraction of Glazier's workforce. Benjamin knew that over 2,000 people worked in the Sunnyview facility alone, and the company had another 20,000 employees worldwide. He guessed that it was only management that had been invited—or required, perhaps—to attend. The line workers who actually assembled and packaged the various electronic components Glazier Semiconductor manufactured were probably at home eating Hamburger Helper or Domino's Pizza.

A considerable amount of effort had been expended to transform the social hall into a shrine to Glazier Semiconductor's history. Large speakers had been set up in the corners to treat the attendees to a wide variety of music that had been popular during Glazier Semiconducter's early days. Bobby Darin's "Mack the Knife" gave way to Doris Day's "Que Sera Sera," which was followed by Jerry Lee Lewis' "Whole Lot of Shakin' Going On." Old black and white photos had been blown up into posters that were hung on the walls all around the hall, and a slide show of color photographs was being projected on one wall. Tables and chairs had been set up in one half of the hall, while the other half was left open to allow people to talk and mingle. Benjamin stood, holding a glass of wine, off to one side of the throng, where he had a good view of the slide show. Interspersed with the photographs were snippets of historical information about Glazier Semiconductor or Sunnyview. He realized after some time that some of the images were black and white photos that had been tinted; it had been so subtly and professionally done that he hadn't noticed at first. Was Jessica responsible for that? An odd combination of pride and anger came over him. On one hand, he had to admire the technical proficiency required to make a black and white photo appear to have been taken in color, but on the other hand it irritated him that someone—even if it was his own daughter—would deliberately alter something from the past. *His* past. What gave her the right?

And yet… the photos *did* look like the Sunnyview that Benjamin remembered. After all, his childhood hadn't been in black and white; the photos were monochrome because of a limitation of the technology of the time. By adding color, Jessica—if it had been her—had actually brought the images closer to fidelity with reality. And it wasn't as if Benjamin had some sentimental attachment to the original photos; he was fairly certain he'd never seen any of them before. So what logical objection could he have to the enhancement? Perhaps it was the introduction of the subjective into the photos: no matter how accurate the colorization had been, the artist had injected part of herself into them. Had that barn really been that shade of red, or was that the shade that Jessica thought it *should* have been? And why did it matter so much to Benjamin?

He had hoped that the presentation would help him reconcile the town of his memories with what he had seen of modern-day Sunnyview, but the slide show left him feeling even more unsettled. The past was spilling over into the present, and the present was intruding into the past, giving Benjamin a sort of chronological vertigo. Making matters worse, the presentation was on an endless loop, repeating about every ten minutes, so that it seemed like the sleepy Sunnyview of his youth was transforming into its modern-day counterpart and then instantaneously regressing to its former self, a universe in microcosm expanding and contracting ad infinitum, ad nauseum. He was relieved when the slide show was halted and the emcee called for the attendees to take their seats.

Benjamin found a placard with his name on it at one of the tables, and introduced himself to the people seated near him. He had to admonish himself for being surprised that he wasn't sitting at William Glazier's table; of course the seats near Glazier would be reserved for VIPs. Benjamin's name had been added to the guest list at the last minute, and he was seated with a seemingly random collection of engineers and managers. Most of them made a point of mentioning their job title to Benjamin as he shook their hands, but Benjamin simply gave them his name. If they were curious as to who this strange old man was sitting at their table, they didn't show it. After the introductions, they contented themselves with shop talk, seemingly oblivious to Benjamin's presence. He had come here to get out of his head and connect with some real people, but he was beginning to think he'd feel less alone watching a movie on cable back at the motel.

Eventually dinner arrived, and Benjamin pretended to be preoccupied with his chicken marsala while the engineers droned on. Just when Benjamin was beginning to think he couldn't take any more talk of LEDs and integrated circuits, the music stopped and the emcee tapped the microphone to get the crowd's attention. He thanked everyone for coming and introduced the CEO of Glazier Semiconductor, James Klassen, who spent five minutes giving a whirlwind tour of the history of the company, from its founding in an abandoned body shop west of downtown Sunnyview to its current status as one of the world's biggest manufacturers of integrated circuits. Klassen then introduced a man who had been one of Glazier's first employees, working for the company from 1953 to 1987. The man, who had to be in his nineties, gave a long, rambling speech about his experience at the company, in a thick Hispanic accent. Benjamin had difficulty concentrating on what the man was saying, and found himself staring at the man's left hand, which was strangely smooth and hairless, as if it had been badly burned at some point. Benjamin heard the man say something about "giving a lot to the company," and he wondered if the scarring on his hand was the result of a workplace injury. A moment of awkward near-silence, filled with whispers and murmurs, followed. The man hurriedly went on to talk about how grateful he was to the company and how much it had given him. He credited Glazier Semiconductor for making it possible for him to buy his house, and for scholarships that helped his daughter get through school. He continued to ramble until the emcee cut his mike and started clapping, prompting the crowd to break into applause as well. Benjamin felt a little bad for the old man, but the man bowed slightly at the applause and walked back to his seat with a smile on his face, apparently unaware of any indignity.

Next up was William Glazier himself, who delivered an emotional speech about his friend Dominick Spiegel, who, besides Glazier himself, was the man most responsible for the success of the company. Spiegel and Glazier had worked together on projects funded by the military during World War II, and their work had laid the groundwork for the invention of the semiconductor in 1947. Spiegel, who had been a medical doctor before his expertise in X-

Ray technology had gotten him recruited into the war effort, was the more personable of the two, but it was Glazier that had seen the commercial applications of the semiconductor—particularly the transistor, which was the foundation of all modern electronic components. Spiegel died in a car accident less than two years after the founding of Glazier Semiconductor, but William Glazier had done his best over the years to make sure Spiegel's contribution was not forgotten. In particular, he had worked to honor Spiegel's work at Sand Hill Children's Hospital, a private charity that had been founded to care for orphans after World War I. Both Glazier and Spiegel had sat on the hospital's board, and Spiegel spent hundreds of hours there doing pro bono work. In 1953, the year after Spiegel died, Glazier created a charitable foundation to build a new children's hospital to replace the dilapidated building that used to sit on the edge of town, near Sand Hill Creek. Glazier's intention was to name the new facility Spiegel Children's Hospital, but Spiegel's widow insisted that her husband wouldn't have wanted his name on the building, so the old name—Sand Hill Children's Hospital—continued to be used—even though the new hospital wasn't near Sand Hill Creek. In 1965, Glazier published a book about the future of computing, which he dedicated to Dominick Spiegel. (It was this book, Benjamin recalled, that originated the concept known as Glazier's Law: the prediction that the number of transistors on an integrated circuit would double roughly every two years.) In 1984, Glazier endowed a chair in Spiegel's name at Stanford.

In fact, as Benjamin listened to William Glazier's speech, he began to feel that it was less about Dominick Spiegel and more about William Glazier's devotion to the memory of Spiegel. It reminded him of the prayer of a televangelist who is more concerned with the approval of his audience than actual communion with the Divine. In twenty-four years on the Portland police force, Benjamin had seen a lot of self-absorbed, guilt-ridden monologues, and William Glazier's speech damn sure fit the pattern. The question was: what was Glazier guilty *about*?

Benjamin cast his gaze around the room, but saw no recognition of the oddness of Glazier's speech in anyone's eyes. Was this just how Glazier talked? Were these people just used to it? Or was Benjamin's radar out of whack? He certainly hadn't been himself lately, so it was quite possible he was hearing something in

Glazier's speech that wasn't there. He'd learned to trust his instincts, but he was in a strange town, and he'd been under some pretty serious emotional duress. I'm tired, he thought. I should go back to the motel and—

Something was wrong. The room had gone silent, and everyone was staring... at Benjamin. Had William Glazier said his name?

"Come on up, Benjamin," said Glazier, for what Benjamin realized was the second time. He felt a tightness in his chest. What the hell was this? Now the televangelist was doing altar calls?

Benjamin looked around uncertainly. "I—" he started.

"It's alright, Benjamin," said Glazier reassuringly. "We're all family here. Jessica may not have worked with us long, but she was one of us, and that makes you family."

Benjamin found himself getting to his feet, and the crowd began clapping politely, smiling sympathetic smiles at him. Benjamin's instincts were poised between fight and flight. He simultaneously wanted to run away as fast as he could and to throttle William Glazier until his eyes popped out. What the fuck did Glazier think he was doing? How dare he?

If anyone else in the hall thought it was odd that a grieving father was being called up to speak to an audience of his dead daughter's former co-workers, they didn't show it. They were all supportive smiles and applause. Benjamin was at a loss about what to do, other than play along. As much as he wanted to tell Glazier to go fuck himself, that would only make the situation even more awkward—and certainly wouldn't help his efforts to determine what had happened to his daughter. In a haze, Benjamin walked to the podium. William Glazier stepped aside, beaming warmly at him.

"I'm not sure what you want me to say," said Benjamin.

"Whatever you like," said Glazier. "We were hoping you'd say a few words about Jessica."

"Whatever I like," muttered Benjamin, stepping up to the microphone. He was sorely tempted to give Glazier what he asked for. He wanted to tell the crowd about the time he'd taken Jessica to the county fair when she was ten. She'd eaten so much ice cream that she didn't touch her dinner, and Benjamin had emptied her plate onto his when her mother wasn't looking. He wanted to tell them about the conspiratorial glances and giggles they'd shared. He wanted to tell them that he loved that little girl more than anything,

59

and he didn't know what had happened to her. That he hadn't lost his daughter yesterday or last week, but rather at some indeterminate point between Katherine being diagnosed with cancer and his drinking getting out of hand. That he would give anything just to go back and pinpoint the last moment that he and Jessica had shared any sort of connection.

Instead, he found himself thanking the crowd for their kind welcome and rambling about how much he appreciated the outpouring of support from the Glazier Semiconductor family. Having stepped out on a limb, he went on to talk about how much Jessica loved working at Glazier Semiconductor, and how meaningful the retrospective project had been to her. "I remember one night we were talking on the phone," Benjamin found himself saying, "and Jessica said, 'Dad, I just feel like I *belong* here.'" He paused and looked out at the audience, who were listening with rapt attention. The eyes of several women near him were glassy with tears. "I know that Jessica is in a better place now," he went on, "but I'm so glad she was able to experience the Glazier Semiconductor family before she passed on. God bless you all."

Benjamin stepped away from the podium and made his way to the exit, as the crowded erupted in thunderous applause. As he pushed open the exit door, they were giving him a standing ovation. Benjamin exited into the dark parking lot, walked behind a Ford Explorer, and vomited his chicken marsala onto the asphalt.

CHAPTER SEVEN

There was a rapping at the car window and Benjamin realized he'd been sleeping. He tried to roll down the window, but the car wasn't on, so nothing happened. Someone was standing just outside but the way the parking lot lights refracted on the glass, he couldn't make out who it was.

He opened the door and stepped out, finding himself face to face with William Glazier's housekeeper, Lucia. "Are you okay?" she asked.

Benjamin nodded. "Yes," he said. How long had he been sitting there? The parking lot was still full, so the event must still be going on.

"I thought that was terrible," Lucia said. "Making you go up there and talk like that. Did he even tell you he was going to do that?"

Benjamin shook his head. "No, but it's okay. I didn't mind."

"It's not okay," said Lucia sternly. "Hijo de puta. He had no right to make you do that."

"Were you at the party?" Benjamin asked. "I didn't see you there."

Lucia glared at him. "I served you your dinner," she said.

"Oh my god," said Benjamin. "I'm so sorry. I didn't—"

Lucia broke into laughter. "I was in the kitchen," she said.

Benjamin wanted to be angry, but something about the way Lucia's dimples quivered as she laughed made it impossible. He found himself laughing too. "Okay," he said. "You got me."

"Lo siento," Lucia said, putting her hand on his shoulder. "I'm so sorry. I'm as bad as Mr. Glazier."

"Not even close," said Benjamin. "You were just having fun. Glazier was—I don't know what Glazier was doing."

"He does that when he feels threatened," Lucia said. "Puts people on the spot. I'm not sure he even knows he's doing it. He's very polite, usually, but sometimes he gets that way. He's been drinking tonight."

"You think he feels threatened by me?"

"I don't know. He's been acting strangely lately. I mean, he's always been eccentric, and people put up with him because he's William Glazier, but lately he's been different. Anxious."

"Your name is Lucia, right?"

"That's right, Mr. Stone."

"Call me Benjamin."

"Okay."

"So you work all day at Mr. Glazier's house, and then he makes you work at company events too?"

"He doesn't make me. It's a chance to make some extra money."

"Are you done for the night?"

"No," Lucia said. "I'll be here for another couple of hours, at least. I just wanted to make sure you were okay."

Benjamin smiled. "I'm okay," he said.

After a pause, Lucia said, "May I ask, Benjamin, why you were talking to Mr. Glazier? Are you investigating your daughter's death?"

"Not officially," said Benjamin. "But I don't know what else to do."

"You could go home."

"I've got to wait until the medical examiner's office releases the body."

"How long will that be?"

"Another two days."

"You should be at home."

"There's nothing for me at home." His candor with Lucia surprised him. Why was he confessing so much to William Glazier's housekeeper?

"I'm sorry," Lucia said. "You don't know anyone in Sunnyview?"

"Not anymore. I grew up here, but everyone I knew is gone."

Lucia nodded. "Alright," she said, as if accepting the inevitability of the situation. "You'll come over for dinner tomorrow."

"To Glazier's house? I'm not sure that's—"

"No, silly. I don't live with Mr. Glazier. To my house. It will be late, though, after I get off work."

"You don't have to do that," said Benjamin. "I'll be fine, really."

"Where will you eat?"

"They have these places called restaurants."

Lucia shook her head. "No. You'll come over to my house. Four thirty-five Walnut Street. Six o'clock."

Benjamin laughed. In Lucia's mind, the matter had clearly been decided. "Okay," he said. "Thank you. Should I bring anything?"

"Just your charming personality," Lucia said. "I need to get back to work. You have a good night, Benjamin."

"Goodnight," said Benjamin, and watched Lucia walk back to the social hall. When she was safely inside, he got in the Buick and started the engine. For the first time since returning to Sunnyview—and for a long time before that, if he was honest with himself—he didn't feel alone.

CHAPTER EIGHT

The boy ran toward the creek, and Benjamin followed, making sure to keep him in view. Benjamin's chest burned, but he pressed on. The boy splashed through the creek and continued to the other side. Benjamin ran to the creek edge and leaped over it, landing awkwardly on the uneven ground and falling to his knees.

Benjamin got to his feet and continued in pursuit. He winced as his weight landed on his ankle; he'd apparently twisted it in the fall. He forced himself to keep on, knowing that following the boy was his only chance of escaping the orchard, but he couldn't keep pace. The boy was getting farther and farther away. Soon Benjamin would be alone in the orchard—a thought that inexplicably terrified him.

"Stop!" cried Benjamin after the boy. The boy stopped for a moment and turned to look at Benjamin. Benjamin halted as well, leaning against a tree and gasping for breath. Benjamin squinted in the bright light breaking through the canopy of leaves, and he realized that the sun was no longer directly overhead. Time had passed, and the sun had moved to the west. Benjamin's relief that he was no longer lost in an endless sea of trees was tempered by a realization of the inevitability of that western pull. For behind the boy was something Benjamin hadn't noticed before: a dark edifice, its twin parapets framing the dying sun.

The boy turned away from him and continued running toward the castle. Dread gripped Benjamin at the thought of the boy reaching the castle. Even being stranded in the infinite orchard was preferable to that. Benjamin limped toward the castle. "No!" he shouted, but his voice was oddly muted. "Stop!" he cried again, but it came out as a hoarse whisper. Benjamin blinked in the blinding sun, blinking away tears. The boy's frame had been swallowed by the black silhouette of stones.

Benjamin spent most of the day at the library, trying to learn more about XKredits.com, Cameron Payne and Farscope Capital, but discovered little of interest. There was a lot of gee-whiz speculation, but very little in the way of hard facts. By the early afternoon, his eyes had completely glazed over. When he realized he'd read the same paragraph about "vertical market integration" six times without comprehending anything, he decided to take a break to get some coffee. His head wasn't bothering him as much today, but he still felt a little hazy, as if he were running low on sleep. The coffee perked him up a bit and he returned to the library to continue his research.

He decided that the XKredits.com/Farscope Capital angle was a dead end. If there was anything there, he wasn't going to find it at the library or on the Internet. It was time to spread the net a little wider.

As he considered what angle to pursue next, he found himself thinking again about Glazier's strange homage to Dominick Spiegel the night before. Was it truly guilt that Benjamin had sensed? And if so, what had triggered that guilt after it had apparently lay dormant for fifty years?

The Sunnyview Library had a fairly extensive collection of books about the history of Sunnyview, Glazier Semiconductor, and Silicon Valley in general. Benjamin gathered a stack of these and began poring through them. He found a book on the early days of Silicon Valley particularly interesting. The seeds for the modern information age, he found, were sown in the 1940s, when Glazier, Spiegel, and a handful of other scientists gathered in the shadow of Stanford University as part of a government-funded initiative to develop Allied countermeasures against enemy radar. After the war, many of the scientists remained in the area, and several of them, including Dominick Spiegel, went to work for William Glazier. The company eventually came to be known as Glazier Semiconductor. Over the next few years, many of the men left to start other companies, some of them blaming Glazier's overbearing personality and eccentric management style. Several of these companies prospered, and they—along with Glazier Semiconductor itself—became the backbone of modern day Silicon Valley.

Benjamin was a bit embarrassed to realize just how little he actually knew about William Glazier, despite his personal connection with the man and the city of Sunnyview. He hadn't understood that Glazier was, as much as any one man could be, the father of Silicon Valley. Nor was he aware of Glazier's less noble pursuits.

For example, in July 1945, the War Department had asked Glazier to prepare a report on the question of probable casualties from an invasion of the Japanese mainland. Glazier concluded:

If the study shows that the behavior of nations in all historical cases comparable to Japan's has in fact been invariably consistent with the behavior of the troops in battle, then it means that the Japanese dead and ineffectives at the time of the defeat will exceed the corresponding number for the Germans. In other words, we shall probably have to kill at least 5 to 10 million Japanese. This might cost us between 1.7 and 4 million casualties including 400,000 to 800,000 killed.

If Glazier was the man who started the Information Age, he was also, to some extent, the man who started the Nuclear Age. Were it not for his recommendation, Truman might not have dropped the bomb on Hiroshima. If Benjamin were looking for reasons behind Glazier's guilt, the deaths of seventy thousand civilians in Hiroshima might be a good start. But why would the guilt suddenly strike now, after fifty-five years?

And Hiroshima wasn't the only sin for which Glazier might seek atonement. In the 1970s, Glazier became intensely interested in questions of race, intelligence, and eugenics. He believed this study was important to the genetic future of the human species, and one point even described it as "the most important work of his career." Glazier argued that the higher rate of reproduction among the less intelligent was having a dysgenic effect, and that a drop in average intelligence would ultimately lead to a decline in civilization. Glazier advocated sterilization for those below a minimum threshold of intelligence, and even donated sperm to a sperm bank in the interest of increasing the quality of the human gene pool.

Glazier's controversial opinions had eventually led to him stepping down as the CEO of Glazier Semiconductor, although he retained a controlling interest in the company. Over the past twenty years he had largely stayed quiet about social policy questions, and the public seemed content to forgive these aberrations in light of Glazier's genius and overall societal contribution as the product of a less enlightened age.

All of Glazier's seemingly unrelated obsessions seemed to stem from one particular aspect of his personality: an obsession with foreseeing—and influencing—the future. Glazier had established himself early on as an uncanny prognosticator of future societal trends based on limited data, which was presumably why the government had come to him with their request for a report on the likely consequence of an Allied invasion of Japan.

But Benjamin found himself continually wanting to go back to the beginning, to find some sort of starting point for the story of William Glazier. He found several biographical sketches, but he wasn't interested in Glazier's birth and schooling in Palo Alto. He was looking for something, a crux of some kind, but he didn't know what it was.

Until he found it.

The government funded-project that Glazier and Spiegel had been a part of during World War II was generally referred to simply as "the Sunnyview Labs," but it had another name in the beginning, one which Glazier himself had come up with: the Glazier Lab for the Research of Electronics, also known as GLARE.

CHAPTER NINE

Benjamin stayed at the library, reading about GLARE, until it was time to leave for dinner at Lucia's. From what he could gather, GLARE hadn't had a significant impact on the course of the war— it wasn't founded until January of 1945, less than four months before the German surrender. But its impact on what was to become Silicon Valley was profound and lasting. The research done at GLARE, and the contributions made by its members over the next two decades, made the South Bay area the global center of information technology.

Was this the "glare" of which Jessica had spoken? And was the homeless man's mention of "the glare" somehow related? The obvious interpretation of the phrase "blinded by the glare," given the organization's purpose, was that it was a reference to the Axis intelligence services being stymied by GLARE's anti-radar technology. But what possible reason could Jessica have to be talking about an obscure and long-defunct World War II counter-intelligence organization? None that Benjamin could think of.

As far as Benjamin could tell, there had been no formal dissolution of GLARE. It had lived on for a few years after the war, but seemed to have disbanded after Dominick Spiegel's death in 1952. There was little information about Spiegel's death; the most comprehensive source of information about the car accident that had taken Spiegel's life was an article in the *Sunnyview Herald*. According to the article, a drunk had run the stop sign at Fremont and Olive, slamming into Spiegel's car and killing him instantly. The accident made the front page of the Herald, and Benjamin supposed it had been a pretty big deal at the time. He didn't remember it happening, though; he had only been ten years old at the time.

"Fremont and Olive," Benjamin said to himself as he drove the Buick across town to Lucia's house. It bothered him that he couldn't picture the intersection. Checking his watch, he saw that he had a few minutes to spare, so he made a detour down Fremont Street. As he neared Olive, he pulled to the side of the street, finding an open parking space next to a meter. He got out and walked to the intersection. Benjamin tried to imagine the intersection with narrower streets and stop signs instead of traffic lights, but he couldn't make the image match anything in his memories. He couldn't ever remember being to this intersection before. How was that possible? He'd lived in this town for years. How could he have a blind spot for this particular intersection?

Shaking his head, he walked back to the Buick. He got in and drove to Lucia's house.

Lucia lived in the Sand Hill Creek area, not far from where his daughter's body had been found. The neighborhood was pretty rough, but Lucia's house was well maintained, from what he could see. The sun was setting, so it was hard to get a good look. Benjamin parked the Buick on the street, walked to the front door and rang the doorbell. After a moment, a young, brown-haired girl opened the door. She looked like she was around eight years old.

"Hello," said the girl, looking brightly up at Benjamin. "Are you Mr. Stone?"

"That's me," said Benjamin with a smile. "Is your mom home?"

The girl turned back inside the house. "Mamá!" she cried. "Mr. Stone is here!"

A short while later, Lucia appeared behind the girl. "Come in, Benjamin," she said. "I see you've met Sofia already. Sofia, go wash up for dinner."

"Nice to meet you, Sofia," said Benjamin, as the girl ran off. Lucia let him into the house. It was small and somewhat cluttered, with toys lying strewn about the floor, but it was clean and cheery. Lucia led Benjamin into the living room, where a man not much older than Benjamin sat in a dilapidated armchair watching *Leave it to Beaver* on television.

"Papá!" shouted Lucia at the man. "Our guest is here."

After a moment, the man looked up at Benjamin, blinking as if he'd just woken up.

"Papá, this is Mr. Stone," said Lucia.

"Call me Benjamin," said Benjamin.

"This is my father, Benjamin. You can call him Vicente."

The man muttered something in Spanish and turned back to the television.

Lucia snapped at him, also in Spanish, and he waved his hand at her. Benjamin noticed an irregular patch of discolored skin on the back of Vicente's hand and forearm where no hair grew. It reminded him of the scars borne by the old man who had spoken at Glazier's party the night before.

She shook her head. "Papá has gotten… how do you say it? Cocky?"

"Crotchety," said Benjamin with a smile.

"Crotchety!" said Lucia, loudly. She turned to her father. "Eres un viejo crotchety!"

Her father continued to ignore her.

Lucia led Benjamin into the kitchen, where she was working on dinner.

"He's been working long hours at the plant," she said apologetically. "They had some problems getting the machines ready to make the new chips, and now they're trying to catch up."

"Your father works at Glazier Semiconductor?"

"Yes," she said. "Twenty-four years now."

"On the assembly line?" said Benjamin. "I'd be crotchety too."

Sofia ran into the kitchen. "All clean, Mamá!" she cried. "Smell!" She held her hands up and Lucia sniffed them. "They smell like flowers!"

Sofia squealed with joy. "Smell, Mr. Stone!" she exclaimed, holding up her hands to Benjamin.

Benjamin sniffed dutifully. "They don't smell like flowers to me," he said.

Sofia looked uncertainly at his eyes.

"They smell like chocolate!" exclaimed Benjamin. "I think I'm going to eat your fingers!"

Sofia squealed again and then stuck out her tongue, licking her fingers. "Do you still want them?" she asked, grinning.

Benjamin made an exaggerated grimace. "No, thank you!" he declared.

"Sofia!" snapped Lucia. "You just washed your hands. Your mouth is full of germs."

"I'll wash them again!" cried Sofia, and ran off.

"Sorry," said Benjamin. "I didn't think—"

"It's no problem," said Lucia. "She likes you. You're very good with children."

"It's easy when they're Sofia's age," said Benjamin. "When they get a little older, I'm clueless."

"Everybody is," said Lucia. "Don't beat yourself up, Benjamin. You were a good father. It isn't your fault what happened to Jessica."

"Yeah," Benjamin said. Maybe not, he thought. But some things *were* his fault. Anxious to change the subject, Benjamin said, "I used to live not far from here. My father sold his orchard to William Glazier in fifty eight. At one point he must have owned half the real estate in Sunnyview."

Lucia nodded. "I guess he used to own all the land around here. My grandparents bought this house from Mr. Glazier in 1950. Mr. Glazier helped a lot of his workers buy houses in this area."

"Helped?" asked Benjamin. "How?"

"When he had a house for sale, he would always tell his employees about it before putting it on the open market. And he would often offer houses for less than market value. Land was a lot cheaper back then, of course, but even so, a lot of employees were able to buy houses that they otherwise weren't able to afford. Mr. Glazier thought making his employees into homeowners encouraged loyalty."

Benjamin nodded appreciatively, but he couldn't help wonder why Glazier had been so interested in instilling loyalty in low-level factory employees. From what he knew about Glazier, the man had believed strongly in the assembly line model of production, in which workers were largely unskilled, interchangeable and replaceable. He'd also been ruthless in busting unions. Benjamin found it hard to believe that Glazier had helped his employees get houses out of a sense of altruism. And of course it wasn't lost on him that the old man who had spoken at the party the previous night had also spoken of Glazier Semiconductor helping him buy a house – and he had similar burn marks on his hands. A cynic might think Glazier had been paying off workers who had been the victims of workplace accidents, but that was a bit much for Benjamin to swallow. There were less obvious ways of buying a worker's silence. There was still something Benjamin was missing.

The four of them ate dinner together in the dining room. Lucia's father said very little, and Benjamin didn't say much either. But that was okay, because Lucia and Sofia—particularly Sofia—had no trouble filling the air with conversation. Benjamin found himself smiling at Sofia's stories of her various exciting and incredible adventures at school and around her neighborhood. Sofia was at the age where fact and fiction mingled freely; she wasn't lying so much as making the truth a lot more interesting. Benjamin particularly enjoyed the part where the neighbor's dog ate Sofia's fingers because they tasted like chocolate. Sofia was more gregarious than Jessica had been at that age, but Jessica had always had a wild imagination as well.

After dinner, Lucia's father went back to the television. "Sofia," said Lucia, interrupting Sofia in the middle of a story about a magic elevator at school that went all the way to the moon.

"Yes, Mamá."

"Go see if Felipe is awake."

"Okay, Mamá." Sofia ran out of the room and turned down a hallway, disappearing from sight.

"Felipe?" asked Benjamin. He had noticed that Lucia wasn't wearing a wedding ring, and he wondered if Felipe was a boyfriend.

"My uncle," said Lucia.

"Oh," said Benjamin. "Does he work nights?"

Lucia shook her head. "He doesn't work."

Sofia came running back into the room. "He's awake, Mamá!" she exclaimed.

"Okay, come help me make him a plate," said Lucia. "Excuse me a moment, Benjamin."

Benjamin nodded. "Could I use your bathroom?"

"Sure. Down the hall. First door on the left."

Lucia and Sofia went into the kitchen, and Benjamin got up and walked down the hall to use the bathroom. When he was done, he stepped out into the hall and noticed a door open a few inches on his right. Benjamin listened for a moment for footsteps, and then stepped quietly down the hall toward the door. He peeked through the crack in the door and saw a man sitting hunched over a large table, muttering quietly to himself. The man wore wrinkled pajamas and he had a thick head of bushy black hair flecked with gray. The table was covered by what appeared to be a model train set, although Benjamin didn't see any trains. Houses, other buildings and the occasional tree dotted a dusty brown landscape.

He heard Sofia saying something to her mother across the house. It sounded like she was leaving the kitchen and coming his way. Feeling a little guilty about his snooping, Benjamin tore himself away from the scene. But as he did, the man looked up from the model and stared directly at Benjamin. Benjamin stopped mid-step, looking back at the man. There was something in the man's eyes, an intensity that Benjamin couldn't quite interpret. But that wasn't what made Benjamin's hair stand on end.

He had seen this man before, outside the Blue Agave restaurant. Felipe was the crazy man who had accosted Benjamin after his meeting with Cameron Payne—the one who had yammered about being "blinded by the glare."

Benjamin looked away, hurrying down the hall.

CHAPTER TEN

Benjamin was more careful this time, leaping the creek at a narrower point. He still tumbled awkwardly to the ground on the other side, but without twisting his ankle. He got to his feet and kept running. This time he would catch the boy before he vanished into the castle. His chest burned and his calves ached, but he was narrowing the gap between him and the boy. Once again, the castle loomed darkly ahead, the orange disc of the sun partially obscured by the building.

"Stop!" cried Benjamin after the boy. The boy stopped for a moment and turned to look at Benjamin. Benjamin halted as well, leaning against a tree and gasping for breath. At his feet he noticed something partially obscured by weeds: a smooth metallic object that glinted in the orange light.

When he looked up, he saw that the boy had resumed running toward the dark castle. "Stop!" Benjamin cried again, but it came out as a hoarse whisper. Benjamin squinted in the blinding sun, blinking away tears. The boy's frame had been swallowed by the black silhouette of stones.

Benjamin spent the morning at the city's hall of records, investigating the purchases of land in Sunnyview from the 1950s to the 1970s. What he found confirmed his suspicions: Glazier had bought thousands of acres, mostly farmland, in the 1950s, and gradually turned it into housing developments. Benjamin would have liked to cross-reference the list of buyers of these houses with Glazier Semiconductor's payroll, but he had no way of getting the company's personnel records. Even if he were still a cop, it would be doubtful whether he could get a warrant for the records under the circumstances. He wasn't sure what he was looking for exactly, or how it connected to Jessica's murder. He had put Lucia's uncle, Felipe, out of his mind. When he had mentioned that he thought he had seen Felipe downtown, Lucia just laughed. Felipe hadn't left the house in more than twenty years.

Felipe was an imbecile, permanently ensconced in a back room of Lucia's house, unable to care for himself, unable to do much of anything but play all day with a model of Sunnyview as it was many years ago. If he had built that model himself, he was a sort of idiot savant, but one with a very limited and impractical predilection. Whatever Felipe's story was, it had nothing to do with Jessica's murder. Benjamin had simply seen someone who looked a lot like him. That was the only explanation. Anyway, obsessing on the matter wasn't going to help him find Jessica's killer.

After Benjamin had perused the records for a few hours, a correlation began to emerge: a high percentage of the buyers of Glazier's houses had Hispanic surnames. The records were full of names like Garcia, Martinez and Lopez, and this was particularly true for houses purchased near Sand Hill Creek. It occurred to Benjamin—and the thought incurred an almost immediate pang of guilt—that maybe this predominance of low income, uneducated immigrants was the reason the Sand Hill Creek area had gone downhill while the Hidden Oaks area had prospered. This trend tended to be self-reinforcing as well: as poor, darker-skinned people moved into an area, the rich, white folks tended to leave, and the quantity of sales tended to cause property values to drop. Other poor Mexican immigrants would look for inexpensive housing near their friends and relatives, and the cycle would continue. The same thing had happened with many other immigrant groups in many other cities in the past – the Irish in New York, the Poles in Chicago, the Cubans in Miami. And often, unless one knew the details of how the first few immigrant families ended up living in a particular area, the ghettoization seemed rather arbitrary. Sometimes it only took a little push, and in this case the push seemed to have been provided by Glazier selling cheap houses to his employees.

And yet, Benjamin still felt like he was missing something. He still had no explanation for why Glazier had begun selling cut-rate houses to his employees—or, for that matter, why he had gotten into the real estate business in the first place. It clearly wasn't to make money, at least not in any direct way, and that was certainly out of character for Glazier. Had Glazier been buying his employees' silence about industrial accidents? Benjamin had come into two long-time employees at the plant, and both of them had chemical burns. Obviously Glazier Semiconductor used some nasty chemicals, and probably hadn't always had very good safety protocols. But there was more to it than that.

As he ruminated on this over lunch at a sandwich shop downtown, his phone rang. He answered.

"Mr. Stone, it's Detective Lentz."

"Yeah," said Benjamin. "What can I do for you, Detective?"

"I wanted to tell you we've made an arrest."

"What?" asked Benjamin, snapping out of his reverie. "Who?"

"The boyfriend. Chris Sandford."

"I thought you'd eliminated him as a suspect."

"I never eliminated him. Anyway, things have changed. We've got evidence linking him to the crime scene."

"Really," said Benjamin. "What?"

"I can't get into that," said Lentz.

"Alright," said Benjamin. "Well, thanks for letting me know."

"Yeah, well, I didn't have much choice."

"How's that?"

"He's asking for you. He won't tell us anything. Keeps saying he'll only talk to you. Do you know why that might be?"

"No," said Benjamin. "I talked to him briefly on Monday, but I have no idea why he'd want to talk to me now."

"What did you talk about?"

"The Giants game," said Benjamin. After a pause: "I asked him about Jessica."

"Covering all your bases, huh?"

"Just trying to be thorough," said Benjamin.

"Yeah? Catch anything I missed?"

"Apparently not," said Benjamin.

"Alright, well, if you want to talk to Chris Sandford, now's your chance. We've got him at the station if you want to come by."

"I'll be right there."

Chris Sandford sat alone in a small conference room, his cuffed hands resting on the table in front of him, tapping his fingers anxiously on the fake wood veneer. Detective Lentz led Benjamin past the uniformed officer guarding the hall into the room.

"Your lucky day, Chris," said Lentz. "Look who I found."

Sandford looked up at them, momentarily confused. After a moment, he nodded in recognition.

"I understand you wanted to talk to me," said Benjamin.

"Yeah," said Sandford, glancing nervously at Lentz.

"Do you mind, Detective?" asked Benjamin.

"Knock yourself out," said Lentz, who seemed resigned to the fact that Benjamin would have more luck getting information out of Sandford than he would. On his way out the door, he shot Benjamin a knowing glance. "Professional courtesy," he said, and closed the door behind him. The implication was not lost on Benjamin.

"He thinks I killed Jessica," said Sandford, his eyes downcast.

"Why would he think that?" asked Benjamin, taking a seat across from Sandford.

"They found her glasses in my car. Underneath the driver's seat, like I'd hidden them there. The frames were broken, and they had sand on them."

"Why were her glasses under your car seat?"

"I don't know!" cried Sandford, seemingly on the verge of tears. "Somebody must have put them there."

"Somebody? Who?"

"How should I know? The people who killed Jessica, probably."

"People? Who do you think killed her?"

"Glazier," said Sandford. "Or somebody who works for him."

"What makes you think that?"

"Jessica found something, when she was working on that historical project for Glazier. Something they don't want public."

"What did she find? How do you know this?"

"I found something," said Sandford.

"What?" asked Benjamin, growing impatient. "What did you find?"

"You can't tell the cops. You can't tell anybody."

"Why not?"

"Glazier owns this town. He owns the cops."

"I don't believe that," said Benjamin. "Glazier is a powerful guy, but if you have some evidence about Jessica's murder, you need to tell Detective Lentz. I can't—"

"I'm not going to tell fucking Lentz!" Sandford cried. There was some motion in the hall, and Sandford went on, in a whisper, "He owns Lentz. He owns them all."

"Alright," said Benjamin. "Tell me what you know. But if you really do have evidence regarding Jessica's murder, eventually I'm going to have to turn it over to the police."

"Fine," said Sandford. "But make copies first. And tell somebody you trust. Somebody outside of Glazier's control. Do you know anybody in the FBI?"

"Slow down, Chris," said Benjamin. "Copies of what?"

"She gave me a combination on a piece of paper. For a storage unit on Coburn and Ninth. I forgot all about it until I found it in my pocket last night. I went over there to see what was in the unit, but I didn't know what to do with all that stuff. Figured I'd call somebody this morning, but then they arrested me..."

"What stuff? What was in the storage unit?"

"Documents," said Sandford quietly. "You'll see. Unit 429. The combination is Jessica's birthday. Get them to somebody outside of Sunnyview, the FBI or somebody. I didn't kill her. You'll see."

"Alright," said Benjamin.

"Don't tell Lentz," Sandford said again. "Don't trust anyone in Sunnview."

Benjamin nodded and got up from the table. He opened the door to room and saw Lentz standing outside. He wondered how much Lentz had heard. Benjamin closed the door behind him.

"Learn anything?"

"Yeah," said Benjamin. "Chris Sandford is paranoid. He thinks everybody in this town is secretly working for William Glazier."

"Including me."

"Yeah," said Benjamin. "Nothing personal. He doesn't trust the cops. Do you really think he killed Jessica?"

"We found her glasses in his car. Broken, and caked with sand. The sand matches the sand from near the creek."

"Is that it?"

"It's pretty damning."

"Unless someone is setting him up."

Lentz snorted. "Now who's paranoid? You think one of my guys put those glasses in his car?"

"How'd you know where to look?"

"Anonymous tip."

"Convenient."

"The tipster didn't tell us about the glasses. He said he saw a tall blond man near the creek on the morning Jessica disappeared."

"Just enough information to get you to search Sandford's house and car."

Lentz shrugged.

"How do you know the glasses are Jessica's?"

"We found a receipt in her apartment. Sunnyview Optical. The prescription and the model match a pair that she bought six months earlier. She was very near-sighted, as I'm sure you know. Never left home without her glasses. But we didn't find them anywhere near the body."

"Why did he take them? Why not leave them with the body?"

"Souvenir? Or maybe he panicked, wasn't thinking clearly. Picked them up and put them in his pocket. Found them there later and stuffed them under the car seat until he could dispose of them."

"Yeah," said Benjamin, unconvinced.

"So did you get anything else from him, other than contracting his paranoia?"

Benjamin shook his head. "Just kept repeating that he didn't do it, thinks he's being framed by Glazier."

"Why was he so insistent on talking to you?"

Benjamin shrugged. "He thinks I'm safe because I'm not part of this town. At least, not any-more."

CHAPTER ELEVEN

Benjamin drove directly to the storage facility on Coburn and Ninth that Chris Sandford had mentioned. He pulled the Buick up to unit 429 and walked to the door. The padlock snapped open when he set the tumblers to Jessica's birthdate, and he pulled open the sliding metal door. Inside were five cardboard boxes.

Benjamin walked inside and removed the lid of the box nearest him, and the scent of very old paper wafted to his nostrils. The box was filled with manila folders holding sheaves of brittle old documents. He pulled out one of the folders and began looking through the papers. If he was hoping for a smoking gun, he was disappointed. The whole stack of papers seemed to relate to the process of oxidizing the exterior of silicon wafers. He stopped to read a section at random.

```
Dry Oxidation

In dry oxidation, silicon wafers to be
oxidized are first cleaned, using a
detergent and water solution, and
solvent rinsed with xylene, isopropyl
alcohol or other solvents. The cleaned
wafers are dried, loaded into a quartz
wafer holder called a boat and loaded
into the operator end (load end) of the
quartz diffusion furnace tube or cell.
The inlet end of the tube (source end)
supplies high-purity oxygen or
oxygen/nitrogen mixture. The "dry"
oxygen flow is controlled into the
quartz tube and assures that an excess
```

```
of oxygen is available for the growth of
silicon  dioxide  on  the  silicon  wafer
surface. The basic chemical reaction is:

Si + O2 → SiO2
```

It continued in this vein for several pages.

"Well, it's dry alright," Benjamin muttered to himself. What on earth made Jessica think these documents were worth sneaking out of Glazier Semiconductor's archives? And why did Chris Sandford think they somehow implicated Glazier in Jessica's death?

By the time he'd taken a sampling of the third box, it was clear that all the documents related in some way to hazardous chemicals used by Glazier Semiconductor in the silicon chip-making process. The documents dated from the 1950s to early 1960s. He found numerous employee accident reports and even internal memos suggesting strategies for downplaying the accidents and the inherently dangerous nature of the chemicals being used. Still, the smoking gun eluded him. Lots of companies handled dangerous chemicals in the fifties and sixties, and back then there was a whole lot less regulation about it. It was hard to believe Glazier would kill Jessica rather than risk this information getting out.

Most of the documents he'd skimmed so far described primarily employee accidents and internal processes. But in the fourth box, he located a few memos and other documents raising broader environmental concerns. As far as he could tell, Glazier Semiconductor employees had simply been dumping these extremely toxic chemicals into holes in the ground. It apparently occurred to only a handful of the hundreds of Glazier Semiconductor employees—and only belatedly, after health concerns began to be raised in the community—that maybe this wasn't such a great idea. Even the documents that indicated an awareness of a potential problem tended to be more interested in the public relations impact of this dumping than the effect on the health of Sunnyview's residents.

The document that gave him chills, though, was the management memo that acknowledged "a high likelihood of toxins leaching into the municipal water supply as a result of the relatively shallow water table," and then went on to state that "no change in disposal procedures is recommended at this time." Sand Hill Creek ran right past the main Glazier Semiconductor plant; it would have been the perfect conduit to transmit chemicals into the city's aquifers. These guys had dumped poison into the city's water supply by the ton, and had never been held accountable for it. He was reading about the potential of the various chemicals to cause cancer and birth defects when the label on a folder at the back of the box caught his eye. It read:

GLARE

Benjamin pulled out the folder. Inside were a few dozen documents, mostly typed on stationary that bore a logo that looked like lightning bolts shooting out of a radar dish. The first document that caught his eye was a memo from Dominick Spiegel, William Glazier's partner. It was dated October 3, 1953, and was addressed to the GLARE Board of Directors. It read:

```
Gentlemen,

I trust that I need not present my bona
fides to you in order to demonstrate my
dedication to the cause. However, in
case you have forgotten, I was a
founding member of this enterprise, and
it was in large part my research that
made GLARE possible. I ask you to
consider these facts, as well as my
current position in both the
organization and the scientific
community, when you read these thoughts.

I did not oppose your efforts to expand
the work of GLARE into areas of research
outside its initial scope; nor did I
oppose your expansion of its purpose to
the containment of the Communist menace.
To the contrary, I applaud these
efforts. I believe it is absolutely
vital that America maintain its edge in
both technology and intelligence.

I must, however, go on record as
opposing the current line of research.
```

```
There is simply no possible ethical
justification for exposing civilians to
this sort of danger, particularly
without their consent. The excuse that
the initial exposure was accidental is
laughable in its childishness. To argue,
three years after
```

"Okay in there?" said a voice behind Benjamin, startling him and causing him to drop the papers in a kind of unintentional pantomime of a Lucille Ball sketch.

He turned to see a man standing expectantly at the door. He was maybe five ten, stocky, forty years old. He wore blue jeans and a button down shirt with the storage place's logo embroidered on it.

"Jesus Christ," said Benjamin, his heart beating three times its normal rate.

"Didn't mean to startle you," said the man. "You been in here for a while."

"Yeah," said Benjamin. "Do you need something?"

"Nope, just seeing if you need anything."

"I'm good," said Benjamin, picking up the papers and trying to put them back in some semblance of order.

"My records say this unit is rented to a Jessica Stone," said the man. "That's the only name on the rental contract."

"Yeah?" said Benjamin, putting the papers back in the folder.

"You wouldn't happen to be Jessica, would you?" the man asked.

"She's my daughter."

"Your daughter know you're in her storage unit?" asked the man.

"My daughter is dead," said Benjamin, picking up the box he had been riffling through. Legally, he had no right to be going through Jessica's possessions, and presumably this guy knew that. If he had to play on the man's sympathies to get the documents out of the storage unit, he was okay with that. He brushed past the man and opened the passenger door of the Buick.

"I'm sorry for your loss," said the man. "But I can't let you—"

"She was murdered," said Benjamin, pretending not to hear, as he set the box down on the passenger seat. "You probably saw it on the news. They found her in the creek. I just wanted to get... a few pictures of her." He slammed the door, walked back to the storage unit, pulled the door shut and locked the door.

"Oh my God," said the man. "I didn't realize...."

"It's okay," said Benjamin. "You didn't know. Anyway, I should get going." He got in the car and shut the door. The man yelled something at him as he drove away, but Benjamin paid no attention. This guy wasn't going to try to stop a grieving father from taking a box of mementos of his dead daughter. Not for ten bucks an hour.

Benjamin pulled out of the parking lot and began driving toward the motel, where he could go through the documents in peace. Hopefully the one box he had taken contained all the information he was looking for, because going back to get the other boxes would be tricky. They might even change the lock on the storage unit.

He stopped at a drive-in on the way to pick up some dinner, and then drove back to the motel. As he opened the passenger door to retrieve the box of documents, he became aware of someone coming up behind him. He turned, but was too slow. He caught a glimpse of a tall man in khaki pants and a green polo shirt, then felt something strike the back of his head. That was the last thing he remembered.

He regained consciousness an indeterminate amount of time later, and for a moment thought he was back in his motel room. But the bed was smaller, as was the room, and the air had a sterile, antiseptic smell. A man was sitting in a chair in the corner of the room. Detective Lentz.

"How you feeling?" asked Lentz.

Benjamin grunted, feeling pain rush into his head as he tried to sit up. He lay back against the pillow. "What happened?"

"You tell me," said Lentz. "A maid found you lying unconscious in the parking lot of the Sandman Motel. She called 9-1-1. Paramedics found my card in your pocket. Any idea who hit you?"

"Didn't get a look at his face," said Benjamin.

"Let me rephrase the question," said Lentz. "Any idea why you were attacked?"

Benjamin didn't reply.

Lentz sighed. He looked tired, like he hadn't been sleeping any better than Benjamin. He leaned forward and looked Benjamin in the eye. "I've been straight with you, haven't I? Went out of my way to give you access. I'll grant you, I had a selfish motive. I thought letting you loose in Sunnyview might yield some results, maybe get this case solved a little quicker. But it doesn't work if you hold out on me, Mr. Stone. Then you're just another civilian fucking up my investigation. I don't need that, understand? You're either helping me solve this or you're an obstacle that needs to be removed."

"I'm telling you," said Benjamin, "I don't know who attacked me. Maybe if you'd spend less time grilling me and more time looking for my daughter's killer—"

"Fuck you, Stone," Lentz snapped.

"Excuse me?" Benjamin said, adrenaline suddenly pumping.

"You don't get to play me," said Lentz coldly. "You and your fucking head games. Always the smartest guy in the room, huh? No wonder Jessica tried to get away from you. You're the most manipulative asshole I've ever met."

"You son of a bitch," growled Benjamin. "You have no right…"

"I have *every* right," Lentz barked. "*I'm* trying to find out who killed your daughter. I don't know what the fuck *you're* doing, but you can either help me or get out of the fucking way."

Benjamin glared at Lentz for a moment. He wanted nothing more than to leap out of his bed and strangle that skinny little fucker. He had to admire the man's dedication, though—and if Benjamin were in his position, he'd have been pissed off too. In fact, Benjamin would never have given the father of the victim as much leeway as Lentz had given him. Benjamin had taken Lentz's acquiescence as a sign of weakness, but maybe him giving Benjamin so much free rein was an indication of Lentz's confidence in his own ability.

The remark about Benjamin being manipulative struck a nerve too. Isn't that what Katherine had always used to say about him? That he used his quick wit to run roughshod over any objections, playing on others' emotions as he saw fit—whatever it took to win. Benjamin had always protested that he couldn't be blamed for having a quick wit. After all, what was he supposed to do, lose arguments on purpose just to be more likeable? On some level, though, he had known that wasn't what she meant, but he rationalized his abrasive behavior until he had alienated most of their friends. The worst of it was how he had treated Jessica. Jessica had the soul of an artist, not a logician. She couldn't hope to stand up to his rhetorical assaults, and finally she had cut him out of her life altogether. He liked to think that he had softened somewhat since she left, but when he heard she was missing, he had snapped back into his investigative persona—the same brutally logical, manipulative persona that had driven her away.

Beyond his personal foibles, though, there was another reason he had been reluctant to level with Lentz: Chris Sandford's insistence that Glazier "owned" Lentz—and presumably the rest of the Sunnyview police department. There was no doubt that Glazier pulled a lot of weight in Sunnyview, and it wouldn't surprise him if he had ways of influencing the outcome of a criminal investigation in this town. Not only that, but Sandford had apparently been onto something with the documents in the storage facility. Benjamin hadn't had time to go through the documents very thoroughly or to process what he had seen of them, but it was pretty clear that Glazier and GLARE had been up to some pretty shady business back in the day. Of course, now he'd probably never know the full story, because whoever had slugged him had undoubtedly taken the box. Maybe if he had leveled with Lentz about what Sandford had told him, they'd have all of those boxes in police custody. The investigation certainly wouldn't be in any worse shape than it was right now. At this point it looked like he didn't have much choice but to trust Lentz.

"Did you find anything else in the parking lot? In my car, or around it?" he asked.

"Why?" said Lentz, without skipping a beat. "You lose something?"

"Papers," said Benjamin.

"Yeah? What kind of papers?"

"Chris Sandford told me about a storage unit in Jessica's name. Said there were documents inside that would exonerate him."

Lentz sighed disgustedly. "And now you've lost them."

"There were five boxes altogether. Four are still in the storage unit. But the one with the damning documents is gone."

"Any idea what was in these documents?"

"A lot of stuff about dumping chemicals at Glazier Semiconductor. Dangerous stuff, carcinogens."

"Recently?"

"The docs I saw were mostly from the fifties, but—"

"Jesus Christ, Stone. The EPA shut that down in the seventies. Do you have any idea how many Superfund sites there are in the Bay Area? Nobody with any sense drinks the groundwater around here. Was there anything else incriminating in the documents?"

"I didn't get a chance to look at all of them, but there seems to have been some kind of cover-up related to the dumping. Dominick Spiegel tried to—"

"I'm sure there was," said Lentz. "Glazier and his money-grubbing pals probably kept a lid on it as long as possible, just so they wouldn't have to spend a few bucks to properly dispose of their waste. But I'm a homicide detective, Stone. I don't investigate cancer deaths."

"What about a murder?" said Benjamin.

"I've already got one of those."

"Another one. I think Dominick Spiegel threatened to go public about the dumping, and Glazier had him killed. Jessica found evidence of Spiegel's threat in those documents."

"I don't suppose you have proof of any of this."

"I had a box full of documents."

"Yeah, well, you don't anymore."

"I'm sorry, Detective Lentz," said Benjamin, through gritted teeth. "I fucked up."

"You have no idea who hit you?"

"Khaki pants, green polo shirt. Tall. White. I didn't see his face."

"Fantastic. I'll just put out an APB on all tall white men with khaki pants. Can't be more than half a million in the county."

Benjamin said nothing. There was nothing he could say. After a moment, Lentz spoke again.

"So your theory is that Glazier had Jessica killed because she was going to go public with these documents?"

"No," said Benjamin. It pained him to say it, but the truth seemed clear to him. "I think she was blackmailing him. She used the documents as leverage to get Glazier to invest in XKredits, and she worked out some kind of partnership with Cameron Payne."

"Wow," said Lentz. "That's… pretty dark."

Benjamin shrugged. "I wouldn't have thought she was capable of it myself, but I'm learning I didn't know my daughter as well as I thought I did."

"Maybe she's more like you than you thought."

"Manipulative," you mean.

"Smart and manipulative."

"I'm not a thief, though. And I didn't raise Jessica to be one."

Lentz shrugged. "It's this town, this place. Money doesn't seem real here. If you're not filthy rich with stock options twenty minutes after you arrive, you start to feel like you're owed something. I've seen it lots of times."

"Yeah, maybe so," said Benjamin.

"Get some rest," said Lentz. "And stay out of trouble."

CHAPTER TWELVE

Benjamin leaped the creek, landing awkwardly on the other side. Regaining his footing, he broke into a run again. He didn't stop to yell after the boy this time, instead focusing all of his energy on catching him. The dark castle loomed in the distance.

Getting within a few paces of the boy, he dove at his legs, throwing his arms around the boy's ankles. The boy went sprawling on the orchard floor.

Benjamin panted heavily, sweat stinging his eyes and his fingers tingling from lack of oxygen, but he held the boy's legs tightly.

"What is that place?" gasped Benjamin.

"Shhh!" the boy hissed, and began kicking wildly at Benjamin. Benjamin struggled to keep hold of the boy's legs, but it was like trying to wrestle an ornery mule. The boy broke free and got to his feet. Exhausted and short of breath, Benjamin dove after him, getting a grip on the back of his pajama tops. He heard button pop and the shirt came loose in his hands. The boy, his brown skin glistening in the orange light of dusk, ran toward the dark castle.

"Please," gasped Benjamin. "Don't go in there."

Benjamin fell on his back, wiping his brow with the boy's pajama top. As he pulled it away from his face, he noticed a nametag embroidered on it. The tag read: *FELIPE.*

Benjamin awoke with a start, finding himself once again back in the motel room. He'd been diagnosed with a mild concussion and released from the hospital. After staying up another twelve hours on doctor's orders, he finally knocked off around four am. It was now past noon. The dream was still fresh in his mind.

The little boy was Felipe, Lucia's uncle. On some level he had known it even before he saw the nametag. He recognized the boy's big, thoughtful eyes. He had seen those eyes overlooking a model of 1950s Sunnyview—and before that, on the street outside the Blue Agave. He'd tried to deny it, but he was sure of it now. Felipe was the man who had first spoken to him about "the glare." And that meant that Felipe was not what he appeared. The realization was unsettling. Benjamin had learned over many years as an investigator not to ignore his gut—and this wouldn't be the first time a revelation came to him in a dream—but this time, it seemed like something else.

He was still thinking about what the dream meant when his phone rang. It was Detective Lentz, asking him to come down to his office. He wouldn't say why, but it didn't sound like good news. He showered and shaved, gulped down a handful of aspirin for his pounding head, got some coffee, and drove down to the Sunnyview Administrative Center. Benjamin's hunch was right: it wasn't good news.

"What do you mean, she's gone?" Benjamin asked. He could hardly believe what Lentz had told him.

"The FBI showed up this morning," said Lentz. "I really can't say any more than that. They took Jessica's body as evidence in a federal case."

"They can't do that!" cried Benjamin. "I don't care if they are the FBI, they can't steal my daughter's body!"

"I'm sorry, Benjamin. I'm not happy about it either. They just showed up at the morgue facility this morning and insisted they needed the body. The Medical Examiner tried to call me, but I was driving in to work at the time. By the time I returned her call, the body was gone. They'd browbeaten a morgue technician into releasing her."

"That's unacceptable," said Benjamin. "The morgue technician should know better than to—"

"She was pretty shaken up," said Lentz. "I don't think they gave her much choice."

"Assholes," grumbled Benjamin. "What's their justification? Who are they investigating? XKredits?"

"I don't know any more than I've told you," said Lentz. "I tried my contact at the FBI office in San Francisco already, but he wasn't talking. I'm going to have to go over his head. I'll let you know as soon as I find anything out."

"What the hell is going on in this town?" asked Benjamin.

Lentz had no answer.

Benjamin got up and left the building. He drove back to the motel.

Not that he didn't trust Lentz, but Benjamin spent the next three hours on the phone with the FBI. It had been a while since he had worked a case with the feds, but he still knew a few people in the San Francisco office. He got the distinct impression all his contacts had been warned about talking to him, however. They wouldn't tell him anything about his daughter or confirm they had an ongoing investigation having anything to do with Glazier or Cameron Payne. Hell, they wouldn't even admit they had sent any agents to Sunnyview that morning. Somebody had put the fear of God into the entire office.

Without thinking, Benjamin grabbed his keys and left the motel room, making a beeline for his car. By the time he got in the car, he knew exactly where he was going: Lucia's house.

He didn't yet know how, but somehow Felipe was connected to everything that was happening in Sunnyview—his daughter's murder, the blackmail, and Glazier's shady past. He was going to confront the man and find out what he knew. He got in his car and drove to Lucia's.

He knocked several times at Lucia's door, but there was no answer. Lucia and her father were undoubtedly at work, and Sofia would be at school. Felipe would be home alone, bent over his model, insensate to the outside world. Unless he was out wandering around downtown again, that is.

Benjamin tried the knob and found the door was unlocked. He called out again, and then opened the door and stepped inside. He shouted a greeting, but there was no reply. The house was completely silent.

He walked through the foyer and down the hall to Felipe's room and stopped in front of the bedroom door. "Felipe?" he asked loudly, more to announce his presence than to evoke a response. There was none, of course. Listening at the door, he heard nothing. It was impossible to tell if Felipe was even inside.

He turned the door handle, pushing the door slowly open. Not knowing the exact nature of Felipe's condition, he erred on the side of being overly cautious. He knew that people with autism could have severely adverse reactions to any unexpected occurrences. Felipe hadn't reacted the last time he'd caught sight of Benjamin, but maybe he had felt safe because Lucia was there. Benjamin wondered how long it had been since Felipe had been forced to encounter a stranger on his own.

Felipe was there, still bent over his model. He didn't seem to notice Benjamin standing there.

"Felipe?" said Benjamin again, more quietly. Still no reaction. Felipe was adjusting the position of a car on his tabletop model. It was a 1950s-vintage Buick Roadmaster, very much like one that Benjamin used to drive. Now that Benjamin got a good look, he realized that the model depicted the town of Sunnyview, circa 1950 or so. It was an eerily accurate model, conforming exactly to Benjamin's memory. If he squinted a little, he could imagine it was an aerial view of the town of his youth—not that he'd ever seen it from that perspective.

The place where Felipe placed the Buick wasn't far from where Benjamin had encountered the homeless man. Benjamin had convinced himself that man was Felipe, but now doubts crept back. It seemed impossible. How would this pathetic man sitting here in his pajamas, whose world existed entirely within the confines of his bedroom, have made his way across town to accost Benjamin? It was clear to Benjamin as he watched Felipe that this model was the only reality he knew.

For an instant, Benjamin was seized by the disturbing idea that he was just a puppet in Felipe's model. It was a crazy thought, but his experiences since he'd come back to town gave it some traction. The feeling that he was part of some grand scheme that he couldn't quite envision nagged at his consciousness. Something was off about this town, and whatever it was, Felipe had tapped into it somehow.

Benjamin stepped slowly toward the table to get a better look at the model. Still, Felipe didn't stir. Having made his adjustment, he now simply stared down at the streets he had populated with strikingly realistic automobiles and tiny people. He seemed to be waiting for something.

Benjamin found his eyes wandering to the intersection of Fremont and Olive, where the newspaper had said Dominick Spiegel had been killed in a car accident. The intersection, just outside the downtown area, and near the edge of the table, was unremarkable. All four corners were occupied by vacant lots. None of the buildings that now stood there yet existed. And yet, despite the complete ordinariness of the intersection, something wasn't right. It was the same feeling Benjamin had gotten when he had explored the intersection two nights ago, but more concrete.

The intersection was wrong. As a kid, Benjamin had ridden his bike down every street in Sunnyview, but he had never been to the intersection of Olive and Fremont, for one simple reason: when he lived there, the intersection didn't exist. When he was a child, Olive Avenue had dead-ended in front of a brick building that had long since been torn down: Sand Hill Children's Hospital. The hospital had been moved a few miles out of town in the 1970s to make room for commercial development, but in 1952—the year of Spiegel's fatal accident—it had stood on the side of the modern-day intersection.

It was impossible. Had Benjamin remembered the newspaper article wrong? He had specifically double-checked the location of the accident before driving to the intersection. It seemed unlikely he could have made such a glaring error. But if he remembered the story correctly, that meant it had been a fabrication: Spiegel couldn't possibly have died at that intersection, because the intersection didn't exist at the time of the accident. That suggested some sort of cover-up, but that idea made no sense either: the error would have been obvious to anyone living in Sunnyview at the time. If you wanted to cover up the details of an accident, claiming the accident had occurred at a nonexistent intersection was probably the absolute worst way to do it.

And why did Felipe's model—which clearly depicted Sunnyview of the 1950s—contain the same error? Why was it missing Sand Hill Children's Hospital? If the model had been designed by anyone else, Benjamin would have chalked it up to over-reliance on the designer's knowledge of modern-day Sunnyview, but it was hard to believe Felipe would have that problem.

95

Benjamin walked slowly around to the edge of the table and reached out with his right index finger, pointing at the intersection. "Right here," he said. "There should be a—"

Felipe screamed. He pulled away from the table, buried his head in his hands, and he *screamed*. It was like nothing Benjamin had ever heard before, like he had shoved an icepick right into Felipe's heart. There was a split-second of silence as Felipe took a breath, and then the screaming continued.

Benjamin backed away, reflexively holding his hands up. "Hey," he said, trying to sound non-threatening. "I'm sorry. I'm sorry, I didn't mean to...."

But his voice was inaudible over the screaming. He debated whether he should try to subdue or calm Felipe, but decided against it. He might just make things worse, and Felipe could very well turn violent if he felt threatened. Benjamin walked slowly out of the room and closed the door. The screaming continued, seeming as loud as ever. Benjamin could only hope that this was an episode of a sort he had experienced before; the neighbors three houses away could probably hear him.

Benjamin made his way quickly down the hall to the front door. But as he reached for the handle, the door swung open toward him. He stopped abruptly, face-to-face with Lucia. Holding her hand, looking terrified, was Sofia.

"Benjamin!" yelped Lucia. "What are you doing here? What is wrong with Felipe?"

Benjamin held up his hands. "I'm sorry, I just wanted to talk to him."

"Talk to him?" yelled Lucia in disbelief, shoving past him. "You can't *talk* to Felipe." Down the hall, Felipe was still screaming.

Lucia turned to Sofia and said, "Sweetie, go in the kitchen and make yourself a snack. I need to take care of Uncle Felipe." Sofia nodded and darted into the kitchen. Lucia spun to face Benjamin. "What are you doing here?" she demanded. "How did you get in?"

"It was unlocked," yelled Benjamin. "I'm sorry, is there anything I can—"

"Wait outside," Lucia snapped.

Benjamin knew better than to argue. As Lucia disappeared down the hall, he stepped outside, closing the door behind him. The screaming was a bit muted out here, but he was sure it could be heard throughout the neighborhood. Hopefully everybody in the area was at work. He sat down on the stoop and waited.

The screaming died down thirty seconds or so later, and after another five minutes Lucia came outside.

"What was that about?" she demanded. "Why were you in my house?"

"I'm sorry," said Benjamin. "The door was open. I just wanted to talk to Felipe for a moment. Shouldn't Lucia be in school?"

Lucia glared at him. "She had a doctor's appointment. I was going to take her back to school after lunch, but now I'll probably spend the rest of the day trying to keep Felipe from flipping out again. I've never seen him that bad. What did you say to him?"

"I just asked him about his model," said Benjamin. "I'm very sorry. I'll go." He got up and began walking toward his car. Lucia didn't stop him. He heard the front door slam behind him.

CHAPTER THIRTEEN

Benjamin returned to the library and confirmed what he already knew: the newspaper article about Spiegel's death definitely placed the accident at the corner of Fremont and Olive, an intersection that didn't exist at the time of the accident. There was only one copy of the article, preserved on microfiche. Benjamin supposed that the microfiche could have been phony, but why would anyone go to the trouble to plant such a bizarre clue? Was someone expecting him to come to this particular library to research a car accident that had occurred over fifty years ago? And why would this hypothetical forger want to mislead him this way? None of it made any sense. The pounding in his head had subsided a bit, but his brain wasn't connecting the dots.

He searched the Internet for information about the crash, but none of the sources he found mentioned the intersection. For a moment he considered driving to another town to check their version of the microfiche, but then he had another idea: he found the phone number for the *Sunnyview Herald* and stepped outside to call them. The story had been written by the paper's news editor, a man named Tony Sabbia. He explained to the woman who answered that he was a retired police detective who was doing some research on Spiegel's accident and asked if she had any information on Mr. Sabbia's whereabouts. She put him on hold and came back a few minutes later with a phone number for him. It was a local number, and Benjamin called it. Twenty seconds later he was talking to Tony Sabbia. Benjamin reiterated his story and Sabbia told him he'd be happy to help out. He gave Benjamin an address near the Hidden Oaks area, not far from where William Glazer lived.

Benjamin stopped for lunch and then drove to Sabbia's house. Tony Sabbia looked to be in his late seventies, which would have put him in his mid-twenties when he wrote the story about Spiegel's death. Pretty young for a news editor, but of course back then Sunnyview was just a tiny farming town. The *Sunnyview Herald* had probably only had three or four employees at the time.

Sabbia met Benjamin at the door and led him into his living room. Sabbia moved slowly, but seemed alert.

"I don't know what I can tell you about that accident," said Sabbia. "It was a very long time ago. Are you writing a book or something? I get calls from people writing books about Glazier once in a while."

"Something like that," said Benjamin. "Were you at the scene?"

"Sure," said Sabbia. "I got there right after the paramedics. Saw them pull Spiegel from the car. Grisly scene. You don't forget something like that."

"Do you remember where the accident happened?"

"Boy, you're really testing me now," said Sabbia. "If you can wait a minute, I've got all those papers in boxes in the garage. That paper doesn't hold up too well, but I've got them wrapped in plastic."

"I was actually hoping you could tell me from your own recollections," said Benjamin. "There seems to be some discrepancy in the records."

"Well," said Sabbia thoughtfully. "It wasn't far from downtown. It was on Fremont, I think."

"Fremont and what?"

Sabbia shrugged. "It was almost fifty years ago. I'm lucky if I can remember where I put my keys these days."

"It's important," said Benjamin.

"I'm sorry," replied Sabbia with a shrug. "I can't remember."

"The story says Fremont and Olive," said Benjamin.

"Okay, then it was Fremont and Olive."

"The problem is, that intersection didn't exist in 1952," said Benjamin.

"What do you mean? Of course it existed."

Benjamin pulled a sheet of paper from his pocket and unfolded it. Before he left the library, he had photocopied part of an aerial photo of Sunnyview from 1948. It showed a large, irregular rectangle where the intersection should be. "That's Sand Hill Children's Hospital," said Benjamin. "The hospital was moved in 1954, but the building sat on that spot until 1976. They had to tear it down to put Fremont through to Jasper. The intersection of Fremont and Olive wasn't completed until 1977."

Sabbia shrugged again. "What do you want me to say? The paper made a mistake. I made a mistake. It happens."

"And nobody noticed? I checked the next several issues of the *Herald*. There were no letters to the editor, no corrections. You printed a story about a car accident at a nonexistent intersection, and nobody in the entire town said anything?"

"Maybe they did," Sabbia said. "Maybe we intended to publish a correction but never got around to it. We were a small paper. Mistakes happen."

"But a mistake like this? How would a mistake like that get in the story in the first place, unless you were hallucinating when you wrote it? Or just making the whole thing up?"

Sabbia bristled. "Are you accusing me of something?"

Benjamin shook his head. "Not at all. I'm just trying to understand this. Something very strange happened here."

Sabbia nodded. After a moment, he said, "You're not writing a book, are you?"

"No, sir," admitted Benjamin. "I'm interested in this on a personal level."

"A personal level," said Sabbia flatly.

"Do you watch the news?" said Benjamin. "You heard about that girl they found dead in the creek?"

"Sure."

"She was my daughter." Benjamin had tried to avoid using his daughter's death to manipulate Sabbia, but he didn't seem to have much choice but to tell him the truth.

"Oh," said Sabbia weakly. "I'm so sorry."

"It's all right," said Benjamin. "I hadn't spoken to her for some time."

"And you think Spiegel's death is somehow related to what happened to your daughter?"

"I have my suspicions," said Benjamin. "Honestly, I was ready to let the police handle it, but things like this keep nagging at me. There's something about Glazier that just isn't right."

Sabbia stared at Benjamin for some time. "Well, you're right about that," he said.

"What do you mean?"

Sabbia sighed. "I spent a lot of time looking into Glazier and his pet projects. You've heard of GLARE?"

Benjamin's ears perked up. "Counter-intelligence program during the war."

"That's what they claimed, anyway," said Sabbia.

"You're saying it wasn't?"

"Sure, it was. But it was more than that. William Glazier was a strange man, with some eclectic interests, and the feds loved throwing money at him. They were terrified about Communism at the time, of course. He was able to indulge a lot of impulses at GLARE, under the guise of fighting Communism."

"Like what?"

"All sorts of things. I'm sure you're aware of his interest in eugenics."

"You're saying Glazier funded genetic research? What are we talking about, Mengele-type-stuff?"

"Like I said, I can't prove anything. I have no hard evidence. But I know what Glazier was capable of. We were friends, after a fashion. I got him drunk one night, and got him to say all sorts of crazy things. Off the record, of course, but he gave me enough information that I decided to do some digging."

"What did you find?"

"Nothing. I said I *decided* to do some digging. I never actually got around to the digging, because the day after my conversation with Glazier, I was visited by a couple of FBI agents. They made it very clear that I was to forget everything Glazier ever told me."

"They threatened you?"

"In those days, the FBI didn't need to threaten. They just showed up and told you what was what. Everybody knew what happened to people who didn't cooperate. I'd be labeled a Communist and a traitor. They'd dig up something from my past, or fabricate evidence against me. At the very least, I'd never get another job as a reporter. I had a family to think of."

"Why are you telling me this now?"

Sabbia shrugged. "I think they've forgotten me. Anyway, my kids are grown and my wife has passed on. I was diagnosed with a

102

brain tumor three months ago. There isn't much they can do to me at this point. How much do you know about Glazier?"

"I've done quite a bit of research in the past few days. I know he had some pretty distasteful ideas. Like the eugenics."

Sabbia nodded. "His real obsession was trying to predict the future."

"Predict it and control it," said Benjamin. "I mean, that's the point of eugenics, right? Control the evolution of the race?"

"Eugenics was mainstream compared to some of Glazier's ideas," said Sabbia. "He was convinced that the human brain possessed the potential for precognition."

"Precognition? You mean literally seeing the future?"

"Yep. He thought that time was simply a matter of perception, and that by altering our perception, we could bridge the gap between the present and the future. This was back when the CIA was testing LSD on Americans without their consent, and I'm sure Glazier had a hand in that. But I wouldn't be surprised if GLARE went far beyond that."

"Meaning what?"

"From what Glazier told me that night, I think they experimented on people. He talked about projecting someone's consciousness forward in time. It sounds crazy, I know. And he was trying to make it sound like it was all theoretical, but he would slip up at times. He was pretty drunk, and I'd switched to soda water after the first couple, so I was still pretty sharp."

"Projecting a person's consciousness forward in time? What does that even mean?"

Sabbia thought for a moment. "Let's say you've got person A, who lives in the year 2000. You send person A's consciousness—their mind, basically, forward a hundred years into the future. In the year 2100, you've got person B, sitting there all unsuspecting, driving his flying car or whatever. All the sudden, person A's consciousness takes over his brain for a few minutes. Person A, in person B's body, looks around for a while, sees what's happening in 2100, and then gets snapped back to 2000 like a rubber band. Person B loses a few minutes of time, maybe crashes his flying car, but otherwise is none the wiser. Meanwhile—well, not meanwhile, but you know what I mean—Person A reports back to his bosses about what he saw in the year 2100."

"That sounds crazy, alright," said Benjamin.

"Glazier claimed to have it all worked out, at least in theory. The way he told it, the only real obstacle was in the human brain itself."

"How is that?"

"Evolution," said Sabbia. "Knowing the future is a selective disadvantage, at least on an individual level. You know how really smart and creative people tend to commit suicide at a higher rate the general population? That's because at a certain point, intelligence becomes a burden. It's a useful trait for the race, because smart, creative people come up with innovative solutions to problems, but it's actually a disadvantage from the perspective of individual survival. Creative people are prone to suicide and self-destructive behavior like alcoholism, not to mention isolation and being ostracized. Enough of these creative types survive long enough to have offspring that the traits are preserved, but these destructive tendencies tend to keep the average IQ of the race below a certain ceiling."

Sabbia went on, "Glazier thought the same thing was true for precognition. He thought that certain individuals were genetically predisposed toward precognition, but that they are exceedingly rare, because such individuals tend to be highly self-destructive. Being able to see the future is too much for a person to take. He also thought these individuals were becoming even more rare, because precognition smacks of the supernatural, and the supernatural has become marginalized in Western society. There used to be a place for shamans and witch doctors, even the Victorian mystics. Not so much anymore. He hoped to find a trigger for these latent abilities, to allow such individuals to project their consciousness into the future. For the good of the race."

"But not so much for the good of the subjects."

"That's the way it goes with people like Glazier," said Sabbia. "The individual gets sacrificed for the greater good."

Benjamin nodded. As much as he was tempted to dismiss Sabbia's comments as the half-remembered rantings of a drunken eccentric, what Sabbia was telling him aligned with what he'd read in Spiegel's letter to GLARE. Had this been what GLARE had really been working on? Precognition? It made sense, given Glazier's apparent obsession with the future, his interest in eugenics, and the political nature of GLARE. The CIA had been involved in all sorts of crazy ideas in the 1950s, including ESP and mind control, but what the government wanted more than anything was *intelligence*. An agency that could see even a day into the future would have a huge tactical advantage over its foes. Most of what the CIA had been up to eventually was made public, but maybe the really top secret stuff was handled by an even more shadowy agency—one that most people had never even heard of: GLARE. If it was true, the real question was: were they successful? Sabbia certainly wouldn't know the answer to that one, though. Spiegel's letter had said something about the "initial exposure" being accidental. Had GLARE happened upon a way to trigger precognition by accident, and then covered it up?

"Who did he conduct these experiments on?" Benjamin asked.

"I don't even know for sure there *were* any experiments," said Sabbia. "This is all speculation, based on the little that Glazier told me. I've thought about it a lot since that day, but I never dared to look very deeply into it. Like I said, I had a family."

"Why are you telling me this?" asked Benjamin. "Do you think GLARE's interest in precognition has something to do with Spiegel's death? Or my daughter's?"

"I think," said Sabbia, "that GLARE, and Glazier in particular, were involved in some very questionable things. Things that may have seemed defensible to some people at the time, but that would look very bad for Glazier, not to mention the government. And Glazier cares for nothing more than his own legacy. So would it surprise me if Glazier had Spiegel killed? Or that fifty years later, there's still plenty he'd like to keep under wraps? Not at all. Maybe it's time the truth came out."

"Why don't you go public?"

"With what? Speculation based on a fifty-year-old conversation?"

"Would you go public if you had more evidence?"

Sabbia shrugged. "Sure. Like I said, I don't have a whole lot to lose at this point."

Benjamin nodded. He was twenty years younger than Sabbia, and he didn't feel like he had much to lose either. But Sabbia was right: they would need solid evidence of wrongdoing if they were going to try to expose GLARE.

"Thank you very much for your time, Mr. Sabbia," he said, getting up. "I'll see myself out."

"You're welcome," said Sabbia, slowly getting to his feet. Benjamin was halfway to the door when he spoke again. "Mr. Stone."

Benjamin turned. "Yes?"

"There's something else … that I just thought of. Not sure if it will be of any help, but it can't hurt."

"What is it?"

"Six years ago, someone else came to me, asking me if I knew anything about secret experiments on children in the fifties."

"Who?"

"His name was Estefan Moreno. A man about your age. He was… that is, I thought at the time that he was insane."

"Why did you think that?"

"He was ranting… almost incoherent. Scared the dickens out of my wife. Talking about Zionists and chemtrails and all sorts of craziness. But a few things that he said—about the "collective unconscious" and precognition—reminded me of Glazier's drunken monologue that night in the bar. In retrospect, I think he was trying to get me to confirm much of what I just told you, but at the time I was more concerned with getting him the hell out of my house."

"So you didn't tell him anything?"

"Well, I didn't have much to tell, and I was a little worried about feeding into the paranoid fantasies of a lunatic. And yeah, I guess I was still a little scared about what the government would do to me if I talked. I'm afraid he left disappointed."

"Do you think he came across the same inconsistency I did, about Spiegel's accident? Why did he seek you out?"

"I don't know," said Sabbia. "He wasn't making much sense."

"Do you have a phone number for him?"

"He's in the book. Still lives here in town. I almost called him many times after June died, but I was never sure what I would say to him—or whether it would make things better or worse."

"I'd like to talk to him," said Benjamin. "Is it alright if I tell him you gave me his name?"

Sabbia shrugged. "Sure. Like I said, I don't have much to lose. Just be careful."

CHAPTER FOURTEEN

Benjamin borrowed Sabbia's phone book to get Estefan's number, and called him from the car as he drove away from Sabbia's house. A woman answered. Benjamin explained that he was doing some research on William Glazier and was hoping to ask Estefan a few questions. The woman told him that was going to be difficult, because Estefan had died six months earlier. Benjamin expressed his condolences.

"What is this about, Mr. Stone?" asked the woman, who claimed to be Estefan's widow. "Who are you?"

Benjamin had been working on a cover story, but something in the terseness of the woman's voice compelled him to honesty. He explained that his daughter had been killed, and that he thought her murder may have been related to illegal activities Glazier had been involved in decades earlier. It was a bold gambit, but if what Sabbia had told him about Estefan's behavior was true, then his widow would likely be well aware of her late husband's eccentricity. And that meant she would either be glad to speak with someone who took his concerns seriously or suspicious that Benjamin was trying to capitalize on Estefan's insanity. If Benjamin was cagey with her, that would only feed her suspicions. If he was completely up front with her and she still refused to talk to him, then she probably wasn't going to be of much help anyway.

It seemed to work. She agreed to speak with him, anyway. She gave him her address—an apartment not far from downtown—and asked him to stop by at two o'clock. That gave Benjamin enough time for a leisurely lunch. He had a sandwich and soup at a café not far away, and then walked to the apartment complex.

Margaret Moreno's apartment was small, cluttered, dirty and depressing. The woman herself seemed like a reflection of her surroundings: tiny, disheveled, and worn out. If Estefan was around Benjamin's age, then presumably she was as well, but she looked far older. She invited Benjamin inside, and they sat across from each other in her little living room. Benjamin had to move a cat and a pile of newspapers to make a place for himself. Margaret showed no sign of embarrassment at the state of her apartment; she simply waited for Benjamin to take a seat.

"You said some reporter gave you my name?" Margaret asked. Her voice was low and husky, like someone who had smoked for a long time.

"Tony Sabbia. Your husband spoke to him once, years ago."

"About what?"

"Well, that's what I wanted to ask you. Do you know why Estefan would have wanted to talk to a reporter?"

"Sure," said Margaret. "He was crazy."

"Crazy how?"

"He was like one of those conspiracy theory types. Thought everything was part of some kind of secret plot. JFK's assassination, the Moon Landing, UFOs.... He was always doing research. He spent a lot of time listening to that AM radio program that's on late at night. You know, the one where they have all the crazies on. He used to call in. I think he got on the air a couple of times, but they stopped putting him on when they realized just how crazy he was. Can you believe that? He spent a lot of time at the library, said he was doing research. If he was talking to some reporter, it was probably because he thought the reporter knew something."

"Knew something about what?"

"That's the question, ain't it?" Margaret said. "The big conspiracy, whatever it was. Sometimes it was the Jews, sometimes it was the Masons, sometimes it was aliens or lizard people. It kept changing, and I never did figure out what the point of all of it was. I loved him, but like I said, he was crazy. Do you really think William Glazier had something to do with your daughter's murder?" The way she asked, it sounded as if she was trying to determine if Benjamin was the same kind of crazy as Estefan.

"It's starting to seem that way," said Benjamin. "Do you know Mr. Glazier?"

"Sure, Estefan worked for him for twenty-five years. At Glazier Semiconductor, I mean."

Another happy Glazier employee, thought Benjamin. "So Estefan was able to hold down a job."

Margaret shot him a bemused glance. "Well, of course he held down a job. He was crazy, not retarded or something."

"So he wasn't delusional?"

"What do you mean?"

"I mean, did he see things that weren't there? Hallucinate?"

"Oh, hell no," said Margaret.

"So when you say he was crazy, you just mean he had some unorthodox ideas. You don't mean he was literally insane."

Margaret's eyes went to the floor, and she was silent for some time. Until now, she had seemed eager to talk about Estefan, as if his "craziness" were some amusing and harmless quirk. But it was clear there was more to it than that. "Estefan wasn't insane in that way," she said. "But he had... issues. His death... it wasn't an accident."

"Do you mean...?"

"He shot himself," she said.

"Oh," said Benjamin. "God, I'm sorry."

She shrugged. "He had problems with depression for as long as I knew him. You ever meet somebody who was uncomfortable in their own skin? That was Estefan. He had a beautiful soul, but he was just never comfortable being himself. At first he tried to hide it, act like nothing was wrong. I told him he should see a psychiatrist, but he hated doctors. I don't think he ever saw a doctor in the twenty years we were married. Tell you the truth, I think all his crazy talk was just a way to take his mind off what was really bothering him."

"So you don't believe there was anything to his suspicions?"

Margaret snorted. "That's what this is all about, huh? You think Estefan knew something about Glazier. Something that has to do with your daughter's death."

"I just want to know what happened," said Benjamin. "I'm following up every lead I can find."

"And you don't trust the police."

"The police have limited resources. She's my daughter."

"I'm sorry about your daughter," said Margaret, "but there ain't no lizard people."

"I realize that," said Benjamin. "I'm not as interested in Estefan's theories as I am in what made him go down that path in the first place. Lots of people suffer from depression. Very few of them seek solace in conspiracy theories. Did something happen to Estefan when he was younger? Some kind of trauma?"

"I didn't know him then," Margaret said. "I can't help you, Benjamin. And I need to get ready for work."

"You work nights?"

"Second shift at the plant," Margaret said, getting to her feet. It was clear what plant she meant. It seemed like everybody in this town who wasn't some kind of entrepreneur or software engineer worked at Glazier Semiconductor. It was probably where she met Estefan.

Benjamin got up as well. "Please, Ms. Moreno. I know this sounds crazy to you, but anything you can tell me about Estefan's childhood—"

"My husband had his problems, but he was a good man. I'm not interested in entertaining any more crazy conspiracy theories. You need to go." She glared at him coldly.

"Did your husband drink water?"

Caught off guard, Margaret regarded him with a puzzled scowl. "Of course."

"Tap water?"

"No," she said. "Only bottled water. He didn't even like me to cook with tap water."

"Did he tell you why?"

"I never asked. I assumed it was another crazy conspiracy theory. Communists putting fluoride in the water or something." She turned as if to walk to the door.

"Your husband wasn't crazy," said Benjamin, taking her arm. "I think something happened to him when he was a child. Something that changed him. My guess is that he spent the rest of his life trying to make sense of it."

She glared at him. "Is this something that reporter told you?"

"No," said Benjamin. "But it's true, isn't it? Something happened to him when he was younger."

"What does this have to do with your daughter?"

Benjamin paused, unsure how much to say. He let go of Margaret's arm. "I think whatever happened to him, he wasn't the only one. It happened to others as well. Other children. I think Jessica found out about it, and that's why they killed her."

"You sound just like Estefan," Margaret said. She may have intended it as an insult, but it came out more like an expression of remorse. Benjamin waited, and she went on, "He wouldn't talk about his childhood. At all. I met his mother once, and asked her about it. She said I was lucky I could get him to talk at all. I guess there was a period where he didn't talk for nearly two years."

"Two years? Did they take him to a doctor?"

"His mother didn't speak much English, so I had a hard time understanding exactly what she was saying. Far as I could tell, they already took him to a bunch of doctors. When he stopped talking, they decided the doctors were doing more harm than good. They kept him home after that. After a while he started talking again, but something about him was different."

"Well, he'd aged two years," said Benjamin.

"She made it sound like it was more than that," Margaret said. "She said when he first started talking again, it scared them more than him *not* talking. Like he was a completely different person."

"They never figured out what was wrong with him?"

"Not that I know of. I don't think Estefan ever saw another doctor. Whatever it was, he dealt with it on his own. I always figured he just had some kind of stroke or something. I saw a show once about how strokes can change your personality."

Benjamin nodded.

"You don't think it was a stroke though, huh?"

"I honestly don't know," said Benjamin. "But I intend to find out."

CHAPTER FIFTEEN

Benjamin drove back to the Sand Hill Creek neighborhood and parked at the end of one of the streets that dead-ended near the creek, not far from where Jessica's body was found. It was the middle of the day, so the neighborhood was mostly deserted. He made his way between two houses and clambered down the shallow ravine toward the creek.

He had come here on a hunch more than anything; he needed concrete evidence tying Glazier to Jessica's death, and he had a vague sense that his subconscious had been trying to tell him something about this place. He had had the dream enough times now that he thought he could recognize that particular bend in the creek when he saw it. He had an inexplicable sense that the place where he had chased the little boy—the young Felipe—was also the place where Jessica had been cornered before she was killed. She had fled some distance down the creek bed before being subdued, but he hoped to find some evidence of a trail down to the creek—evidence that had thus far evaded the police. Benjamin would leave the police work to the police; at this point, he was going on sheer intuition.

Most of the time there was no water in Sand Hill Creek, but it was spring, and there had been heavy snowfall in the mountains. Even so, it wasn't much of a creek: just a narrow rivulet of water cutting through a shallow ravine that ran between two housing developments. The whole area was overrun with scraggly weeds.

Sitting down on a small boulder, Benjamin removed his shoes and socks and rolled up his pant legs, then stepped into the cold water. He trudged down the creek until he came to a line of police tape strung between two trees. A large area surrounding the creek had been taped off, and foreboding warning signs hung from trees in two languages and facing every possible direction, giving no semi-literate individual any excuse for failing to comprehend that this was a crime scene, and that trespassers would be dealt with harshly. Benjamin thought of lifting the tape and trudging inside to get a better look, but thought better of it. Lentz was already pissed at him, and violating the man's crime scene was not going to further endear Benjamin to him. Besides; it was unnecessary. Lentz and his men had scoured this area already, and would have found anything there was to find. If they had missed something, it was well outside of the taped area. Benjamin stood perusing the scene for a moment. Long metal stakes with flags tied to them had been placed in several places in the creek; as he got closer, Benjamin noticed small numbered tags had also been affixed to the stakes. Presumably these corresponded to a note in Lentz's files. There was one near a muddy footprint. Another where Jessica had struck her head on a rock. Another where she had died.

Benjamin turned and made his way back upstream. He didn't know for sure which way Jessica had been running, upstream or down, but his gut told him to head back the way he'd come. He passed the rock where he'd left his shoes and socks and kept going. The water was shallow enough that if he paid some heed to the rocky creek bed, he could traverse it without much trouble. Jessica could have run quite a distance in such shallow water before slipping and falling, allowing her killer to catch her.

When he'd walked a good hundred yards from the tape barrier, he began to wonder if he was deluding himself. There was no good reason to believe the bend in the creek he'd seen in his dream even existed. With Sabbia's talk of precognition, and all the weirdness he'd experienced of late, he'd somehow convinced himself that his dreams were evidence of some sort of supernatural perspective on Jessica's death. But the clarity of the creek in the dream was probably evidence of nothing more than a lot of wasted days playing in this creek as a child. In fact, his dreams depicted the creek not of today, but of his youth: unspoiled and surrounded by apricot orchards. The path taken by the young boy no longer existed; today it would take Benjamin through living rooms, carports and above-ground pools.

And then he saw it. There was no doubt: it was the very spot Benjamin had first fallen, and then leaped over, while chasing the boy. It existed. It was real. And it was identical to his dream. Was it possible that the creek had changed so little over the past fifty years? It seemed inconceivable, but then, erosion was a very slow-moving force. The real question, though, was: what did it mean? Was this just an arbitrary memory, or was his subconscious—or something else—trying to tell him something?

Benjamin climbed onto the edge of the creek and up the shallow ravine, tracing the path he had taken in the dream, but in reverse. He followed the remembered path fifty feet or so through the scrubby weeds to a redwood fence that ran along the back of someone's yard. He wasn't sure what to do next. The dream had given him a sense of this place's importance, but that was about it. He didn't know what he was looking for.

As he turned and began back toward the creek, he noticed something metallic behind a clump of brush. He leaned over and picked it up, using the edge of his shirt sleeve to gingerly lift it without smearing any fingerprints—or leaving any of his own. It was an aluminum water bottle. On the bottom, in permanent marker, were the letters *JS*.

Sloppy of Lentz's people to have missed it, but then he was nearly a hundred yards from the crime scene, and he'd walked right past the bottle at first himself. The bottle appeared to be empty; he unscrewed the top and confirmed that it was bone dry. Jessica hadn't brought water to drink—she'd brought an empty bottle to take a sample of the creek water. She was trying to determine whether Glazier Semiconductor was still dumping chemicals into the creek. Presumably her plan was to take a sample and bring it to a lab for analysis. Had she decided to go to the authorities after all? Or had she simply been looking for more leverage against Glazier?

It seemed unlikely to Benjamin that Glazier Semiconductor was still dumping illegally; the EPA was pretty strict about that sort of thing these days. You couldn't just pour hundreds of gallons of solvents into a creek anymore. But somehow Jessica had gotten the idea that the dumping was still going on. And someone had either been very interested in stopping her, or had been following her and seized upon the opportunity to kill her. Benjamin tended toward the latter theory.

He cradled the bottle in his shirt as he made his way back down the creek, stopped to put his shoes and socks back on, then returned the way he came. Behind his car was parked a late model black Lincoln. Two suited men stood near it. One of them pulled a badge from his jacket as Benjamin approached. Even from thirty feet away, Benjamin could read the big blue letters at the top: FBI.

"Benjamin Stone?" said the man.

"Yep," replied Benjamin.

"I'm Agent Hill. This is Agent Kassel. We'd like you to come with us, please."

"And if I'd rather not?" asked Benjamin.

Agent Hill eyed the water bottle Benjamin was holding. "Then we arrest you for removing evidence from a crime scene."

CHAPTER SIXTEEN

"Care to tell me what you were doing at my crime scene?" asked Agent Hill. He sat across from Benjamin in the conference room of the Sunnyview administrative center. Agent Kassel sat on one side of Hill, and Detective Lentz was on the other. Lentz didn't look happy.

"Care to tell me why it's suddenly your crime scene?" asked Benjamin. "This is a local murder case."

"We've taken over, as of an hour ago," replied Hill. "This is now a federal investigation."

"Really," said Benjamin, looking at Lentz. Lentz averted his eyes. "Why is that?"

"That's not something I need to tell you," said Hill. "Why were you at my crime scene?"

"I wasn't at your crime scene," said Benjamin. "I was *near* your crime scene. And I found something the cops missed. You're welcome."

"Convenient," said Lentz. "A water bottle belonging to the deceased. And you knew right where to look."

Benjamin snorted. "So, what? I went back to the crime scene three days later to pick up a piece of evidence I forgot about? Why would I do that? How would the water bottle tie me to Jessica's murder, if I had killed her?"

"Maybe you thought your prints were on it."

"And were they?"

"I'm not going to—"

"Of course not," Benjamin continued. I bet you found one set of prints on that bottle, and they belonged to Jessica. Tell me, Agent Hill, if I'm the criminal mastermind you think I am, why wouldn't I have wiped the bottle down the second I picked it up? I'll tell you why I didn't: I was trying to *preserve* any prints that might be on the bottle, in case it would help the police figure out who killed Jessica."

"Just helping out," said Hill.

"She's my daughter," Benjamin seethed. "So, yeah, I'm doing what I can."

"How did you know where to look for the water bottle?"

"I didn't. I got lucky."

Hill regarded him skeptically. "We followed you to the crime scene," he said. "You were there less than half an hour. You're expecting us to believe you just walked right to the spot where Jessica dropped the bottle by accident?"

"I don't know what to tell you," said Benjamin. "That's what happened. I don't suppose you're going to tell me why you've been following me."

"No," said Hill. "We're not. Did you know that your daughter owned thirty million shares of XKredits?"

"No," said Benjamin. "I just found out that she had an interest in the company two days ago. If you say it was thirty million shares, I have no reason to doubt you."

"You're sure you didn't know about the shares before Jessica was killed?"

"Pretty sure, yes."

"And did you know that you're Jessica's only known living blood relative?"

"Can we just cut to the part where you accuse me of killing my own daughter for her money?"

"Why, Mr. Stone?" asked Agent Hill. "Is that what happened?"

"You know goddamned well it isn't," said Benjamin.

Agent Hill shrugged. "Let's just say it doesn't look good. You've got a solid motive, and now we find you snooping around the crime scene."

Benjamin didn't reply. If the FBI were going to arrest him, they would have done it by now. They were trying to scare him. The question was: why?

Agent Hill got up from the table, and Agent Kassel followed suit. "I think we're done here, Detective Lentz. Mr. Stone, try to stay out of trouble." They left the room without another word.

"What the hell was that about?" asked Benjamin. "How long have they been following me?"

"No idea," said Lentz. "I've been completely shut out. First they took Jessica's body, and then they showed up here, saying they were taking over the investigation. Oh, and they've taken Cameron Payne into custody."

"What are they charging him with?"

"Hell if I know. I don't even know where they're holding him."

Benjamin found himself scanning the room for cameras and microphones.

"Room's clean," said Lentz, reading his mind. "We don't have a real interrogation room. This is the only listening device." He picked up the phone that sat in the center of the table and unplugged the cord. "Better?"

Benjamin nodded. "Maybe I'm paranoid, but I don't trust those guys one bit. This is a murder case. How are they claiming jurisdiction?"

"Interstate fraud. They think Jessica's murder is linked to the funding of XKredits, like you said."

"Isn't that an SEC thing? Why is the FBI involved?"

"Exactly," said Lentz. "It smells like bullshit to me. A half-assed cover story."

"So what are they really after?"

"You tell me," said Lentz.

"What's that supposed to mean?"

"It means I think you know more than you're telling me. How *did* you know where to find that water bottle?"

"Jesus," said Benjamin. "Not you too. I didn't kill my daughter. I'm trying to help you find out who did."

"I know that, Stone. Give me some fucking credit. But you're holding out on me. I never would have told you as much as I did if I had known you were going to lie to me and run around playing detective behind my back. Hell, I've got the FBI for that."

Lentz was right. He was getting nowhere on his own. The only way he was going to find out what had happened to his daughter was to level with Lentz.

"It is funny, the way they're handling this," Benjamin said.

"What do you mean?"

"Did they even ask for a briefing about Jessica's murder?"

"No," said Lentz. "Took all the case records, but didn't ask me a damn thing."

"It's like they already know what happened," said Benjamin. "They know why Jessica was killed, and who killed her. They aren't trying to solve her murder."

"What are you saying?" asked Lentz. "The FBI is covering up something?"

"That agent mentioned the possibility of me inheriting XKredits stock from Jessica," said Benjamin. "That's the second time somebody has brought that up. The first time, it was Glazier."

"You think Glazier tipped them off? Trying to divert suspicion from him?"

Benjamin shook his head. "They have no case against me. They'd have to prove I knew about the stock, which of course I didn't. And in any case, that stock is going to be worthless in a few days. Not much of a motive. All they have is a water bottle conspicuously lacking my fingerprints. This wasn't a serious attempt to frame me. They're just trying to scare me off. Keep me from poking around anymore."

"So how is Glazier involved?"

"He's feeding them information. Glazier isn't a suspect. He's working with the FBI."

"In exchange for what? Immunity from prosecution?"

"Maybe," said Benjamin. "But I'm betting it goes deeper than that. Glazier has been working with the feds for a long time. I suspect they have shared interests."

Lentz sighed. "This is where you lose me. Glazier's company got away with dumping some chemical in the creek fifty years ago, and the government is so embarrassed about letting him get away with it that they're willing to cover up a murder to keep word from getting out? That dog won't hunt, Stone."

"There's more to it," said Benjamin. He was hesitant to tell Lentz his suspicions about Glazier, because he was pretty sure it would make him sound like a lunatic. But what choice did he have? He had to at least try to convince Lentz of the soundness of his theory.

"I'm listening," said Lentz.

"Okay," said Benjamin. "You wanted me to level with you, so I'm going to level with you. But some of this is going to be a little tough to swallow."

"You've got the floor," said Lentz. "But I reserve the right to call bullshit."

"You know who Dominick Spiegel was?"

"Sure," said Lentz. "Glazier's old partner. Died in a car accident."

"Right," said Benjamin. "Except I don't think it was an accident. I think Glazier had Spiegel killed because Spiegel threatened to go public about what they were doing."

"You mean the dumping?"

"It was more than dumping," said Benjamin. "The impression I got from Spiegel's letter was that the chemicals in the water had caused some sort of… biological anomaly in some of the people exposed to it."

"Like what? Cancer? Birth defects? You're saying they knew the water was making people sick and they didn't do anything about it?"

"That was part of it, probably. But I think there was something else. Spiegel's letter mentioned 'subjects,' like people were being exposed to these chemicals on purpose. The letter said the 'initial exposure' was an accident, but it implied that later exposures were intentional. I think they accidentally produced a desirable effect of some kind, and then decided to capitalize on the accident by replicating it. Or increasing it."

"What effect?"

"Honestly," said Benjamin, "I don't know. It has something to do with a government-funded project called GLARE that was started during World War II. Some kind of counterintelligence program that was initially developed to stop the Nazis, but was redirected after the war to focus on the Communist threat. You're too young to remember, but the paranoia about Communism back then was insane. The government would do just about anything if they thought it would help defeat the Communists. Hell, you've heard of Operation Paperclip, right? They basically brought hundreds of Nazi scientists to the U.S. to keep them out of Soviet hands. And then there was Project MKUltra, the mind control project. Those guys did all sorts of twisted things to people.

Torture, brainwashing, giving people LSD without their consent...."

"Yeah, I'm familiar with that stuff. What's your point, Stone?"

"My point is that there were a lot of shady, government-funded projects going on in the forties and fifties, and GLARE was the shadiest. We don't even know half the stuff the MKUltra guys did, because most of the documents were destroyed by the CIA. And those were the projects that were officially sanctioned by the CIA. GLARE was so sensitive that as far as I can tell, even the CIA didn't know what the people working there were doing. I can only guess, but we know for sure that Glazier was involved, and if you read some of the things he was saying at the time... well, it wouldn't be a surprise if GLARE was working on some pretty hair-raising stuff."

"Testing on civilians. Dumping chemicals in the water to see what they would do to people. You think this whole town was subject to some kind of experiment?"

"Like I said," Benjamin replied, "I just don't know. But I'm convinced that Glazier had Spiegel killed to cover it up. And fifty years later, Jessica figured it out, and he had her killed too."

"But Cameron Payne was in on it as well, right? Why didn't Glazier have him killed too?"

Benjamin nodded. "I've been thinking about that. I think something changed the equation. Jessica may have had an attack of conscience. That would explain why she was down at the creek. She was trying to determine if the dumping was still going on. She was okay with keeping the lid on a fifty-year-old murder, but if people were still being poisoned...."

"Yeah, okay," said Lentz, nodding. "For one reason or another, Jessica had second thoughts."

"Maybe she goes to Payne, tries to convince him they need to go public."

"But Payne, being the asshole he is, doesn't care. He just wants his money."

"Right. She goes to the creek to take a sample of the water. Maybe Payne comes with her, pretending to be sympathetic. And he kills her."

"And Glazier is in on it?" asked Lentz.

"Maybe, maybe not. Seems a little sloppy for Glazier. But he's part of the conspiracy, so he's as guilty as Payne. Payne tells him what he's done, and Glazier freaks out. He thought he could solve this problem on his own, the way he solves every problem—by throwing money at it. But Jessica's murder attracts too much attention. So he calls in his old pals in Washington to bail him out. The FBI swoops in, confiscates all our evidence, and takes Cameron Payne into custody."

"You think it was Hill and Kassel who attacked you and took the GLARE documents?"

Benjamin shook his head. "Again, too sloppy. That was Payne, trying to keep control of things. He's a loose cannon. No wonder Glazier had his friends lock him up."

Lentz was silent for a while. "Well," he said at last, "it's a nice story. I'm not sure I buy it, but it certainly would explain some things. Unfortunately, if it's anywhere close to the truth, we'll probably never know."

CHAPTER SEVENTEEN

Feeling tired and defeated, Benjamin returned to the motel. His cell phone rang the moment he stepped inside the room. It was Lucia.

"Benjamin, are you busy?" she asked.

"No," he said. "Why?"

"Felipe is still agitated. I can't seem to calm him down. What did you say to him?"

"I swear, Lucia," replied Benjamin, "I just asked him about his model. There was a discrepancy—"

"A what?" she asked.

"A mistake. Something in his model. A mistake I'd seen someone else make. It's hard to explain. I thought Felipe might know something. It was stupid. I'm sorry."

"Know something about what?"

"Honestly, I don't think I could explain it if I tried. Just something I noticed about his model. Like I said, stupid."

"Well, something you said made an impression on him. He keeps saying your name."

"My name?" asked Benjamin. "I didn't even *tell* him my name."

"He keeps saying 'Stone, Stone, Stone.'"

"Maybe it's a coincidence."

"Felipe hardly ever talks," Lucia said. "When he does, it's usually just mumbling about the placement of something in his model. Now suddenly he starts saying your name over and over, right after... whatever happened between you two?"

"I don't know what to tell you," said Benjamin. "I tried to ask him about his model. That's it. I'm certain I never said my name." A long pause followed. "Is there something I can do?"

"I don't know," said Lucia after a moment. "I think... I think he wants to tell you something."

Benjamin didn't reply. Lucia clearly wanted his help figuring out what was wrong with Felipe, but she was trying to maintain her air of disapproval. "If you don't think it will make things worse," he said at last, "I could come over and try to talk to him again."

Another long pause. "Could you?"

"Of course," said Benjamin. "I'll be right there."

When Benjamin arrived, Felipe was the same as he ever was. He simply stared at his model, without moving or speaking. He seemed to have no interest whatsoever in Benjamin.

"I don't understand it," said Lucia, as they stood in the doorway observing him. "He was rocking, and holding his head, and kept saying 'Stone, Stone, Stone.' Sofia was terrified. But he stopped just before you got here."

Benjamin didn't know what to say. "Should I try talking to him? I don't want to upset him again."

"I think it will be okay," said Lucia.

Benjamin nodded. "Felipe," he said quietly. "Did you have something to tell me?"

But Felipe made no sign of having heard him.

"Felipe," Benjamin said a little louder. "Lucia said you were saying my name. You were saying 'Stone, Stone, Stone.' Is that because you wanted me to come here? Did you want to say something to me?"

Felipe simply stared at the model, paying Benjamin no heed.

Benjamin turned to Lucia and shrugged.

"Well, at least he's quiet now," said Lucia. "I should check on Sofia."

She walked down the hall to the living room, and Benjamin followed. Sofia was curled up on the couch, clutching a pillow tightly.

"Felipe is better, Sofia," said Lucia. "You don't need to worry about him."

Sofia didn't respond.

Lucia sat down next to her, putting her hand on Sofia's knee. "Niña, qué pasa? Are you worried about Felipe?"

Sofia shook her head. Tears began to roll down her cheeks. "I keep seeing them, mamá. When I close my eyes, I see them."

"See what, mi cielo?"

"The buildings," said Lucia. "I can't stop seeing them."

Lucia sighed. "I'm sorry, sweetheart. I know. We'll figure it out. The doctors will help you."

Sofia nodded, but didn't seem convinced.

"I need to make dinner, mi niña. Do you want to watch some TV?"

She nodded again, and Lucia turned on the television. *Blue's Clues* came on, and Sofia was suddenly enraptured.

Sofia nodded to Benjamin and turned to go into the kitchen. He followed.

"What was that about?" said Benjamin quietly, once they were in the kitchen. Sofia was oblivious to them. "She sees buildings?"

Lucia sighed. "She's been having nightmares. She says she sees airplanes flying into two very tall buildings. At first I thought it was just something she saw on television, but the nightmares seem to be getting more vivid, and now she's says she's seeing them when she's awake."

So Sofia was having dreams too, thought Benjamin. Visions of some other place, some other time. Maybe just a fantasy constructed from flashes of things she saw on the news, but maybe something more.

"When did this start?" asked Benjamin.

"A few days ago," said Lucia. "The first dream was the night before I met you at Mr. Glazier's house. I didn't think anything of it at first, but they keep getting worse. I took her to the doctor this morning, but he wasn't much help. He referred me to a child psychologist. We're supposed to see him tomorrow."

Benjamin nodded. "Sofia has a vivid imagination," he said. "Jessica was the same way. She used to get all worked up about the craziest things. The things in her head were so real, she sometimes had a hard time distinguishing them from reality. She grew out of it. I'm sure Sofia will be fine. The psychologist should be able to help."

"I hope so," said Lucia. "I've already got my hands full with Felipe. And I'm worried Sofia...." She didn't need to finish the thought.

"You're afraid Sofia is going to end up like Felipe."

Lucia bit her lip, but didn't reply.

"It's really not my place to say," said Benjamin, "but I think you're borrowing trouble you don't need. Sofia is a very bright, very sociable little girl. I honestly don't think you have anything to worry about. There's nothing wrong with her." As he said it, Benjamin realized he believed it. There wasn't anything wrong with Sofia. Most likely she just had a powerful imagination. And even if the dreams were something more, it only meant that Sofia could see things others couldn't. That wasn't a disability; it was a gift. But then he remembered what Sabbia had said: Being able to see the future is too much for a person to take. What did that mean, exactly? That if Sofia possessed the gift of precognition, she would ultimately become self-destructive? Or was there another path?

"Felipe wasn't always like that," said Lucia.

"What do you mean?"

"He was a perfectly normal, happy child. That's what Papá says, anyway. He says something happened to Felipe when he was around Sofia's age. He changed. Became very quiet and started to spend all day in his room. Wouldn't participate in school. They took him to doctors, but no one could help. Finally they just left him alone. He's been like that ever since. He lives in his own fantasy world."

"There's no reason to think that's going to happen to Sofia," said Benjamin. "She's not Felipe. And psychology has come a long way since the 1950s. The doctors will help her, I promise."

Lucia nodded glumly. "I hope you're right," she said. "Well, I should start on dinner. Papá will be home soon. You're welcome to stay, if you like, but you have to stay out of my kitchen." She managed a weak smile at him.

"Do you mind if I try talking to Sofia?" he asked. "I know I don't have a great track record...."

"Don't feel bad about Felipe. He just gets worked up sometimes. You didn't know. And yes, please, talk to Sofia. She likes you."

Benjamin smiled and walked back to the couch. He sat down next to Sofia and watched *Blues Clues* with her for a while.

"I like Steve," said Sofia after some time. "He's cute."

"Yeah, he seems like a nice guy," said Benjamin. "Good with dogs. And salt shakers."

Sofia was quiet for a moment as the two of them watched Steve trying to puzzle out a clue. It reminded him of sitting on the couch with Jessica on his lap, watching Barney the dinosaur. He hated that big purple dinosaur, but he treasured those moments with Jessica.

"Do you see the buildings too?" asked Sofia.

"The buildings in your dream?" asked Benjamin. "I don't think so. What do they look like?"

Sofia shrugged. "Like buildings. Two of them. Really tall. The airplanes hit them. One of the buildings falls down. Then there's lots of smoke, and I can't breathe. That's when I wake up. Except now I see them when I'm awake too."

"Where are you, in the dream?"

"A big city. I'm late for my job. In the dream, I work in one of the buildings. But I never get there, because of the airplanes."

Benjamin shuddered, thinking about what Sabbia had said about someone projecting one's consciousness into the body of someone in the future. It sounded uncannily like what Sofia was describing. In her dreams, it wasn't Sofia witnessing the airplanes hitting the building. She was someone else. A woman who worked in the city.

It was a ridiculous notion, Sofia somehow unintentionally projecting her consciousness into the future, to witness an event that hadn't yet happened. And yet, he couldn't help reflecting on his own dreams, which had inexplicably led him to the water bottle Jessica had dropped while fleeing her murderer. His dreams had given him insight only into the past, but they were no less unexplainable for that. How much harder was it to believe that Sofia was seeing into the future? He'd heard anecdotes about people having dreams foretelling train wrecks and other accidents. But airplanes hitting buildings?

"How many airplanes are there?" he asked Sofia.

"Two," replied Lucia. "The first one hits one of the buildings. And then a little bit later, another airplane hits the other building."

A strange sort of accident, thought Benjamin. Maybe some sort of terrorist attack?

Lucia's father came home not much later, grunted a welcome, and sat down in his chair. He flipped the station to the news and Sofia went to her room. The newscaster was talking about Cameron

129

Payne's disappearance and the uncertain future of XKredits. He then segued into another story, about the collapse of several other high-profile startups in Silicon Valley. A talking head dismissed the string of bankruptcies as a "momentary correction" that would have little impact on the financial juggernaut of Silicon Valley, but Benjamin sensed a deep uneasiness hiding behind the man's words. The same intuition that had seen through Glazier's performance at the anniversary banquet was now communicating the unspoken message behind the talking head's words: the "dot com boom" was over.

Benjamin got up and helped Lucia set the table. She made lasagna, which was delicious. But this time there was little laughter and no talk of Sofia's prodigious imagination.

CHAPTER EIGHTEEN

Benjamin leaped the creek, managing this time to land without losing his footing. He kept going, pursuing the boy at top speed. The dark castle loomed in the distance.

Getting within a few paces of the boy, he dove at his legs, throwing his arms around the boy's ankles. The boy went sprawling on the orchard floor.

Out of breath and shaking with adrenaline, Benjamin scrambled forward and grabbed the boy's right wrist, twisting it behind his back. This time, he wasn't going to get away.

But then the boy screamed. It was the same scream he had heard at Lucia's house, the same ear-piercing, soul-wrenching howl. More than just sound, it was like some kind of visceral vibration that threatened to tear Benjamin's brain apart. And it just kept going, and going, and going. Benjamin realized he had no choice: he was going to have to let the boy go.

The screaming stopped the moment he did. The boy flipped onto his back and scrabbled away from him, those familiar eyes glaring at him in anger or terror.

"Please," gasped Benjamin. "I'm trying to help you."

The boy didn't reply. He got to his feet, trying to catch his breath.

"What is that place?" asked Benjamin.

The boy shook his head. "Shhh!" he hissed. With that, he turned and ran, disappearing once again into the blackness.

The dream weighed on him more heavily this morning. In the past, it always seemed like there was a chance he could keep the boy from going into the castle, but now he realized it was impossible. Not just impossible to prevent, it was predetermined. The boy was always going to end up in the castle. That's how the dream was always going to end.

He didn't know why it bothered him so much. Even if the boy in the dream was Felipe, why did the dream matter? What was the castle? What was going to happen to Felipe there? The answer had to be in the dream, but Benjamin couldn't imagine what it was. There were no obvious clues. Just the same scene, over and over.

While he was trying to puzzle this out over breakfast at a nearby Denny's, Lentz called.

"Good morning, Detective," said Benjamin. "Any luck getting anything out of the FBI?"

"None," said Lentz. "I had my boss call them this morning. They're stonewalling us. Now they're claiming it's a matter of national security."

"Figures," said Benjamin. "That's the go-to excuse for the feds when they're covering up something embarrassing."

"Yeah, I gotta admit," replied Lentz, "your wacky conspiracy theory is getting more believable all the time. That isn't what I called to tell you, though."

"Yeah? Then why did you call?"

"Chris Sandford," said Lentz. "He's talking."

"Talking? You mean he confessed?" He wouldn't put it past Glazier or his FBI cronies to have somehow manipulated Chris Sandford into confessing to a crime he hadn't committed. Even in jail, he doubted Sandford was completely beyond Glazier's reach.

"No," said Lentz. "Actually, it might be better if you just come down here."

"Alright," said Benjamin. "Be there as soon as I can."

Benjamin paid the bill and walked to his car. Ten minutes later he was back in the conference room, sitting across from Chris Sandford. Lentz sat next to Benjamin. Sandford seemed even more anxious than the last time Benjamin talked to him. His hair was disheveled and his eyes were bloodshot. It didn't look like he had slept since he'd been taken into custody.

"Why don't you tell Mr. Stone what you were telling me," said Lentz to Sandford.

Sandford nodded. Evidently he'd either decided Lentz wasn't in on the conspiracy or that there was no point in trying to hide what he knew anymore. "It's bigger than I thought," he said. "I thought it was just the cops, you know? Maybe the government. But it's the whole *city*. He runs it. He runs *everything*."

"Who, Glazier?" asked Benjamin.

Sandford nodded again. "I've been having these flashes. They started a while back, but now I'm seeing things more clearly. I see it. Sunnyview, I see it for what it is. I mean, it's not even a city. It's, like, a *construct*."

Benjamin shot a glance at Lentz, who nodded, as if to say, "Keep listening."

"What do you mean, a 'construct?'" asked Benjamin.

"I can't explain it," said Sandford. "It's like a mass delusion. I mean, it's real enough to the people in it, but only because they're in it. They're not real either. Most of the time I'm one of them, but sometimes I can see it, like, from the outside."

"And why is Glazier doing this?" asked Benjamin.

"I don't know," said Sandford, shaking his head. "I think it's like an experiment. We're like rats in a maze. Except we're not even real rats! We're just, like, the *idea* of rats."

Benjamin was becoming frustrated. He wanted to think Sandford knew something about the conspiracy, but so far all of this just sounded like the ravings of a sleep-deprived, paranoid narcissist. None of it was going to help him find his daughter or get justice.

"How is he doing it?" Lentz interjected. "Tell Mr. Stone what you told me."

Sandford nodded. "Something in the water," he said. "That much I know for sure. They dump chemicals in the water, near the creek. It filters through the sand and gets in the water supply."

Lentz gave Benjamin a meaningful glance, but Benjamin shrugged. It was a coincidence, sure, but diabolical entities dumping mind-altering chemicals into the water supply was standard conspiracy theory stuff. Sandford could have gotten that idea anywhere. And his logic was faulty.

"So everything we're experiencing right now is part of an experiment?" asked Benjamin.

"Exactly," replied Sandford.

"And this whole city is an illusion?" asked Benjamin.

Sandford nodded.

"But the creek running through it is real?"

Sandford opened his mouth as if to say something, then closed it again. He clearly hadn't thought this through. "I don't know how it all works," he said at last.

"Okay," said Benjamin. He turned to Lentz. "I think I've heard enough." Lentz looked like he wanted to protest, but didn't say anything. Benjamin got up and walked out. Lentz followed him. A uniformed officer waited in the hall.

"Put him back in the holding cell for now," said Lentz. The officer nodded and went into the room. Lentz followed Benjamin outside.

"You don't think it's a little weird," Lentz said, "Sandford coming up with that story about chemicals in the water? I mean, the rest of it is out there, I'll grant you, but how do you explain the water thing? Isn't that exactly what you were saying about this GLARE operation? They dumped chemicals in the water?"

Benjamin stopped and turned to face Lentz. "So now suddenly you believe in a big, malevolent conspiracy running Sunnyview? Because of what that nutcase said?"

Lentz stared at him. "I don't get you, Stone. Yesterday you were trying to sell me on this conspiracy, and now you're calling Chris Sandford a nutcase because he corroborates your story?"

Benjamin bit his lip. Lentz had a point. Was he being hostile to Sandford's story because it didn't make sense, or because it sounded so much like his own? Up to this point, Benjamin had felt like he had some control over the narrative—that maybe whatever seemed to be happening in Sunnyview somehow revolved around him. In a strange way, he had found comfort in his own psychosis—the idea that there was something wrong with him, but that the world outside him continued to make sense. But now he was being confronted with the evidence of the reality of the conspiracy, and it unnerved him.

"Alright," Benjamin said. "So what do you make of his story? Are you saying you believe it?"

"Not all of it," said Lentz. "Of course I don't buy that crap about having visions of the behind-the-scenes workings of the 'real Sunnyview.' My thinking was that he overheard something Jessica said to Payne or Glazier, and he's just now remembering it, though a fog of self-delusion. In other words, I think it's partial confirmation of your theory that Jessica was killed to cover up Glazier's past sins."

"Yeah," said Benjamin, without enthusiasm. "But your investigation is stalled while you wait for the feds to figure out what to do with XKredits, and you may recall that you barred me from pursuing the investigation on my own. In any case, the more I try to make sense out of what happened to Jessica, the less sense it makes."

Lentz nodded. "Truth is, I'm as frustrated as you are by this case. I guess I thought having Sandford talk to you might trigger an idea for a different way to approach it. But you're right, it's just more unsubstantiated hearsay."

"You going to let Sandford go?"

"I'm going to have to. Between his personal history with Jessica and the glasses, we've got a pretty good case against him, but...."

"But you don't think he did it."

"No. If he's involved at all, he was being manipulated by someone else, most likely Glazier or Payne. And if that's the case, we're better off letting him go and keeping an eye on him, see if he tries to make contact with either of them. But frankly I don't see it happening. I get the feeling that he's told us everything he knows."

"And a lot of stuff he doesn't," said Benjamin. "Not to mention that you have no corpse, which could make things awkward during the trial."

"Yeah," said Lentz. "The feds have pretty well fucked us both on this case. Anyway, I'll call you if I hear anything."

Benjamin got some lunch and then went back to the library. Whatever the FBI was doing, it had to have something to do with Glazier and GLARE. GLARE was not just something that happened in the past; in some form it lived on, and Glazier was still involved. Benjamin could feel it in his bones. There was something deeply rotten about that program, something that had caused the government to keep it even more deeply buried than Operation Paperclip or Project MKUltra. Something that was still going on.

He spent the next couple of hours researching the history of chemical dumping in the Sunnyview area. As much as he hated to admit it, he was starting to think he had dismissed Chris Sandford's ravings too quickly. Sandford had gotten under his skin, and not because he had been wasting Benjamin's time. On some level Benjamin feared that Chris Sandford was just a little farther down the continuum that Benjamin himself was on. The line between his dreams and reality had begun to blur, and the past, present, and future were getting all jumbled together. And the craziest part of Sandford's story, the part that would have once rung warning bells in Benjamin's mind, was the one part he was fairly certain was true: at some point, evil men had poisoned Sunnyview's water supply with brain altering chemicals. Everything else was just details.

What had Sandford said exactly? That Sunnyview was a "construct," whatever that meant. Some sort of mass delusion, Benjamin supposed. But he got the impression that Sandford didn't even think the people experiencing the delusion were real. *We're like rats in a maze. Except we're not even real rats! We're just, like, the idea of rats.*

Solipsism, thought Benjamin. The idea that everything is illusory except for me. Except that Chris Sandford thought Chris Sandford was also part of the illusion. He, Benjamin, Lentz, Jessica—they were all ideas in someone else's mind. Glazier's, evidently.

No, Benjamin couldn't quite get there. Glazier was a powerful man, but he was just a man. And Benjamin wasn't an idea in anyone's head. If he were, what would be the point of trying to solve a murder, or to figure out what was really going on? An idea would never be given free rein, would never be able to penetrate the secrets of the mind that created it. And Benjamin couldn't accept that. Wouldn't accept it.

His rejection of Sandford's solipsism wasn't the result of philosophical rumination so much as a feeling in his gut. There was an answer here, somewhere. He could feel it. His dreams pointed toward it, and the clues—frustrating and contradictory as they were—were helping him get there. He just needed to trust his gut, and trust the deductive process he'd used to solve hundreds of crimes in the past. The answer was here in Sunnyview, and he was going to find it.

He wasn't going to find it at the library, though. He spent another three hours combing through old newspaper stories about dumping, class action lawsuits, the EPA and Superfund, but nothing that remotely connected to GLARE or any other aspect of his daughter's murder. No, his gut told him the answer wasn't to be found in old newspaper articles.

He left the library and went for a walk, strolling downtown and trying to imagine it as it once was, a sleepy farming town surrounded by orchards. Orchards like the one he had grown up on, backing up against Sand Hill Creek. The creek that GLARE had polluted.

Benjamin had spent thousands of hours playing in and around that creek as a child. He had resisted thinking about it until now, but the truth was, if anyone could have been expected to experience adverse effects from exposure to the creek water, it was Benjamin. But he had rarely been sick a day in his life. Even at fifty-eight, Benjamin was remarkably healthy, the only overt sign of his age being a little occasional stiffness in his joints. And he certainly hadn't had any obvious mental or psychological problems. Had he?

That was the problem with mental illness; you couldn't trust your brain to diagnose it. But he'd passed a psych examination to become a cop, and he'd managed to hold down a job with the Portland police for thirty years. Sure, he'd had some problems with depression and drinking, but he'd never experienced hallucinations or anything like a psychotic break. By any reasonable standard, he was a normal, psychologically healthy individual. On the other hand, there were psychotics who had imagined extremely convincing and detailed pasts for themselves. How could he possibly know that he wasn't one of them?

He shook his head, arresting that train of thought. That way led to Sandford's pointless solipsism. No, he had to trust his own experiences and his reasoning. Somehow the two would bring him to an answer.

Benjamin was still contemplating this thought when he saw a young boy with brown skin and black hair darting across an intersection to the other side of the street. He was wearing pajamas.

Felipe.

It couldn't be, Benjamin thought. Felipe was a grown man. What Benjamin was seeing had to be some sort of hallucination.

137

The stress of his daughter's death was getting to him, making him see things. But the little boy in the pajamas continued running down the street away from Benjamin, looking very real indeed. And if Benjamin didn't pursue him, he would never know for sure.

Benjamin crossed the street, barely dodging a Lexus whose angry driver honked and swore at him, and ran after the little boy. Nobody else seemed to notice the boy running down the street in bare feet and pajamas, which lent weight to the notion that he was a figment of Benjamin's imagination. Even with bare feet running on pavement, the boy was as fast as he was in the dream, and Benjamin struggled to gain on him, dodging pedestrians as he ran. Finally Benjamin stopped, cupping his hands over his mouth.

"Felipe!" shouted Benjamin, as a trio of window-shopping women stopped to stare at him. He thought he saw the boy slow for a moment, but then he continued running. Benjamin cursed and ran after him.

His heart pounding in his chest, he gradually gained on the boy. The boy crossed an intersection and kept going, oblivious to the flashing *Don't Walk* sign. Traffic rules didn't apply to ghosts, thought Benjamin. It occurred to him as he approached the corner that Felipe was heading west toward the creek, just as he had in the dream. Where was he going? In the dream, he had been running to the dark castle beyond the creek, but there was no castle in modern-day Sunnyview. Benjamin was halfway across the street when he heard an unmistakable voice calling out to him from across the street to his right.

He knew it was her before he even turned to look. It was impossible, but it was her. Jessica.

She stood on the corner, wearing the same blouse and pants she was wearing the day she died. Her hair was damp and matted. Another hallucination, thought Benjamin. Soon I'm going to be imagining phantoms on every corner.

It was the last thought that went through his mind before he was struck by a car and thrown to the ground.

CHAPTER NINETEEN

The car hadn't been going fast; when the light changed, it had rolled forward a few feet before the driver noticed Benjamin stopped in the middle of the street. The car stopped and the driver, a swarthy young man with a long beard and turban, threw open his door and ran to check on Benjamin. Benjamin was dazed and embarrassed but unhurt. He waved off the turbaned man and stepped back to the curb. People on all four corners of the intersection were staring at him, and he nervously walked back the way he had come. Jessica was nowhere to be seen.

Things were getting out of hand. The dreams had been bad enough, but now the visions were spilling over into real life—not unlike Sofia's visions. But his visions weren't of the future; they were of the past. Was he going insane? How would he know? If I see things that aren't real, but I know they aren't real, am I still going crazy?

Why was he seeing these things, these people? Why Felipe? As crazy as it was to see his dead daughter standing on a street corner looking like she had just crawled out of the creek bed, at least the vision of Jessica made some sense from a psychological standpoint. The vision of Jessica might have been a manifestation of his guilt over his daughter's death. But what was with his fixation on Felipe? He had never even known Felipe as a young boy. Why did he keep seeing him? And why had Jessica not appeared until now? Maybe it was a symptom of the progression of his madness, but it seemed to him that Jessica's appearance had been an afterthought, or even a response to his vision of Felipe.

Yes, he thought. Thesis and antithesis. Two competing ideas fighting it out in his subconscious. Felipe had wanted Benjamin to follow him, but Jessica had stopped him. Why? Did she not want him to know what happened to Felipe? Did she want the evils of GLARE to remain hidden? Did she want her own murder to go unsolved?

Well, if that's what she wanted, she was going to have to try a little harder. He wasn't going to give up so easily. He wanted nothing more than to get in the Buick, drive back to Portland, and try to get on with his life, forgetting all about Sunnyview. But there was still something about GLARE, something about Jessica's death that he didn't understand. And there was something about himself, something about who he was, that he had yet to understand. Until he did, he would never be able to leave Sunnyview behind.

He returned to the motel and lay down, but was unable to sleep. When he closed his eyes, he saw his daughter standing on the street corner, her clothes wet, an unreadable expression on her face. "What do you want me to do, sweetheart?" he murmured aloud. "Just tell me what you want me to do."

This thought was still tormenting him when his phone rang. It was Lucia, asking him if he wanted to come over for dinner again. Benjamin accepted the invitation, maybe a little too eagerly. He hadn't realized how desperate he was not to be alone. Maybe it was foolish to think that being around other people would protect him from any more unsettling visitations, but it was worth a shot. Besides, he was growing to like Lucia and her family—even her crotchety Papá. And he got the impression she liked him as well. He hadn't allowed himself to give much thought to his future beyond solving Jessica's murder, but he wouldn't mind eating dinner with Lucia and her family every night. The only flaw with that idea was Felipe. Benjamin was still convinced that Felipe knew something about Sunnyview, something that had to do with Jessica's death. As long as Felipe was around, Benjamin didn't think he'd ever be able to fully let go of his suspicions.

Dinner was delicious as usual, and the mood at the house was a little more positive than the night before. Sofia had seen a child psychologist, who had prescribed her a low dose of an anti-anxiety medication. The psychologist had also scheduled an MRI for Sofia the next morning. He assured Lucia that it was merely a precaution to make sure there were no neurological problems contributing to Sofia's condition. Lucia was clearly worried, but trying to put on a brave face for Sofia. Sofia, being the perceptive child she was, saw right through this. "It's okay, Mamá," she said. "They're just going to take a picture of my brain. Taking pictures doesn't hurt."

Lucia smiled and laughed. "No, mi cielo. You're right. Taking pictures doesn't hurt."

CHAPTER TWENTY

Benjamin leaped the creek, managing to land without losing his footing. He kept going, pursuing the boy at top speed. The dark castle loomed in the distance.

Getting within a few paces of the boy, he dove at his legs, throwing his arms around the boy's ankles. The boy went sprawling on the orchard floor.

Out of breath and shaking with adrenaline, Benjamin scrambled forward and grabbed the boy's right wrist, twisting it behind his back. The boy screamed again, the same horrible scream Felipe had emitted at Lucia's house. It was too much to take. Once again, he had to let the boy go.

The boy flipped onto his back and scrabbled away from him.

"Please," gasped Benjamin. "I'm not going to hurt you. Just tell me what that place is. The dark castle."

The boy shook his head. "Shhh!" he hissed. He got to his feet and ran, disappearing once again into the blackness.

Benjamin sat up, his fists clutched in frustration. There had to be a reason for the dream. Something he was missing. He obsessed over it as he showered, shaved, and got dressed, going over and over it in his mind, trying to identify something in the dream that might give him a clue as to the meaning. Why was the boy running to the castle? What was inside? And why did it make Benjamin so afraid? Three times he'd asked the boy what the castle was, but the boy hadn't answered.

No, that wasn't true, Benjamin realized. The boy—Felipe—had said "Shhh." Every time. Benjamin had assumed that the boy was afraid to talk about it, but maybe Benjamin had been misinterpreting him. Maybe Felipe *was* answering him.

Benjamin grabbed a pen and notepad from the nightstand and scrawled on it:

SHH

Except the way Felipe said it, it was more drawn out. Three Hs, Benjamin decided.

SHHH

A chill crept up his spine. He scribbled below this:

SHCH

"Shhh," said Benjamin. That's how a young child, unfamiliar with abbreviations, might pronounce that string of letters, if he ran across them on a nametag or written onto a tag on his pajamas. SHCH. Sand Hill Children's Hospital. The building that sat on the reported location of Spiegel's fatal car accident. The intersection that didn't exist. The dark castle of his dreams.

Of course. Glazier had moved the hospital to a newer, larger building shortly after Spiegel's death, supposedly to honor his friend's memory. But what if his real motivation was to expand on the work that GLARE had begun? With Spiegel out of the way, GLARE had free rein to experiment on Sunnyview's most vulnerable citizens: the children.

Benjamin still didn't understand how it was possible for Spiegel's accident to have occurred at an intersection that didn't exist at the time of the accident. It was like the universe had conspired to tell him something terribly wrong had happened at that place. His dreams had been telling him as well, but he had been too confused to understand. In the dreams, Felipe had vanished inside the castle. Is that what had happened to Felipe? Had he been subjected to some sort of experiments at the hands of GLARE, in the name of national security? Lucia said that he had been a normal child until something happened to him, when he was around Sofia's age.

144

Sofia. Benjamin's heart sank. Lucia had said Sofia was scheduled for an MRI this morning. She hadn't said where, but he had a sickening feeling he knew. Somehow the bastards at GLARE had found out about Sofia's visions, and they were planning on capitalizing on her abilities. Benjamin couldn't let that happen. He couldn't let Sofia turn out like Felipe.

He called Lucia, and cursed himself for his denseness while the phone rang twice, three times, four times… and then Lucia picked up.

"Hello?" she said.

"Lucia, it's Benjamin."

"Hello, Benjamin. Can this wait? I've got to get Sofia to her appointment. I'm already running late because she's being difficult."

"That's what I called about," said Benjamin. "You can't take her to that place. Sand Hill Children's Hospital."

"How did you know where her appointment is? I didn't—"

"Lucia, you need to trust me. There's something very wrong with that place. You can't take Sofia there."

"Can we discuss this later? It was lucky that I could get Sofia in on such short notice."

"No!" Benjamin cried. "Please, Lucia. Reschedule the appointment. No, don't do that. Just stay home. I'm coming over."

"Benjamin, you're talking crazy. I'm not going to miss this appointment. Please do not come over."

"Felipe," said Benjamin. "He was there as a child, wasn't he?"

Lucia didn't reply.

"I know he was," said Benjamin. "He had the same thing Sofia has. Visions of another time, another place. They did something to him, made him the way he is. That's what's going to happen to Sofia if you take her there."

The line was silent for a moment. "That is a horrible thing to say," said Lucia coldly.

"I know, and I'm sorry," said Benjamin. "But it doesn't have to be that way. There's nothing wrong with Lucia. She doesn't need a doctor. She just has… an overactive imagination. We can help her learn how to deal with it. But you can't take her to that place. Please, I'm begging you, for Sofia's sake. Don't take her there."

There was another long pause. Then Lucia asked, "Are you going to explain to me how you know all of this?"

"Yes," said Benjamin, although as he said it, he wondered if he even *could* explain it. "I'll be right there. I'll explain everything. Just don't leave the house."

"Fine," said Lucia. "Hurry up, before I change my mind."

Benjamin hung up, grabbed his keys and ran out the door. He got in the Buick and drove to Lucia's house. But when he got there, Lucia's car wasn't out front, and a man wearing a suit was sitting on the front porch steps: Agent Hill. Benjamin parked on the street and walked toward him. "Where are they?" he demanded. "Where are Lucia and Sofia?"

"Agent Kassel went with them to Sofia's appointment. She said you tried to talk her out of going. We explained that you are a very dangerous, unbalanced man, and that it would be better for them not to be around when you showed up."

"You son of a bitch," growled Benjamin. "Glazier put you up to this, didn't he? What does he want with Sofia?"

"Good question," replied Agent Hill, getting to his feet. "Why don't you ask him yourself." He walked past Benjamin to his car. Benjamin stood and stared at him.

"Well?" said Hill. "Are you coming or not?"

Benjamin walked to the car and got in.

Twenty minutes later, Benjamin was back on William Glazier's back patio, sitting across from the old man. Agent Hill stood silently by the door.

"So you've got FBI agents working as your personal goons now," Benjamin observed.

"They don't work for me," said Glazier flatly. "We share the same goals."

"Covering your ass," said Benjamin.

Glazier sighed. "Is that what you think this is about?" he asked. "Keeping me out of trouble? Because I assure you, Mr. Stone, I was never in any danger. I'm very well insulated against any possible harm."

"The twenty million dollars you gave to Cameron Payne would seem to indicate otherwise," said Benjamin. "Seems like you were pretty anxious to keep him and Jessica quiet."

Glazier shrugged. "Sometimes the best tactical move is the liberal application of cash. When the situation changes, tactics have to change."

"Is that what the murder of my daughter was?" said Benjamin, unable to hide his rage. "A change in tactics?"

"Not that it's going to make you feel any better," said Glazier, "but that was Payne acting on his own. And I assure you he won't be making that sort of mistake again."

"You're still to blame," said Benjamin.

"Fair enough," replied Glazier. "I'll be judged for my sins in time, no doubt. But everything I did was for my country and the survival of the human race."

"Including performing experiments on young children. That was the point of GLARE, right?"

Glazier looked impressed. "Just how much do you know about GLARE?" he asked.

"I know it started as a counter-intelligence program during World War II, but after that it morphed into a more general program to counter perceived threats to U.S. interests. I know that Glazier Semiconductor was dumping dangerous chemicals into Sunnyview's water supply for years, and that either accidentally or on purpose, you triggered some sort of mutation in some of Sunnyview's residents—children, mainly. Something that allowed them to see visions of the future. Visions that GLARE used to gather intelligence about future threats. You got on the board of Sand Hill Children's Hospital so that you'd be in a position to identify children with this mutation, study them, and experiment on them in order to determine how to fully take advantage of their gift. Your partner, Dominick Spiegel, grew a conscience at some point and threatened to go public. You had him killed. You then donated a large sum of money to Sand Hill Children's Hospital in order to move it to a new building to expand the program. How am I doing?"

"Alarmingly well," said Glazier. "Tell me, Benjamin, how did you come to learn all of this?"

"Old-fashioned detective work," said Benjamin.

"And the occasional flash of insight," said Glazier.

"Hunches will only get you so far," replied Benjamin. "It's still going on, isn't it? Maybe you've gotten more careful about how you deliver the chemicals to your subjects, but you're still experimenting on children."

"Yes and no," said Glazier. "We stopped dumping chemicals in the water supply in the seventies. But the mutation is passed down from one generation the next. We have a system in place for flagging individuals who show signs of precognitive ability. They get referred to Sand Hill, where we attempt to quantify the level of precognition. Usually it goes no further than that. But occasionally we find a child who is truly gifted. Those are the ones who can fully project their consciousness into the future."

"Like Sofia Sanz."

"I'm hearing promising reports," said Glazier. "But I'm not much involved in the day-to-day operations anymore. I understand her visions show her a possible terrorist attack. Airplanes hitting buildings."

"Probably just an accident," said Benjamin.

"Two different planes hitting two different buildings, very close together? Unlikely. The trick is going to be to figure out where and when it happens. That's the maddening thing about this. After fifty years, we still have very little control over what the subjects see. Some of them are projected mere days into the future, others years. We once had a subject who was able to project himself nearly fifty years ahead. But the information the subject brings back is often trivial. Usually the subject is only able to witness a few minutes of the future, and frequently there isn't enough context to determine when or where the events occurred. We've had a few successes, but they've been few and far between. Hopefully Sofia Sanz will be one of the exceptions."

"What are they going to do to her?"

"They're not going to harm her, if that's your concern," said Glazier. "Sometimes they use pharmaceuticals to treat anxiety or to increase concentration. Hypnosis sometimes helps. Mostly they'll just listen."

"The way they 'listened' to her great uncle?"

"Felipe," said Glazier, with a nod. "He was a tricky one. Very strong precognitive ability. Sadly, we never got any useful information out of him. But our methods were much cruder back then."

"You reduced him to a shell of himself. He never had a chance at a normal life."

"We did what we did in the interest of national security. Believe it or not, Mr. Stone, this country does have enemies. This program has done more to keep us safe than any other single government agency, and I won't apologize for it."

"You keep people safe by kidnapping little girls?" said Benjamin.

"It rarely comes to that," said Glazier. "But if it did, I wouldn't hesitate. Are you familiar with the term Autumn Forge?"

"Doesn't ring any bells," said Benjamin.

"Not surprising," said Glazier. "It isn't nearly as well-known as, say, the Cuban Missile Crisis. Some analysts—including me—believe Autumn Forge is the closest we ever came to war with the Soviet Union. "

"And you're going to tell me that GLARE prevented that war?" asked Benjamin.

"It's impossible to know for sure," said Glazier. "This isn't an exact science. There are no control groups. We can never know for sure what didn't happen as a result of what we did. But I can tell you that one of our subjects, a girl named Marina Evans, foresaw what appeared to be the aftermath of a nuclear strike in Eastern Europe in late 1983. Using the information Marina provided, we were able to work with the CIA to trace the cause of the strike to the Soviets misinterpreting NATO troop movements in Finland. At the time, the United States had underestimated Soviet paranoia regarding a nuclear first strike by the west, so we explained the situation to President Reagan. He sent a communique to Yuri Andropov reassuring him the U.S. had no intention of starting a war, and scaled back our maneuvers in Finland. As I said, it's impossible to know for certain what might have happened if we hadn't acted on that intelligence, but I think it's likely we saved millions of lives."

"Is that why you brought me here?" Benjamin asked. "To sell me on the benefits of your wonderful program?"

"I thought you deserved to know the truth," said Glazier. "After all that you've gone through. But yes, I also hoped to help you see the big picture."

"All I see is you taking advantage of children," said Benjamin.

Glazier shrugged. "It's the nature of our work. Our successes go unnoticed, and our sins will eventually be revealed. History can judge me."

Benjamin found himself laughing.

"Did I say something funny?" asked Glazier.

"You don't have any intention of letting history judge you," Benjamin said. "My daughter uncovered part of your unsavory history, and you had her killed."

"As I said, that was—"

"Yeah, sure," said Benjamin. "Cameron Payne acting alone. Convenient for you, though. And then there was that bullshit story in the *Herald*. I still don't know how you pulled that off."

Glazier's brow furrowed. "I'm not sure what you mean," he said.

"You rewrote the story about Spiegel's death, after the fact. Somehow managed to replace every existent copy of that issue of the *Sunnyview Herald* with a fake story. For somebody who wants to be judged by history, you put a hell of a lot of effort into covering up what really happened to Spiegel."

"I'll admit I wasn't eager for the truth about Spiegel to come out," said Glazier, "but only because it would have led to unwanted scrutiny of GLARE, handicapping our efforts to keep this country safe. But I never faked any news stories."

"Okay," said Benjamin, unconvinced. "Well, the next time you don't fake a news story, find someone who has a better grasp on the geography of Sunnyview in the 1950s. The intersection where Spiegel was supposedly killed? It didn't exist in 1952."

Glazier regarded Benjamin, a puzzled expression on his face. "Dominick Spiegel was killed at the intersection of Fremont and Olive. Did the *Herald* report otherwise?"

Benjamin studied the old man. Was Glazier playing him? Or had he simply read the erroneous report so many times it had replaced the truth in his mind?

"Fremont and Olive is what the *Herald* reported," said Benjamin. "As you well know."

"And you're saying that intersection didn't exist in 1952?"

"Playing dumb doesn't suit you," said Benjamin. "You know better than anyone what was on that spot in 1952."

Glazier stared at him for some time, not speaking. "Yes," he said at last. "Of course. I must have remembered the accident incorrectly."

"Hazard of being a pathological liar," said Benjamin. "Are we done here?"

Glazier nodded, studying Benjamin with an inscrutable expression. "Yes," he said. "I believe we are."

CHAPTER TWENTY-ONE

Agent Hill drove Benjamin back to Lucia's house to get his car. Lucia's car was still gone. Felipe was probably inside, but Hill made it pretty clear Benjamin wasn't going to be allowed near the family again. Sofia was too valuable to GLARE or whatever they were calling it these days to let that happen. Once again, Benjamin was stymied in his efforts to find the truth. He'd come to Sunnyview to determine what had happened to his daughter, but had run into an impenetrable wall set up by the national security apparatus. He didn't have a chance in the face of that. And whatever thoughts he might have had about seeing more of Lucia in the future had been dashed as well. He was considering packing his suitcase and heading home when his phone rang. Lentz.

"What is it, Lentz?" said Benjamin tiredly. "The FBI is impounding my car?"

"I need you to get over here," said Lentz. "Your friend Lucia and her daughter are here. Lucia is pretty upset."

Benjamin stood. "Where?"

"At my house. Lucia called the office. She mentioned your name, so they transferred her to me. She said the FBI showed up at her house earlier, were saying you were some kind of nutcase. Agent Kassel went with her to her daughter's appointment, supposedly to protect them from you, but she said they seemed real interested in making sure she got to that appointment. Stone, what do these people want with a little girl?"

"She's one of their research subjects," said Benjamin. "Or will be, if Glazier's people have their way. Did they make the appointment? How did they get away from Kassel?"

"Yeah, they met some doctor at Sand Hill Children's Hospital. Didn't say too much about it, but they both seem a little wigged out. Somehow they managed to ditch Kassel afterward and get to a phone booth."

"Alright," said Benjamin. "I'll be right over. What's the address?"

Lentz gave it to him. Benjamin knew the area; it wasn't far from downtown. Benjamin grabbed his suitcase and jogged to the car. He threw the suitcase in the trunk, got in and fired up the engine. Ten minutes later he was at the address Lentz had given him. It was an older working class neighborhood, a step or two up from the Sand Hill Creek area where Lucia lived.

He ran to the door and knocked. Seconds later, Lentz opened the door a crack. He was holding his gun.

"Stone, come in," said Lentz. He was calm but clearly on edge.

Lucia and Sofia sat on a couch in his living room. Benjamin thought he saw Lucia hug her daughter a little tighter as he approached.

"Hey," Benjamin said quietly. "It's just me. Are you two okay?"

Lucia nodded. "What is going on, Benjamin?" she asked. "That FBI agent, he said you were crazy. But he knew about Sofia's appointment. Did you tell him?"

Benjamin shook his head. "It's the people running the hospital," he said. "They have friends at the FBI. I think they're interested in Sofia because of her visions. How did you get away?"

"I told Sofia she could have a candy bar if she was good at the doctor's. But then on the way home, I told her we didn't have time because we didn't want to make Mr. Kassel late. Sofia didn't take it well."

"Because you promised!" Sofia said accusingly.

"I know, mi cielo," said Sofia, hugging her. "I'm sorry, I had to say that to get the man to go away." She smiled at Benjamin. "Sofia started crying. Mr. Kassel felt bad and said we could stop at the 7-Eleven. When he went in the store, I drove away and called the police. Detective Lentz said to meet him here. Why are they so interested in Sofia?"

"The visions she has," Benjamin said. "They think she's seeing the future."

"The future?" said Lucia. "That's crazy. She's just a little girl." She looked to Lentz as if wanting confirmation. Lentz just shrugged.

"I don't pretend to understand what's happening here," he said. "But it does seem like the feds are trying to cover up something pretty big. Something involving William Glazier."

"Mr. Glazier?" Lucia asked. "What does he have to do with this?"

"He started a project back in the 1940s to take advantage of children with special abilities," said Benjamin. "Children like Sofia. And Felipe. Felipe was one of the first. I don't want to give them a chance to do to Sofia what they…" He trailed off, looking at Sofia, who seemed to be nodding off on the couch. "What did they do to her at the hospital?"

"They gave her some tests," said Lucia. "And we talked to a doctor, Doctor Zanders. He asked Sofia a lot of questions."

"About the buildings she sees? The airplanes?"

"Of course," said Lucia.

"What kind of questions?" asked Benjamin. "Did it seem like he was trying to figure out why she was having these visions, or was he asking for a lot of details about the visions? Like what the buildings looked like, and whether she saw any street signs, that sort of thing?"

"No," said Lucia softly, shaking her head. "No, I don't believe any of this. It's crazy. People seeing the future? Mr. Glazier doing experiments on children? No. This all started when you showed up, Benjamin."

"Me?" asked Benjamin, surprised. "This has been going on long before I got here. I didn't make Felipe the way he is."

"Don't talk about Felipe," Lucia snapped. "Felipe was fine before you got here. Ever since you arrived, he's been acting strange, agitated. And Sofia's nightmares started right after you came to town. There's something about you, Benjamin. I don't know if it's completely your fault, but there's something not right about you."

It hurt Benjamin to hear Lucia talking this way. She was the one person in this town that had seemed to always think the best of him, despite his own doubts. Now that she was attacking him, he came to realize how much he'd come to rely on that support.

"Please, Lucia," he said. "I only came here to find my daughter. I didn't—"

"Your daughter, who ran away and wouldn't talk to you. What did you do to her, Benjamin?"

Lentz was beginning to look very uncomfortable. He seemed to want to intervene, but feared making things worse.

"Jesus, Lucia," said Benjamin. "What kind of person do you think I am? I told you I wasn't a great father, but I never intentionally hurt Jessica. I came here hoping to find her, hoping to make things right...."

"Well, you haven't," said Lucia. "You just keep making things worse. You need to leave this town, Benjamin. Things are never going to be right here until you leave."

"Lucia," said Benjamin. "You can't—"

"Oh my God," Sofia suddenly said, her eyes wide open. "What is happening to me?"

"Sofia," said Lucia, still holding her daughter close. "It's okay. I'm with you. We're at a friend's house. A policeman."

Lentz smiled and nodded at Sofia, trying his best to look reassuring.

"Oh my God," said Sofia again, recoiling from her mother's touch. "Oh my God." She pulled away from Lucia and got off the couch. She stood for a moment, looking dizzy and uncertain.

Lucia leaned toward her and reached out to take her daughter's hands, but Sofia pulled away again. "Sofia," said Lucia. "What's wrong? Did you have another bad dream? About the airplanes hitting the buildings?"

"The towers," said Sofia. "The planes hit the towers. I was late for work. I saw them hit, and then the north tower fell down. I ran, but then I got caught in the dust cloud."

"No, Sofia," said Lucia. "It was just a dream. It wasn't you."

"It wasn't a dream!" Sofia cried. "I was there! I tripped on something and fell down. There was so much dust and smoke, I couldn't breathe. I thought I was going to die, but then...."

Benjamin and Lentz exchanged baffled looks. Something about Sofia's voice had changed. Not so much the tone of her voice, but the cadence and word choice was wrong.

"I was in the hospital," Sofia said. "How did I get here?"

"I drove us here," Lucia. "Remember? We left the hospital with Mr. Kassel."

"No, it's not right," Sofia said, closing her eyes and burying her head in her hands. "Who are you? I don't understand. I shouldn't be here!"

"Sofia," said Benjamin, kneeling down in front of her. "Sofia, is that you?"

Sofia gazed into Benjamin's eyes, then looked down at her hands. Her eyes rolled back in her head and she slumped to the floor. Benjamin did his best to break her fall.

"Get away from her!" Lucia screamed, shoving Benjamin out of the way. She tried to embrace Sofia, but Sofia squirmed away, still screaming hysterically.

"What did you do?" Lucia demanded.

"I didn't—" Benjamin started.

"This is all your fault!" Lucia shrieked, going to Sofia's side. "Get away from her!"

Benjamin stood up and backed away. Sofia looked up at him, a puzzled expression on her face. "Mamá?" she said. "Why are you yelling? Are you angry at Mr. Stone?"

Lucia glared at Benjamin. Lentz caught his eye, motioning toward the kitchen. Benjamin followed him out of the room.

"What was that all about?" Lentz asked.

"I could tell you what I think," said Benjamin, "but you're going to think I'm crazy."

"We're well beyond that," said Lentz. "The girl," said Lentz. "It was like she turned into a completely different person."

"That's a remarkably astute observation," Benjamin said with a nod.

"What the hell are you saying?" asked Lentz.

Benjamin sighed. "Lucia has a gift, although it may be more correct to call it a curse. She seems to be able to project her consciousness into the future."

"Project her...?" said Lentz, eyeing Benjamin dubiously.

Benjamin continued, undeterred. "Her mind actually moves forward in time to occupy the brain of another person living sometime in the future. She sees what that person sees. Her consciousness eventually snaps back into the present, but she retains memories of what this other person experiences in the future."

"Okay," said Lentz, "you're right. That does sound crazy."

"I know," said Benjamin. "But that's what this is all about. That's why the FBI is here, why Glazier's people are so interested in Sofia. They think she's an intelligence asset. They think she can help them foresee and prevent events that occur in the future. And they may be right."

Lentz shook his head. "I don't know that I buy the part about seeing the future, but something strange is definitely going on, and they certainly are interested in Sofia for some reason. But does she get like this after all these visions? She turns into someone else?"

"No, this is new," said Benjamin. "I think something they did at the hospital may have triggered it."

"Triggered what exactly?"

Benjamin shrugged. "Hell if I know. I'm just conjecturing, based on very limited information."

"We need to get her to a doctor."

"Not in this town," said Benjamin. "I'm not sure how much good a doctor can do her anyway. "She seems okay now. Hopefully she'll grow out of it." He thought of Felipe and Estefan. Or maybe not.

"Looks like our friends in the FBI found us," said Lentz, looking out the window. A black Lincoln had pulled up in front of the house.

"So now what?" asked Benjamin. "We can't let them have Sofia."

"I don't plan to hand her over," said Lentz. "As far as I'm concerned, unless they have an arrest warrant for her, they've got no business with Sofia."

"Good," Benjamin said. They watched Agents Hill and Kassel exit the car and begin walking toward the front door. Their guns were holstered.

"They're not coming in with guns blazing," said Lentz. "Let's hope they listen to reason. I'm going to move Lucia and Sofia to the back room just in case, though."

Benjamin nodded, and Lentz escorted the two out of the living room. Benjamin hoped things didn't get violent, but they would be safer if they were out of the line of fire. Lentz returned as a knock sounded on the door.

"Not interested," yelled Benjamin through the closed door.

"Mr. Stone?" Hill said. "Is that you? We're just here to talk."

"We're not giving you Sofia," Benjamin yelled.

"We're not here for Sofia," called Hill. "Please, Mr. Stone. Could you open the door?"

Benjamin glanced at Lentz, who had drawn his gun. He nodded to Benjamin. Benjamin opened the door.

"Mr. Stone," said Hill. He glanced at Lentz. "Detective Lentz. I assure you, the gun is not necessary. We're just here to talk."

"Alright," said Lentz. "Let's talk." He held onto his gun, but pointed it down at the carpet.

Hill and Kassel stepped inside, Kassel closing the door behind them.

"I don't know what we have to talk about," said Benjamin. "Unless you've got an arrest warrant, you can't take Sofia. You don't want to press that point."

"We're not here for Sofia," said Hill again. "We're here for you, Mr. Stone."

"Me?" said Benjamin. "What do you want with me?"

"Mr. Glazier has taken an interest in you," said Kassel. "He said to tell you it was something he read in the newspaper."

Benjamin studied Kassel for a moment, wondering if Glazier had explained to them what he was referring to. Benjamin decided he hadn't. These guys were just Glazier's errand boys. How powerful *was* Glazier, that the FBI did his bidding without question? More importantly, what did this development mean? Had Glazier been straight with him when he'd claimed ignorance of the story about Spiegel in the *Herald*?

"If I go with you, you'll leave Sofia alone?"

"Those were our instructions," said Hill. "Mr. Glazier seems to think you have information relevant to matters of national security."

Lentz shot a puzzled look at Benjamin. Benjamin shrugged. "I think Mr. Glazier is going to be disappointed in how much I actually know. But if you give me your word you'll leave Sofia alone, I'll cooperate."

"You have my word," said Hill.

Whatever that's worth, thought Benjamin. But he nodded to Lentz, and Lentz reluctantly holstered his gun. "I hope you know what you're doing," Lentz said quietly.

"Not a clue," said Benjamin, turning his back on the two men. "But if there's still a chance for Sofia to have a normal life, I'll do whatever I can. There's a guy in town named Tony Sabbia. Used to be a reporter for the Herald. He knows about Glazier. Some of it, anyway. Take Lucia and Sofia to him. Tell him what I told you. They can't silence all of us. And tell Lucia I'm sorry."

"For what?" Lentz asked.

"I don't know," said Benjamin. "Everything."

CHAPTER TWENTY-TWO

Benjamin got into the back of the black Lincoln. Hill drove, while Kassel rode in the passenger seat. Benjamin didn't have to ask where they were going. They'd be taking him to Sand Hill Children's Hospital to meet with the doctor who had examined Sofia. As valuable as Sofia's visions were to GLARE, something Benjamin had said to Glazier convinced him that Benjamin possessed still more vital information. But what?

Assuming that Glazier hadn't been lying about the story in the *Herald*, that meant... what? The story had been real? Sabbia had published a story about a famous scientist dying in a car accident at a nonexistent intersection, and nobody had noticed the error? It was impossible, an irreducible flaw in the history of Sunnyview. It reminded him of the sort of flaws that often marred eye witness testimony in criminal investigations: a witness would give an extremely detailed, convincing account of a series of events, but in the course of fact-checking the story Benjamin would run up against an obvious error—one on which the rest of the account depended. Memory was a funny thing, often sketchy and replete with errors; the mind would fill in gaps with convincing fictions that became part of the witness's reality.

But in this case, it was as if the error in recollection had affected the entire town. Some sort of collective delusion had taken hold, in which no one questioned an accident that couldn't possibly have happened the way it was officially recorded. Benjamin had brought the error to the attention of Glazier, and Glazier clearly believed that it meant something. But what? And what did it mean that Felipe's model shared the error? Was that just another symptom of the delusion, or was it something more? Benjamin found himself entertaining the absurd conclusion that the entire town of Sunnyview existed only in the mind of Felipe Sanz. It was a ridiculous idea. How could I be a figment in someone else's imagination? Whatever else is true, I know that I exist, and my experiences are real.

But if the error wasn't the result of one person's imperfect recollections, then it was apparently the result of a collective delusion that seemed to affect the entire city of Sunnyview. Where did that delusion come from? What motivated it? Was there some memory that was so abhorrent to the residents of the city that they had somehow unconsciously collaborated to blot it out?

This wasn't a new idea: Benjamin remembered reading about Carl Jung's theory of the "collective unconscious" when he was in college. Jung's idea was that there existed a set of unconscious attitudes that were inherited by members of a culture; that in a sense, these attitudes created the reality of the culture's members. Past occurrences were interpreted through a filter of pre-rational patterns of thought, so that two different cultures might have completely different interpretation of the same historical event.

But what was happening here seemed to be a quantum leap beyond the mere framing of events according to pre-existing attitudes. Somehow the people of Sunnyview had unconsciously decided to ignore a completely obvious contradiction. Whether the oversight was the result of a malevolent conspiracy by GLARE, the faulty memory of a single individual, or a collective delusion, the question remained: why such an obvious flaw? The error had evidently just been sitting around in a newspaper for over fifty years, waiting for Benjamin to find it. And how had nobody else noticed it until now? Why was Benjamin the only one who had seen through the delusion? What was so special about him?

Whatever it was, he suspected it was why Glazier was so interested in him. Somehow he had seen something that nobody else had noticed, in over fifty years. It seemed like an obvious mistake, but maybe it was only obvious to *him*. And yet, when Benjamin pointed out the error to Glazier, Glazier had apparently seen it as well. So it wasn't that only Benjamin could see the contradiction. Others could see it as well, but only after Benjamin pointed it out. None of it made any sense.

As the car made its way toward the hospital, Benjamin wondered if this is how the prophets of the Old Testament felt. Most people thought of prophets as people who foresaw the future, but mostly what the prophets did was remind people of things they were already supposed to know. That is, they pointed out errors in the people's thinking; contradictions that they were trying to remain ignorant of. The story rarely ended well for the prophet. Was that his fate? To be punished by Glazier for pointing out the error? He would find out soon enough, he supposed.

Efforts to gather more information from Hill and Kassel proved pointless; either they didn't know anything or they had been instructed not to say any more than was necessary to get Benjamin in the car. Benjamin suspected it was the former; these guys threw around "national security" like it was some kind of shibboleth, marking them as members of an elite group of protectors, but in reality it was more like a badge of ignorance. All they knew was that what Glazier wanted, Glazier got. And in this case, he wanted Benjamin Stone.

Agent Hill at least seemed a bit irritated at having been demoted to Glazier's stooge; his jaw was set tightly and his knuckles were white on the steering wheel. He turned left onto Main Street, gunning the engine, obviously impatient. The Lincoln's engine roared as it shot down the street.

In the distance, a woman stood motionless in the middle of the street. Hill was staring straight ahead, and Benjamin couldn't imagine the agent didn't see her. But he continued to accelerate, apparently oblivious. The car was going close to forty miles an hour.

"Hey," Benjamin snapped, leaning forward between Hill and Kassel. He pointed at the woman, who was now less than a hundred yards away.

"Sit down!" Kassel barked. "Don't make me—"

"Jesus Christ," Benjamin growled. "Watch out!"

But Hill remained oblivious, continuing to accelerate.

In the split second that Benjamin reacted, he realized both who the woman was, and why Hill didn't see her. She isn't real, Benjamin told himself. She's a hallucination.

But it was too late. He had launched himself forward between the seat, pulling the steering wheel sharply to the right. Jessica watched placidly as the car veered to the right, missing her by inches. Her damp hair didn't even rustle in the breeze.

The car fishtailed, sliding perpendicular to its vector of motion. Agent Hill tried to correct, but the Lincoln's mass fought against him. The car's right tires left the ground and the vehicle rolled. The next thing Benjamin knew, he was lying crumpled against the roof of the car.

Taking a moment to get his bearings, he realized that Hill and Kassel were still in their seats, hanging upside down from their seatbelts. Both front airbags had deployed. The rear windshield had spider-webbed into a thousand pieces, and it only took a couple of kicks for Benjamin to detach it from the frame. He crawled onto the street and stood up. He was shaking with fear and adrenaline, but other than a few scuffs and bruises, he was unhurt.

Several other cars had stopped, and a ring of onlookers had formed. Benjamin was vaguely aware of people asking him if he was hurt, but he ignored them. He was straining to see beyond the ranks of onlookers to get a glimpse of Jessica. Was she an illusion? Maybe. But she had appeared to him for a reason, and he wasn't going to let her get away this time.

"My daughter," he mumbled. "Jessica."

The people let him pass. In the distance he heard sirens. Hopefully Hill and Kassel weren't seriously injured, but Benjamin couldn't worry about them right now. He needed to find Jessica.

Benjamin strode past the gawkers and gridlocked traffic to the section of road where Jessica had appeared, but she was nowhere to be found. Once again, the apparition had vanished. Benjamin looked around frantically, but there was no sign of her.

There was no longer any doubt that he was losing his sanity. He could no longer tell what was real and what was an illusion. Maybe he'd been deluded to think he ever could. And yet, it had been his perception that had interested Glazier. He was the only one who saw Jessica's ghost, just as he had been the only one to see the flaw in the account of Spiegel's death.

No, not the only one. There was one other: Felipe. Somehow, Felipe had known about the flaw as well. He'd incorporated it into his model. But how? Benjamin was convinced that if he could find the answer to that question, he'd be able to figure out what was happening in Sunnyview. Somehow Felipe had seen the truth, and it had driven him mad, just as it was now threatening to drive Benjamin mad. Maybe if Benjamin could determine precisely what had happened to Felipe, he could find the cure for his own insanity before it was too late.

Benjamin made his way toward downtown, where he flagged a cab. He had the driver drop him off back at Lentz's house. The house was quiet; hopefully Lentz had taken Sofia and Lucia to Sabbia as he'd asked. Part of him wanted to go there and make sure they were okay, but there was nothing he could do for them, and Lucia was convinced that everything that was happening with Sofia was somehow Benjamin's fault. Maybe she was right. In any case, they were better off without him.

He got in the Buick, drove back to Lucia's house and parked on the street in front. He got out, walked to the front door and knocked several times. There was no response, as he expected. He turned the knob and the door opened. He walked inside. The house was quiet.

Benjamin walked down the hall to Felipe's room, and knocked on the door. Again, there was no answer. He opened the door.

Inside, Felipe sat motionless in front of his model. Benjamin approached slowly, not wanting to spook him again. This time, he wouldn't point out the flaw. He would do his best to approach Felipe on his own terms. If he was right about Felipe, he knew something important about Sunnyview—something that perhaps in his own way, he'd been trying to communicate. Benjamin just had to figure out what that was.

"Felipe," said Benjamin.

Felipe met Benjamin's gaze, the expression on his face peaceful. "Felipe," he said. Then he was silent, as if waiting for a cue from Benjamin.

"Felipe, is there something…" Benjamin started.

"Felipe, is there something…" Felipe repeated, echoing Benjamin's uncertain tone.

Benjamin found himself fighting irritation. Why was Felipe doing this? Was he teasing Benjamin, or did he simply lack the ability to engage in a normal conversation? Was this sort of mindless repetition the closest he could come?

He started again: "Is there something about Sunnyview that you…"

165

"Is there something about Sunnyview that you…" Felipe dutifully repeated.

Benjamin gritted his teeth. Somehow he had to get past this impasse, figure out how to communicate on Felipe's level. But how? He surveyed the model of Sunnyview, looking for something of significance. But other than the one flaw, it simply looked like a remarkably accurate model of the Sunnyview of Benjamin's youth. Benjamin was tempted to ask Felipe about the flaw, but that didn't go so well last time. There had to be some other way to communicate with him. But seconds turned into minutes, and Benjamin still hadn't a clue. Felipe simply stared at his model, oblivious to Benjamin's discomfort. Finally Benjamin couldn't take it anymore.

"Felipe, do you know something about…"

"Felipe, do you know something about…"

"God damn it!"

"God damn it!"

"I'm a fucking moron."

"I'm a fucking moron."

Benjamin couldn't help laughing at Felipe's deadpan response, but any humor in the situation was quickly negated by the mechanical barking laughter that followed. Overcome with anger, Benjamin gripped the edge of the table, and overturned it. Houses, shops, cars, trees and pedestrians flew everywhere. Hundreds, if not thousands, of hours of work simply destroyed. Felipe's conception of Sunnyview was no more.

For a moment Benjamin stood, wavering between shame at what he had done and anger—anger at Felipe, at Glazier, at Cameron Payne, at the FBI and their bullshit stories about "national security." And most of all, at Sunnyview itself. He hated this city. Hated what it had become, hated the fact that a town of real people doing real work had been supplanted by narcissistic assholes blowing sunshine up each other's asses. If only he could do to the Sunnyview around him what he had done to Felipe's model.

Felipe seemed strangely unperturbed by the destruction. The table lay on its side, next to a pile of debris, but Felipe continued to stare straight ahead, as if the model was still there. Benjamin couldn't be sure, but he thought he saw a smile playing at the corner of Felipe's mouth.

Benjamin lunged forward, gripping the front of Felipe's pajamas. "What is it?" Benjamin demanded. "What do you know? Tell me what you know!"

But Felipe now seemed to stare right through Benjamin. He made no response of any kind.

Benjamin pulled back and slapped Felipe across his cheek. Felipe reeled and he blinked several times, but remained silent. His mind seemed to have receded somewhere Benjamin couldn't reach. Whatever chance Benjamin had of communicating him was lost. Felipe was gone.

Benjamin turned, walked back down the hall and out the front door. He stood for a moment in defeat, staring down the street toward the creek that had claimed his daughter's life. So this was it. The end. He would never know for sure why his daughter died, would never know the truth about GLARE. He was a fool to think otherwise. The FBI agents didn't even understand what was going on in this town. Maybe nobody did—including Glazier. Maybe that was the real deep, dark secret of Sunnyview: that the flaw ran all the way through this town, from the 1940s to the present, and if you pressed too hard, looked too deeply, the complex tapestry of lies would unravel, leaving incompatible strands of memory that ultimately signified nothing.

In his career as an investigator, Benjamin had had to accept that some cases were unsolvable, and this certainly felt like one of those times. The only difference here was that he suspected that there was no solution out there, that no matter if he had endless time and unlimited resources, he would still never find the truth. It was actually a small consolation: he hadn't failed as an investigator; he'd been set up, given a question that had no answer. The only thing to do now was to try to move on.

CHAPTER TWENTY-THREE

Benjamin started the Buick and drove to the freeway exit just east of downtown. There were no answers for him in Sunnyview. It was time to go home. He could fight the FBI for custody of Jessica's body just as well in Portland as here.

He pushed down a pang of regret as he steered the Buick onto the freeway—whether it was about how he'd handled his investigation or other sins he'd committed long ago. He had plenty to feel regretful about, but none of it was going to do him any good now. He needed to let the past go. And the first step was getting out of this town.

His spirits began to rise as the car moved away from Sunnyview. It felt like shaking off a bad dream. Ever since he'd arrived in Sunnyview, he felt like he'd been sinking deeper into a morass of guilt and ambiguity. It would be good to get back home to something that felt more real.

But as he watched for the turnoff to Interstate 680, which would take him through northern California to Oregon, he noticed something was wrong. Somehow he'd missed his exit and made a circle, coming back around to the Sunnyview exit. Must have taken the business loop, he thought. That's what happened when you weren't focused on what you were doing.

He passed the Sunnyview exit and kept going, being careful this time to watch for the correct turnoff. But a few minutes later, he found himself once again passing the Sunnyview exit. An disconcerting sensation began to take hold of him. Was he missing time? Had he driven in a circle and then forgotten doing it? If so, then perhaps what he'd assumed was insanity was really some sort of brain damage. Did he have a stroke at some point after coming to Sunnyview? That would explain the headaches and sleepiness, and maybe the hallucinations—if not the rest of the weirdness he'd experienced. Unless the apparent weirdness was also the result of his faulty memory. Again, the solipsistic trap: if he couldn't trust his own memories, then reasoning his way out of this situation was going to be impossible.

So: assume your memories are accurate, as far as possible. He passed the Sunnyview exit, checking his watch as he did so. It read 3:43. At 3:48, he found himself approaching the Sunnyview exit again. It was impossible. He couldn't have made a circle around Sunnyview that quickly. And he was absolutely certain he'd never exited the freeway. He'd seen exactly one exit: the one for Sunnyview.

This time, he checked the display on his phone, which read 3:49 as he passed the exit. The phone's time was synchronized with satellites; maybe it was possible to manually set the time, but Benjamin had no idea how. At 3:54, he approached the Sunnyview exit again.

"What in the hell..." Benjamin murmured to himself. Either he had completely lost his mind, or he was on an endless loop of freeway with only one exit. There was no way off this road except Sunnyview.

He got into the right lane and slowed, pulling onto the shoulder. When the car was stopped, he threw it into park and got out. Cars continued to zip past, their drivers oblivious to the trap they were in. Or was the trap only for Benjamin? Did this loop somehow exist only for him? Were the other drivers speeding merrily to their destinations while Benjamin was doomed to circle Sunnyview for eternity?

He paced back and forth on the shoulder, occasionally casting a glance over at the cars zooming by. He hadn't really been paying attention, but he didn't think he was seeing the same cars passing by over and over. No, it was just regular freeway traffic—people going wherever they would normally go at four in the afternoon. What would happen if he flagged down one of the cars? Could he hitch a ride out of here? Or would the psychosis transfer itself to the driver of that car as well? Did the other drivers even exist? Were these cars just phantoms, like the ghost of Jessica he had seen? There was one way to find out, but Benjamin wasn't sure he was ready to try that yet. The only possible result of that test—whether a car slammed into him or went right through him—would be a confirmation of Benjamin's insanity: either he was hallucinating or he was suicidal.

He got back in the Buick and made the loop again. This time, though, he took a deep breath and took the exit. This seemed to be what the universe—or his psychosis—wanted from him, and it seemed pointless to resist. Whatever Sunnyview was, it wasn't done with him yet.

Not knowing where else to go, he returned to the motel. In his hurry to leave town, he hadn't checked out, so he figured he'd try to get his bearings first. Despite the increasingly bizarre nature of his experiences, he still couldn't quite bring himself to accept that there wasn't some sort of rational explanation for it all. If he could just splash some cold water on his face and then just sit and think for a minute, it would all become clear. It was a laughable thought, but he clung to it up to the moment that his hand went through the doorknob. He pulled his hand away, blinked and shook his head. Was his depth perception failing him now? He tried again, and again his hand passed through the doorknob, as if it was just an immaterial projection. Either that or *he* was.

He reached out to touch the door, but his fingers went through it as well. Am I dead? He wondered. Am I a ghost, like Jessica? Is that why I could see her? Is that what she was trying to tell me? But when did I die? And why am I still here? Have I been cursed to roam this city as a phantom for eternity?

No, that didn't seem right either. Whatever was happening to him, it was a gradual progression. He'd sensed that something wasn't quite right about Sunnyview not long after he arrived, and that sense had become a certainty in the past couple of days. The insubstantiality of the door in front of him was unsettling, but somehow not entirely unexpected. But what did it mean?

He took a deep breath, closed his eyes, and took two steps forward. When he opened his eyes, he was inside the motel room. He'd gone right through the door and hadn't felt a thing. An involuntary shudder passed through him. What was happening to him? Or was it happening to the town of Sunnyview? How could he know?

Benjamin walked right through the bed and continued through the far wall, emerging on the far side of the motel. A few rooms down a maid was wheeling a cart away from him.

"Hello," Benjamin called. But the woman didn't respond. She opened the door to a room and went inside, leaving the cart parked outside. Benjamin walked to the cart and peered inside the room. The maid was pulling sheets off the bed. "Excuse me," he said. Still she didn't respond. He reached out to touch the cart, and his hand passed through it.

Benjamin felt himself beginning to panic, and forced himself to breathe deeply. Feeling his breath on his hands, and his heart beating in his chest, gave him some measure of reassurance. I am real, he told himself. I am alive. This much I know to be true.

Somehow he had gotten out of phase with the rest of reality. He existed, and the motel existed, and they somehow overlapped in space, but they no longer occupied the same plane of being. This was troubling enough, but there was more to it than that: his world had shrunk to the size of Sunnyview. What did the computer geeks call it? Virtual reality. It was like he was stuck inside a computer simulation, and the computer hosting it only had enough memory to render a single city. But now the computer was going haywire, and the simulation was breaking down. The only problem with this theory was that even with his limited knowledge of technology, Benjamin was certain that no computer in existence could render a simulation anywhere near this size or resolution. And when would he have entered the simulation? When did his false reality begin?

Benjamin walked around the motel, refusing to walk through it in what was probably a vain effort to retain his own sanity. He walked across the empty parking lot to the Buick, half expecting his hand to go through the door handle when he reached out to it. But the door—and evidently the rest of the car—remained solid. He got behind the wheel and started the car. Whatever mysterious physics had taken over the motel had apparently not yet affected his trusty old Buick. Perhaps because the Buick had originated outside the simulation, as Benjamin had? Again, there was no way to know.

As he pulled away from the motel, Benjamin thought he saw the building flicker slightly, becoming almost transparent for a moment. Just my imagination, he thought, and then found himself laughing at the thought. It seemed like just about everything was his imagination these days.

The streets were nearly deserted, as if the effort to maintain the illusion of vehicles and pedestrians on the street had become too much for whoever was running this show. Benjamin guided the Buick toward downtown, noticing the flickering effect on several other buildings as he drove. Imagination or not, the town of Sunnyview seemed to be becoming less real before his eyes. The effect was less pronounced toward the center of town, though; it was as if the whole simulation, or hallucination, or whatever it was, was eroding from the outside in. What was that old poem he read in school?

Turning and turning in the widening gyre
The falcon cannot hear the falconer;
Things fall apart; the center cannot hold

There was more to it than that, but that was all Benjamin could remember. Figures, he thought. Memory fails me once again.

As he watched the buildings flicker, he realized there was another reason the faltering of the illusion seemed less pronounced downtown: behind the modern façade were the buildings Benjamin remembered from his youth. The Blockbuster reverted momentarily to the Sunnyview Drugstore, and the organic grocery store became Jacks' Farm Service for a split second. Was this the reality the illusion had been hiding? Somehow he was back in Sunnyview of the forties or fifties, and the image of modern day Sunnyview had been superimposed on it? But how? The technology to do something like that didn't exist in 2000, much less in the fifties. And just as importantly, why? Was this all for his benefit? What possible reason could there be for subjecting him to such a vast, meticulously detailed illusion? Who would do something like that?

The answer hit him with all the solidity the buildings around him lacked: GLARE. It had to be. Somehow they were behind this. That's why Glazier had been interested in him. Because he saw things others couldn't. Just like Sofia. And Felipe. Felipe with his incredibly detailed model of 1950s Sunnyview. What did Felipe see when he looked at the model? Benjamin wondered. Did he see the town as the model portrayed it, or did he see it as Benjamin had

173

seen Sunnyview until a few hours ago, with a false image of a future Sunnyview superimposed on it? And what did Felipe see *now*?

Once again, he was struck with the unavoidable sense that Felipe was the key. Whatever was happening in this town, it somehow all came back to Felipe. What would he find if he returned to Lucia's house? Would Lucia and her family still be there? Would they be able to see or hear him? Would Felipe be there? And would it be the aged Felipe, or the young boy who had been subjected to GLARE's testing?

Benjamin turned down Fourth Street, toward the Sand Hill Creek neighborhood where Lucia lived, nearly rear-ending a parked Studebaker in the process. The car was in beautiful shape, but it was hard to tell whether it was still relatively new or if it had been painstakingly maintained for fifty years. Benjamin had been too surprised to look whether it had been bearing a plate identifying it as a classic car. He was tempted to stop and take a closer look—and see whether it was more solid than the motel he had just left—but decided that getting to Lucia's house was more important.

He couldn't be certain, but it seemed like the buildings in this area were less flickery, more solid. Was the illusion becoming stronger the closer he got to Lucia's house? Was that the epicenter of the simulation? If Felipe really was the key, then... was Felipe somehow generating the illusion of modern-day Sunnyview? It was an absurd idea, but it gave Benjamin hope that he might reach Lucia's house before it too became a phantom.

The houses in the Sand Hill Creek neighborhood seemed more substantial, and Benjamin even passed a few pedestrians in the street. He honked at one and got no response, but he wasn't sure if the man couldn't hear him or was simply ignoring him. Benjamin decided not to try to run him down to press the point.

He pulled up to Lucia's house, which looked as real as ever. He ran up to the front door and knocked. That is, he tried to knock, but his hand went right through the door. He was too late. Even if Lucia and her family were home, they'd be unable to see him. To them, he would be an insubstantial ghost. But maybe he could learn something here anyway. Felipe held the secret. Maybe if he could observe Felipe without Felipe seeing him, he could piece together this puzzle.

He walked through the door into the house, where he saw Lucia's father sitting in his chair, watching the news. He took no notice of Benjamin, but then he'd seemed oblivious to Benjamin whenever the television was on. Benjamin cleared his throat, but still the old man didn't stir.

"Hello," Benjamin said at last. No response. Either I can't be seen, or Lucia's father is determined not to see me. Benjamin heard the clank of a pan from the kitchen.

He shrugged and walked across the room toward the kitchen. He paused a moment as he got to the door, confirming that it presented no resistance, then continued through to the other side. In the kitchen, Lucia was cooking dinner while Sofia sat at the table doing her homework.

"I'm sorry," Benjamin found himself saying—a reflexive response to his intrusion. But of course they couldn't see him. At least, he assumed they couldn't, until Sofia turned her head and looked right at him.

He looked back at her, trying to determine if she really could see him.

"Someone is here," said Sofia after a moment.

"What do you mean?" asked Lucia. "At the door?"

"No," said Sofia, getting off her chair and walking toward Benjamin. "In the kitchen. I can see him."

"You're getting too old for these games, Sofia," Lucia said, stirring a pot on the stove. "You need to do your homework."

"But Mamá, I see him!"

Lucia stopped stirring and turned to look at Sofia. "Is this one of your... visions?" she asked.

Sofia shook her head. She was standing less than two feet from Benjamin, looking right in his eyes.

"Hello, Sofia," he said, feeling anxious and a bit foolish. He'd never been a ghost before, and wasn't sure how to behave.

"He knows my name," said Sofia. "Who are you?" she asked.

"It's me, Sofia," he said. "It's Benjamin."

"He says his name is Benjamin," Sofia said.

"Sofia, stop it," said Lucia. She had moved away from the stove and was reaching toward Sofia as if to pull her away from unseen danger.

"It's okay, Mamá," said Sofia. "I don't think he's going to hurt us." She put out her hand, and it passed right through Benjamin's knee. "I don't think he *can* hurt us." She looked Benjamin in the eye again. "Are you a ghost?" she asked.

"I... I don't know," said Benjamin. "Something... strange is happening to me. You don't remember me?"

Sofia shook her head. "You're a confused ghost," she said.

"I guess I am," he said. "You don't remember me, but I remember you. You're Sofia. You like chocolate. And you have a very vivid imagination. Sometimes when you close your eyes, you see airplanes hitting buildings."

"Mamá, he knows about my visions!" Sofia exclaimed excitedly.

Lucia took hold of Sofia's shoulders. "Sofia, there's no one there," she said, her voice breaking. "Please, Sofia, you need to stop this. Let's go see what Papá is doing."

"But Mamá, I want to talk to the ghost!"

Lucia said something in Spanish that Benjamin didn't catch. Then she said, "Papá was right. I need to take you to see a doctor."

"No!" Benjamin cried, and Sofia backed away, startled.

"What is it, sweetie?" asked Lucia. "Are you alright?"

"I'm sorry," said Benjamin. "But Sofia, you can't go to the doctor. Tell your mamá you can't go to the doctor."

"He says I can't go to the doctor," said Sofia.

"Come, Sofia," said Lucia, grabbing her daughter by the wrist. She pushed the kitchen door open, dragging Sofia behind her. Benjamin followed them. "Papá!" Lucia cried. "Something is wrong with Sofia."

"Mamá, stop!" cried Sofia. "You're hurting me!"

Lucia's father, still enraptured by the TV, grumbled something in Spanish. His voice was oddly muffled, as if he were speaking through a wall. Benjamin looked at him, and saw that he had begun to flicker like the buildings. Lucia too. He was losing them. And soon, he would lose whatever tenuous connection he had with Sofia.

"Sofia," he said, crouching down next to her. Sofia didn't seem to hear. She was trying to wrest her arm from her mother's grasp.

"Papá," said Lucia faintly. "Turn that off! Necesito tu ayuda. Sofia está..." her voice trailed off, an incomprehensible muffle of syllables. The sound from the TV was muted as well; it reminded

Benjamin of the voices of the teachers on the Charlie Brown cartoons.

"Sofia!" Benjamin shouted, looking into the girl's eyes.

She looked up with a start, squinting at his face. "Benjamin?" she said. "I can hardly hear you."

"I know," he shouted. "Please, tell your mother. No doctors! Don't let them take you to…" But Sofia was now looking through him, and he could see that his words were no longer registering.

Lucia and her father were gone, and the television had gone dark. The walls around him were flickering, and gradually losing their opacity. Beyond them he saw not the stucco houses of Lucia's neighborhood, but only trees. The vast apricot orchards that had once occupied this ground, many years ago. Soon the illusion would deteriorate completely, and with it his chances of ever finding out the truth.

Felipe, he thought. I have to talk to Felipe.

He raced down the hall and through the half-transparent door to Felipe's room. But Felipe wasn't there. The room was empty, except for a pretty young woman with damp hair and clothes, who stood staring at him, as if she had been waiting for him.

"Jessica," he said, despite himself.

CHAPTER TWENTY-FOUR

"Hi, Dad," Jessica said. She was neither reproachful nor forgiving. There was an air of serene acceptance about her. He wanted to go to her, to hug her, but something held him back.

"What are you doing here?" he found himself asking. "What is happening to me? Am I dead?"

"Dad, you need to stop this," Jessica said.

"Stop what?" Benjamin demanded. "I just want to know what is happening. Is this whole town some kind of hallucination? Am I going crazy? Am I dead?"

"No," she said. "You're not dead."

"But you are," he said. "Cameron Payne murdered you."

"In a manner of speaking," she said.

"What the hell does that mean? Please, Jessica. Just tell me what's going on. Am I losing my mind?"

"No," she said. "Your brain is doing its best to understand things that are incomprehensible. The past, the present, the future. All at once. You aren't going to be able to make sense of it, Dad. You need to stop trying. Just let it be."

Only the faintest outlines of the house remained now. Benjamin and his daughter were standing in the middle of an orchard. Rows of well-pruned apricot trees ran on either side of them.

"Do you see what I'm seeing?" asked Benjamin, looking around him. "The city is disappearing. Why?"

"The past, present and future are just different points of view," said Jessica. "Your point of view is shifting. It's best if you just accept it."

"I tried to leave, but this city won't let me. Why, Jessica? What does it want from me?"

"It doesn't want anything," Jessica said. "Dad, this isn't a problem you can solve. This city isn't a puzzle for you to rearrange until it makes sense."

"I don't care about Sunnyview," said Benjamin. "I care about you. I came here for you."

"No," said Jessica. "You came here for you. You came here because you feel bad about the way you left things between us. About how you shut me out when Mom was sick. You thought that solving my murder could make you feel better about yourself. But it won't."

"Please, Jessica," Benjamin pleaded. "I have to do something. I have to try to make things right."

Jessica shook her head. "It's too late for that," she said. "You need to let go of the past. Just live. Just be."

"Let go of the past," Benjamin echoed, surveying the orchard around him. "I'm *in* the past. How can I let go of it?"

"This is *a* past. You need to let go of *your* past."

Benjamin couldn't help laughing. He was losing his mind for sure. He was hallucinating a time long since past, and his dead daughter was talking to him in New Age truisms. "What year is this?" he asked.

Jessica looked around, and seemed to be taking in the same scene as Benjamin was experiencing. "June fourteen, 1950," she said. "Almost exactly fifty years before you came back to Sunnyview."

"But this isn't real," said Benjamin. "It's some sort of illusion, or projection."

"Everything is an illusion," said Jessica. "It's a matter of perspective. Your reality is comprised of your perceptions."

"Uh huh," said Benjamin. He was starting to get the impression that Jessica—or whoever it was standing before him—was putting him on. She was giving him pseudo-mystical non-answers, trying to retain an aura of mystery while hiding what was really going on. But wherever he was, whatever was happening to him, the rules of logic still applied. Somehow he was going to catch her in a contradiction, force her to tell him the truth.

"You're saying that what I'm experiencing right now is the year 1950?" he asked.

"Yes."

"And a few minutes ago, I was experiencing the year 2000?"

"Yes, Dad, but—"

"And they are both illusions? Or both real, depending on your perspective."

"Essentially, yes. But Dad—"

"Then why can't I change the future? Why can't I prevent you from being murdered fifty years from now?"

Jessica sighed again. "Dad, I keep trying to tell you, this isn't a puzzle you can solve. Yes, you can change the future, but you can't change *your* past. It's *your* past that is tripping you up, preventing you from letting go. No matter what you do, your past is going to follow you."

"Because my memories stick with me," Benjamin said. "But if I find myself forty years from now, keep myself from going to pieces, get a handle on the drinking before it gets out of control, be there for you and your mom…." He broke off, unable to continue. When he'd started, he was just trying to poke a hole in the Jessica-apparition's nebulous narrative, but the vision of Katherine in the hospital bed, her head wrapped in a scarf, her flesh pale and gaunt, was too much for him.

"Dad," said Jessica gently. "You are who you are. You did what you did. It's okay. Accept it. Move on."

With some effort, Benjamin regained his composure. "Who are you, really?" he asked.

"I'm your daughter," Jessica replied.

"No," he said, shaking his head fiercely. "My daughter is dead. I don't know who you are, but you're not going to get in the way of me bringing Jessica's killer to justice. I don't fully understand what all this is yet," he said, waving his arms to indicate the orchard around him, "but I know GLARE is behind it, and they aren't going to be able to get away with it forever. They've got some way of creating mass delusions, of preventing people from seeing the truth. But I've seen through them. I found a flaw in the illusion. Maybe that's why everything is going haywire now. I started pulling on a loose thread, and the whole thing is unraveling. I'm going to expose Glazier and this program, and I'm going to make sure Cameron Payne is dead or in prison."

"You can't do that, Dad," said Jessica. "It won't help me. It won't bring me back."

"You are not Jessica!" Benjamin howled. "You're part of this hallucination, this delusion, whatever it is. A tool of GLARE. Glazier's puppet. Hell, you could *be* Glazier for all I know. All you've done since I first saw you is try to get me to drop this investigation, to get me to give up. First you distracted me when I was chasing the boy, Felipe, and then when the FBI agents were taking me to…." He trailed off, realizing the truth. "That's it, isn't it? Sand Hill Children's Hospital. That's where I'll find the answers. The answers you don't want me to find."

"You're right, Dad," said Jessica. "I did try to keep you away from that place. But not because I don't want you to find the answers. I kept you away because you weren't ready for the answers yet. You weren't ready to let go."

"Bullshit," Benjamin snapped. "You are *not* my daughter. You're a projection. Glazier fucking with my head, trying to distract me, keep me from finding the truth."

"Remember my ninth birthday, when I wanted a Paula Panda?" Jessica asked. "Mommy bought me a stuffed panda, but it wasn't a Paula Panda, so I cried and cried. Mommy said I was being ungrateful, but you decided you were going to save the day. You took me to three different toy stores looking for the Paula Panda I wanted."

"And we found it," said Benjamin, despite himself. "You—Jessica was so happy."

"I was happy to go home," said Jessica. "The one we found wasn't the Paula Panda I wanted. I already had the purple one. Mommy knew that. That's why she bought me another panda. But you were so set on finding the right one that I pretended the purple one was the one I wanted."

Benjamin stared at her, not understanding. Was she telling the truth? Or was this some trick of Glazier's?

"Don't you see, Dad?" Jessica said. "You were trying to solve the problem, to fix everything. But Mommy had already gone to every store in town. She tried to tell you, but you wouldn't listen. I think the only reason she let you take me along to the stores was to punish me for being ungrateful. It worked. By the time we got to the third store, I wanted to go home so bad that I pretended to be thrilled to find the purple bear."

"Why are you telling me this?" Benjamin asked. "I know I wasn't a great father. If Glazier's plan is to wear me down by—"

"That's not the point, Dad. I loved that you cared enough to find the Paula Panda for me. But you got so wrapped up in it, it got a little scary."

"I get it," Benjamin said. "I can't fix the past. But I can still bring Cameron Payne to justice. I can still stop Glazier. If you really are my daughter, you'll understand that I can't just let this go."

"It's because I'm your daughter that I understand how difficult it is for you," said Jessica.

Benjamin shook his head. "You want me to let Glazier and Payne off the hook? Then tell me they weren't responsible for your death. Tell me I was wrong about them, and I'll drop it." If this apparition really was the work of GLARE, then presumably it would jump at the chance to assure him that Glazier had nothing to do with Jessica's death—which would only confirm to Benjamin that he was being manipulated. But Jessica, or whoever it was, didn't play along.

"You weren't wrong," she said. "I thought I could use Glazier to make me and Cameron a lot of money. But the more I looked into GLARE, the guiltier I felt about it. They just poured all this shit into the water, and when they found out it was causing birth defects, they covered it up because they thought some of the defects might prove useful to them. When I first uncovered what they were doing, I assumed it was all in the past. But I couldn't find any indication that they had ever stopped. Sure, the EPA eventually made them stop dumping, but the truth about what GLARE was doing never really came out. It kept me up at nights, wondering if they were still experimenting on kids. I finally told Cameron about it, and he pretended to be sympathetic. He was the one who suggested we take water samples from the creek. He asked me to meet him down there, and then he hit me over the head with a rock. I ran, but couldn't get away. He shoved me down and kept hitting me until I stayed down. I should have known not to trust that asshole."

"The FBI is holding him now," said Benjamin. "Or they will be, back in 2000." He was having a hard time figuring out how to talk about a reality he didn't understand, where time didn't seem to exist in its ordinary sense. But he pressed on, clutching tightly to what he could make sense of. "I suspect they're going to put him in witness protection, because he knows too much about GLARE. He's going to get away with your murder, Jessica. Unless you help me. If you really are my daughter, and if you really know everything you seem to know, then you can help me find Cameron Payne and bring him to justice. We can stop Glazier together."

Jessica shook her head. "No, Dad. That isn't going to happen. I'm not here to help you solve a mystery. I only came to tell you to let go. Stop fighting."

"At least tell me what's going on," Benjamin pleaded. "What is all this? Was Sunnyview of the year 2000 an illusion? Or is *this* the illusion? Am I still in the year 2000, but imagining that it's fifty years earlier?"

Jessica sighed. "You think I'm keeping something from you, not telling you what's really going on. But I've been trying to tell you. You've been experiencing Sunnyview in 2000. Currently you're experiencing Sunnyview in 1950. Neither of them is real. Neither of them is an illusion. They're just perceptions."

"I don't accept that," said Benjamin. "I am somewhere right now. I exist in a particular time. What I'm asking you is: what is the actual date, where I am, right now?"

"*Where* you are depends on *who* you are, Dad."

"You know who I am," he said.

"Yes, but do *you* know?" she asked.

"Don't be ridiculous," Benjamin said. "I'm Benjamin Stone. Fifty-eight years old. Retired police detective from Portland."

"In that case," said Jessica, "you're in Sunnyview in the year 2000. All of what you're currently experiencing is a hallucination. And you're going to want to ignore this." She raised her hand as if to indicate something to her right. Benjamin looked in that direction, but saw nothing.

"Ignore what?" Benjamin asked. Was this another diversion? But then he saw it: something moving among the trees in the distance. No, not something. Someone.

Felipe. The young boy from his dream, running in through the orchard on a path that would take him past Felipe and Jessica. He was nearing them, and soon would pass within five rows of Benjamin. If he was going to catch Felipe, this was his chance.

But the boy was a hallucination. He wasn't real. Even Jessica said so.

But then she wasn't real either.

He was clearly losing his mind. Maybe he'd already lost it. He could no longer tell what was real and what was an illusion. Was he imagining that he was in the middle of an orchard, or had he been imagining Sunnyview of the year 2000? Or were both of them illusions? If he followed Felipe now, what would happen? Would Felipe finally lead him to the answers he sought, or would he plunge even deeper into madness? Was there a difference?

He wanted to ask Jessica, but there was no time. And he knew what she would say: the boy wasn't real. Ignore him. Let go. But what did that mean? Remain in the orchard forever, never knowing what was real? No, he couldn't do that. If he had a chance to know the truth, he had to take it, even if it meant embracing his insanity.

Benjamin turned and ran after the boy, knowing that he'd never see Jessica again. Whether or not she was real in any sense, he couldn't do what she asked of him. He couldn't let it go. Not yet. Not while there were still answers to be found. Not while there was a chance to bring Jessica's killer to justice.

The boy ran toward the creek, and Benjamin followed, making sure to keep him in view. Benjamin's chest burned, but he pressed on. The boy splashed through the creek and continued to the other side. Benjamin ran to the creek edge and leaped over it, landing awkwardly but managing to keep his footing. It was just like the dream.

He slowly gained on the boy, and didn't waste time yelling at him to stop. When Benjamin was nearly on him, he dove forward, throwing his arms around Felipe's ankles. Felipe yelped, falling hard to the ground. His joints aching from the impact, Benjamin forced himself to scrabble forward, keeping Felipe pinned. Gripping the boy's shoulder, Benjamin took his knees off his back and turned him over. Looking at the boy's face, there was no doubt: it was a younger version of the man he'd met at Lucia's house—and met on the street before that. His dark hair was matted with sweat, and his chest heaved as he gasped for air. He looked frightened, but not surprised. He knew that Benjamin was going to get the truth out of him eventually, in some iteration of the dream. Or whatever this was.

"What is happening?" Benjamin gasped, sweat dripping from his chin onto Felipe's pajamas. "What is all this?"

"You shouldn't be here," the boy replied. "I have to go back. You don't. Get out of here, while you can."

"No!" Benjamin growled. "I'm not going anywhere until I get some answers. What is that place? The castle. Why are you going there?"

"It's not... a castle," Felipe said, still breathing heavily.

Not in the mood for more semantic games, Benjamin motioned toward the dark castle that he knew loomed to the west, ready to snap at Felipe. But as Benjamin looked at it, his perspective shifted. The sun had disappeared behind the edifice, and what he had seen as a black fortress silhouetted against the sky was now taking on new detail. It wasn't a castle at all, just a large and rather mundane-looking building. Only the sheet metal letters affixed to the top of the building were foreboding. They read:

Sand Hill Children's Hospital

This is where Felipe had been leading him all along. And not just Felipe. Everything had been leading him to this place, at this time. Even Spiegel's impossible car accident. The building didn't exist in 2000, which meant he was experiencing Sunnyview of the past. This is where GLARE evaluated Sunnyview's children, using their visions for gathering intelligence about future threats to national security.

"Why are you going back?" asked Benjamin. "After what they did to you?"

"I don't have a choice," said Felipe. "They always pull me back. But you need to go. You don't belong here." Felipe sat up, and Benjamin didn't restrain him. He no longer seemed interested in running.

"Where is here?" Benjamin asked. "Where am I? Is this 1950, or 2000?"

"You're in between," said Felipe, futilely brushing at the splotches of dirt on his pajamas. "You can't stay here. You have to go back."

Benjamin got to his feet, staring at the building just beyond the end of the orchard. "I told you, I'm not leaving until I know what's going on."

"If you stay, it will be too late. You'll never be able to go back."

"Why not?" asked Benjamin.

"Because," said Felipe in frustration, "this is all in your imagination. It's not real. If you stay, you'll be lost. You'll never find your way back."

"I don't care about going back," said Benjamin. "I care about stopping GLARE. And putting the men who killed my daughter in prison."

"You can't do both," said Felipe. "If you stay here, you can't do anything about the men who killed Jessica."

So Felipe knew about Jessica. He knew everything. Benjamin had been right: Felipe was the key.

"But then I'll never know the truth," said Benjamin. "Is that right? I'll never know what all this is? What's really happening? And GLARE will never stop."

"You've done what you could," said Felipe. "The truth is coming out. The truth of what GLARE has been doing for fifty years."

Benjamin stared at Felipe. The way he talked, it was hard to believe he was an eight-year-old boy. It was a bizarre inversion of Benjamin's experience with the seemingly infantile middle-aged Felipe.

"So they get to keep doing this for fifty years? Poisoning the water? Experimenting on kids? I don't accept that. If this really is 1950, then we can shut them down. Now, before they hurt more kids."

"Lots of people will try to shut them down," said Felipe. "People more powerful than you. A lot of them will get killed. No one will listen to you. GLARE is too big. They're too strong. I will try to stop them, but you have to go. Now, before it's too late."

But Benjamin had made up his mind. "No," he said. "I need to know. And if there's a chance I can stop them, I need to try."

"Even if you have to go in there?" asked Felipe, indicating the hospital.

"Why do I have to go in there?" asked Benjamin. "Why don't you just tell me the truth?"

"Because we're out of time," said Felipe. "I'm sorry. I tried to warn you."

"Felipe!" said a voice from the orchard behind them. Benjamin spun to face the voice. It was two men, dressed in orderly uniforms bearing the initials SHCH.

"We've been looking for you, Felipe," said one of the men. "It's time to come back." Oddly, the man seemed to be talking to Benjamin.

"I'm not..." Benjamin started, and turned to look at Felipe. But Felipe was gone. Vanished, like the vision he was.

The men approached him. He saw that one of them had a syringe. Alright, thought Benjamin. I'm old, but I think I can still fight off two pudgy hospital orderlies. But as the men approached, they seemed to be growing larger, and soon they were towering over him. Baffled, Benjamin swung at one, but his fist thudded into the man's gut with little effect. Huge, soft hands gripped his wrists, and a wasp stung his arm. Everything went black.

CHAPTER TWENTY-FIVE

Benjamin awoke in a room lit only by gray light filtering through a barred window of frosted glass. Sitting up, he determined it was a hospital room—sparsely furnished, with no television, and painted pale institutional green. He wore only gray cotton pajamas.

It was impossible to tell where he was, or when. The décor of the room was minimal and might have dated from the 1950s, but that didn't mean much. The room seemed to lack overhead lighting; the only light source other than the window was a small incandescent lamp on a nightstand next to the bed. There was a small bathroom adjoined to the room.

Benjamin slid out of bed, feeling the cool tile on the bottom of his feet. Next to the bed rested a pair of sandals, and he slid them on his feet. He walked to the window, but the frosted glass made it impossible to see anything but indistinct greenish and bluish blobs. He heard the door to the room open behind him, and he turned.

A middle-aged woman in an old-fashioned nurse's outfit stood in the doorway. She glanced at a clipboard. "Benjamin?" she asked.

Benjamin didn't reply.

"The doctor is ready to see you now."

"Where am I?" asked Benjamin.

"You're in a hospital."

"What hospital?" he asked. He resisted the urge to ask what year it was.

"Please, Benjamin," the woman said. "The doctor is waiting." She stood waiting for Benjamin to walk past her into the hallway. After a moment, he did. Probably better to follow the path of least resistance until he understood better what was happening.

The woman led him down the hall to a door bearing a placard that read DR. ADAM HOLST. She opened the door into a small but well-appointed office. A slightly built man who seemed to be in his mid-thirties sat behind a wooden desk. On the desk were several books and a writing pad, but no computer or other electronic devices. On the other side of the desk were two dark green leather chairs.

Benjamin stepped inside, followed by the woman. She stepped past him, handing the clipboard to the man. He glanced at it, nodded, and motioned at one of the chairs. "Please," he said. "Take a seat."

The woman turned, closing the door behind her. Benjamin sat.

"How are you this morning, Benjamin?" asked the man.

"Honestly, Doctor?" said Benjamin, "I'm a bit confused."

"Perhaps I can help with that," replied the doctor. "Do you remember me?"

"No," said Benjamin.

"My name is Doctor Holst. I work here at the hospital."

"Sand Hill Children's Hospital?"

"Yes," said Dr. Holst, seeming a bit surprised. "That's correct."

"Why am I in a children's hospital?"

"You're a... special case," said Dr. Holst. "We work mostly with children, but we focus on psychological disorders. You are sick, Benjamin. We've been trying to make you well."

"What's the date?" Benjamin asked.

"June fourteen, 1950," said Dr. Holst. It was the same date Jessica had given him.

"How long have I been here?"

"Nearly a week," said Dr. Holst. "You and I have talked every day since you arrived. You have no memory of this?"

"No," said Benjamin.

"But you know the name of this place."

"I... dreamed about it," said Benjamin. If Holst was to be believed, the whole time he thought he had been in Sunnyview, he'd actually been in a mental hospital.

"Yes," said Dr. Holst. "We've been talking about your dreams. Did you have the dream again, about your daughter?"

"My daughter," Benjamin echoed. It seemed like years since he had found her body in the creek. But it hadn't been a dream. Had it? He was no longer sure what was real and what was illusion. If he really was in a mental institution in 1950, then he couldn't have seen his daughter dead in 2000. "They killed her," he said.

"Who killed her?"

"Cameron Payne and William Glazier."

Dr. Holst nodded, and jotted something in a notepad. "Yes," he said. "You've mentioned them before. This Glazier, he is some sort of business magnate?"

"I don't understand what's happening to me," said Benjamin. "I was born in 1942. How can it be 1950 now? I saw my daughter dead in the year 2000."

"You're going to experience some temporal dissonance for a while," said Dr. Holst. "I can help you through it, but you have to trust me."

"Help me through it how? I'm half-expecting to wake up any minute back in the year 2000."

"You're awake now, Benjamin," said Dr. Holst. "But I understand your confusion. If you can tell me exactly what you've experienced over the past few days, I can help you separate what is real from your delusions."

"Just tell me whether my daughter is dead," said Benjamin.

Dr. Holst regarded him stolidly for a moment. "I'm afraid Jessica is gone, yes."

"But how?" Benjamin asked. "If she died in 2000, and it's 1950 now...?"

"That's one of the things I'm hoping to help you understand," said Dr. Holst. "Shortly before you were brought here, you had a psychotic break. You've been experiencing extended delusional episodes since then. I've been doing my best to help you separate reality from fantasy. But if I'm going to do that, I need you to explain to me everything you've experienced over the past few days. Do you understand?"

Benjamin nodded. He understood what Dr. Holst was saying, and no doubt it was at least partly true. At least some of what Benjamin had been experiencing recently was delusion. But what parts were real, and what was illusory? And could he trust Dr. Holst to help him determine which was which?

"Are you saying that everything I've experienced recently was only a dream?"

"The dreams began before your break," said Dr. Holst. "Before you were brought here for treatment. They became increasingly vivid and intense, and since arriving here you've experienced several waking visions as well. At this point, it seems that you are no longer retaining any memories of your waking life. The dream is all that exists for you. You don't remember our sessions, for example, and you seem to have no memory of being in this hospital. But your unconscious mind is aware of this place, and it seems to have crept into your dreams. That's a positive sign. It gives us a bridge to connect the dream and reality."

Benjamin couldn't deny the logic. He wasn't entirely certain he wasn't dreaming right now, but the hospital was a constant. It existed both in the present and in what Holst claimed was a dream. Presumably that meant that it, at least, was real. What other commonalities were there to be grasped?

"Tell me about this William Glazier," said Dr. Holst. "He seems to be an important figure in the dream."

"I met him once when I was a child," said Benjamin. "He bought my father's land. He's something of a legend. Invented the semiconductor. He also… that is, in the dream, he was involved in the work of this hospital." He found himself adopting Dr. Holst's language, even though he didn't really believe his memories of Glazier were dreams.

"Really," said Dr. Holst. "That's quite interesting."

"Because Glazier is real as well," said Benjamin.

"The chairman of this hospital's board of directors is a man named David Stockton, but he shares some traits with your William Glazier. Your unconscious mind seems to have seized upon your anxiousness about being in this hospital and projected that anxiousness onto this fictional character, William Glazier. Your mind created a villainous version of Mr. Stockton, who is responsible for the death of your daughter."

"You're saying Glazier didn't kill Jessica."

"As far as I know, William Glazier doesn't exist. David Stockton does, but it's highly unlikely he murdered your daughter."

"Why?"

"Why do you think he did?"

"Jessica uncovered evidence of a conspiracy Glazier was involved in. A secret, government-backed program."

"What sort of program?"

Benjamin regarded Dr. Holst, uncertain how much to tell him. Was GLARE real? If it was, then Dr. Holst was likely part of it. If it wasn't, then it was a key element in his delusion. "Precognition," said Benjamin. "They were experimenting on children in an attempt to predict future events."

"Why?"

"To alter the future, I suppose," said Benjamin. "To stop tragic events from happening and change the course of history. You're saying no such program exists?"

"Not that I'm aware of," said Dr. Holst. "Which isn't to say it *doesn't* exist—or won't exist, in the year 2000—but you have to admit it sounds improbable."

"Then who killed my daughter?" Benjamin asked.

"Who do you think killed her?"

"I told you," said Benjamin. "Cameron Payne. And indirectly, William Glazier."

"Even though I've told you these people don't exist."

"You told me to tell you what I experienced."

"And now I'm asking you to reflect on that experience. Knowing that William Glazier doesn't exist, and that Cameron Payne probably doesn't either, who do you think killed Jessica?"

"Assuming that some of the things I know for certain are false, what do I think? That's an impossible question to answer."

"But you *have* to answer it, Benjamin. You need to feel your way through your memories for the truth."

"Why don't you just tell me what happened?" Benjamin demanded. "Why the games? How is it possible that it's 1950 now when I have five decades of memories since then? What is happening to me? Just tell me what is happening!"

"I've tried," said Dr. Holst. "Yesterday. And the day before that. Every day since you've been here, in fact. But every time I tell you, you shut down. You retreat into your fantasy world, where I can't reach you. I've come to the conclusion that there are certain things you have to work out for yourself. I can't do it for you. So please, Benjamin, humor me. Tell me who killed Jessica."

"Cameron Payne and William Glazier."

"Because she uncovered the truth about a secret government project to conduct experiments on children in order to predict the future."

Benjamin said nothing.

"Am I misstating what you said?" asked Dr. Holst, leaning forward and looking Benjamin in the eye.

"No," replied Benjamin. "That's accurate."

"But you hear how absurd that sounds, right?"

"Yes. But sometimes absurd things happen."

Dr. Holst nodded. "Presumably, then, I'm part of this conspiracy. Correct? I'm one of the evil scientists conducting dangerous experiments on children for nefarious purposes?"

"Presumably," said Benjamin.

"And what does that make you, Benjamin? How do you fit into this?"

"I don't know."

"I think you do," said Dr. Holst. "Follow the narrative where it leads. If I'm helping to run this secret program, then who are you?"

"I'm a retired police detective," said Benjamin. "I'm 58 years old. My name is Benjamin Stone."

Dr. Holst sighed. "Fine," he said. "You're a retired police detective. You came to town to find your estranged daughter. A daughter who hated you, and showed no signs of wanting to reconcile with you."

"Jessica didn't hate me," Benjamin said.

"What did she tell you the last time you saw her?"

"She was angry," Benjamin said. Had he told Holst about the argument he'd had with Jessica before she stormed out that day? "She didn't mean that."

"How did you find her?"

"Detective Lentz called me."

"When her body was found, you mean."

"That's right."

"And you never talked to Jessica before that?"

Benjamin glared at Dr. Holst. "What are you getting at?"

"Who are the most likely suspects in a murder such as this?"

"Boyfriend," said Benjamin. "Or a family member. But that isn't what happened."

"No," said Dr. Holst, dryly. "Because Jessica was murdered to cover up a top secret government program."

"You want me to think I killed Jessica," said Benjamin. "That I made up this whole thing about GLARE to avoid responsibility for my actions." The word slipped from his mouth before he had a chance to stop it. Holst made a note.

"I want you to ask yourself which is more likely," said Holst. "That you had a psychotic break and killed Jessica, or that she was killed to keep the lid on a secret conspiracy to conduct experiments on children in order to predict the future."

"This is bullshit," said Benjamin. "I didn't kill my daughter. She was dead before I ever came to Sunnyview."

"When you came to Sunnyview in the year 2000, you mean."

"Yes, God damn it."

"But it's 1950 now. If you were 58 in 2000, how old are you now?"

"Stop it," Benjamin growled. "Just stop! You're trying to make me think I'm crazy!"

"I'm trying to get you to understand that you are asserting certain facts that can't possibly be true. You had a psychotic break, caused by the death of your daughter."

"I would never kill my daughter!" Benjamin cried.

"I know you wouldn't, ordinarily," said Dr. Holst. "But something happened to make you violent. I think you had a dissociative episode. I want to help you understand why that happened. But I can't do that if you're not honest with me."

"I did not kill Jessica!" Benjamin roared.

"Okay," said Dr. Holst. "Let's explore the idea of this secret program to predict the future."

"You're going to humor me, you mean," said Benjamin.

"I'm on your side, Benjamin," said Dr. Holst. "I want to help you determine what is true and what is illusion. I assume that's what you want as well. So tell me what you've experienced, and I will do my best to be objective and help you work through it. Does that sound fair?"

Benjamin glared at Dr. Holst. If Benjamin didn't trust Holst before, he certainly didn't now. It was clear the man had an agenda. He was trying to convince Benjamin he had killed his own daughter. But why? If he was part of GLARE, how did convincing Benjamin that he had killed his daughter help them? Any avenue Benjamin's mind tried to travel ended up somewhere that he didn't want to be. He was adrift in a sea of conflicting memories, and he desperately needed some sort of anchor.

"GLARE is real," he said, as much to himself as to Dr. Holst. "They experimented on children, put chemicals in the water supply. Jessica found out about it, and they killed her."

"What is the purpose of GLARE?" Dr. Holst asked.

"It's an intelligence-gathering operation," said Benjamin. "They use their subjects to pinpoint future events. The information is passed on to the government, so they can prevent them, or prepare for them."

"What sorts of events?"

Benjamin thought about what Glazier had told him, and about Sofia's and Estefan's visions. "Large scale tragic events," he said. "Catastrophes."

"Like hurricanes?" asked Dr. Holst. "Or earthquakes?"

Benjamin shook his head. "No. The subjects seem to focus on human-caused events. Wars, terrorist attacks, that sort of thing. I'm not sure why. Maybe it's easier to predict those sorts of events."

"You met one of these subjects?"

"Yes," said Benjamin. "A girl named Sofia." Actually, he had met two subjects and the widow of a third, but he didn't feel the need to give Dr. Holst all that information quite yet. "Sofia saw airplanes hitting buildings."

"How old was she?"

"Eight, I think."

"And she was a subject of this 'GLARE' program? In the year 2000?"

"She was," said Benjamin, again not feeling the desire to elaborate.

Dr. Holst nodded and jotted something down. "Where did she see this happening? Where were the buildings the airplanes hit?" he asked.

"I don't know," said Benjamin. "Nor do I know when it happens. I didn't grill her for specifics."

"Of course not," said Dr. Holst. "But you must see how this Sofia's experiences mirror your own. If Sofia is a manifestation of your own confusion about reality, understanding what she saw may help you make sense of your own circumstances."

Benjamin nodded slowly, regarding Dr. Holst as he scribbled away at his pad. This situation was starting to feel all too familiar. Benjamin had been through hundreds of interviews like this, but usually it was in an interview room in a police station, and he was the one holding the notepad.

"Sofia wasn't the only subject I met," Benjamin said. "There was also a man named Estefan."

Dr. Holst's response was almost imperceptible, but he couldn't hide it completely. His pencil paused on the paper for a moment, as if he had lost his train of thought. He quickly finished the line, but Benjamin had already seen his tell. Dr. Holst recognized the name.

"Oh?" Dr. Holst said, faking nonchalance. "Did this Estefan have visions of the future as well?"

"Estefan was insane," said Benjamin. "He had what I think you would probably call a 'psychotic break.' One day he woke up, and he was a different person. It was too much for him to take."

"Interesting," said Dr. Holst. "It's possible that this Estefan represents—"

"Estefan doesn't *represent* anything. He was a kid that GLARE experimented on."

"GLARE is a delusion, Benjamin. I've been trying to help you see that."

"No," said Benjamin, his instincts kicking in. He was certain now that Holst had been lying to him. Maybe not about everything, but he certainly wasn't giving Benjamin the whole truth. "You've been playing me. Trying to confuse me about what's real, so that you can squeeze me for information. I didn't kill my daughter and you know it."

"Then who did?" said Dr. Holst.

"Cameron Payne. William Glazier. GLARE."

"GLARE doesn't exist. Neither does William Glazier."

"I don't believe you," said Benjamin.

"Please, Benjamin," said Dr. Holst. "You have to trust me."

"Because you're all that I have, right?" asked Benjamin. "You're my tether to reality. But it isn't true. You're not all I have. I've seen things, patterns that point to the truth. Some of what I've experienced is delusion, but not all of it. The truth lies underneath it all, and I can glimpse enough of it to know you're lying. GLARE is real, and you're the proof. You're using me to gather intelligence. I'm one of your subjects."

"What makes you say that?"

"Sofia," said Benjamin. "And Estefan. I've seen what GLARE does to people. I recognize the signs."

"These people exist only in your imagination," said Dr. Holst. "They are manifestations of your psychosis. You can't—"

"So my 'dream' is only real when you need it to be," said Benjamin. "Is that it? You make me doubt my own memories, so that I'll spill them to you, and you can sort through them for what you need?"

Dr. Holst stared at him for some time. "Are you sure that you want to go down this road, Benjamin? I'll acknowledge that I have my own agenda, but I do have your interests at heart. I'm trying to protect you."

"From what? The truth?"

"Yes," said Dr. Holst.

"I'm not afraid of the truth," said Benjamin, although he sounded more certain than he felt. Part of him wanted to retreat back into the uncertainty of delusion.

"Alright, then," said Dr. Holst, getting to his feet. "Come with me."

"Where are we going?" asked Benjamin.

"To see the truth."

Benjamin hesitated, but got to his feet. He followed Dr. Holst out of the room and down the hall. Dr. Holst knocked on a door and waited for a moment, but Benjamin heard no response. Dr. Holst opened the door, peeked inside, and then motioned for Benjamin to enter. Benjamin did, and Dr. Holst followed, closing the door behind him.

The room was nearly identical to the one in which Benjamin had awoken not long before. But in this room sat a small figure, silhouetted against the gray glow from the frosted window pane. The figure didn't stir as Benjamin and Dr. Holst entered.

"Estefan," said Dr. Holst. Still the figure didn't move. Dr. Holst turned to Benjamin. "You've met Estefan, yes?"

Benjamin nodded dumbly. Was it possible? This was the same Estefan? The one whose widow Benjamin had met?

"Wie geht es dir heute?" asked Dr. Holst.

The figure stirred slightly, but didn't respond. Dr. Holst turned back to Benjamin. "Estefan arrived a week before you did. We had high hopes for him, but it seems we pushed him too hard. I tried to warn David, but he wouldn't listen. We've been getting a lot of pressure from Washington to produce results."

Benjamin was dumbfounded. On some level he had hoped he was wrong, that there was some other explanation. But Estefan was another point of commonality, a confirmation of the truth in his "dreams." GLARE was real. Estefan was real. Estefan had seen the future, and somehow it had driven him mad.

"You spoke to him in German," Benjamin said.

"It's the only language he is fluent in. He knows some French, very little English. No Spanish, as far as I can tell. I speak some German, but we have a translator on staff for our sessions together. Not that it does us much good."

"But… he grew up in Sunnyview, to Spanish-speaking parents. How can he have forgotten how to speak both English and Spanish?"

"The better question," Dr. Holst said, "is how did he learn to speak fluent German?"

Benjamin nodded slowly. He suspected he knew the answer, but he was hesitant to speak it. "He isn't Estefan," he said at last.

"That's correct," said Dr. Holst. "In a manner of speaking, anyway. Estefan projected himself into the future, taking on the point of view of an elderly woman in East Berlin, about forty years from now. We were able to ascertain a fair amount of detail about her life, but no actionable intelligence. We use various drugs to help improve recall and vividness, and we kept increasing Estefan's dosage in hopes of getting useful information. One day he woke up speaking German. It would be funny if it weren't so tragic."

Benjamin considered Dr. Holst's statement. He was tempted to think that Holst was referring to the loss of potential intelligence, but he sensed there was more to it than that. Holst really was saddened by what had happened to Estefan.

"What's his… her name?" Benjamin asked.

"I don't know," said Dr. Holst. "She won't talk to me. She talks sometimes, but doesn't seem to be fully aware of where she is. Doesn't acknowledge people around her. The shock of finding herself in a hospital in a foreign country, four decades in the past...."

"In the body of a young boy," Benjamin added.

"Yes," said Dr. Holst, turning from Estefan to Benjamin. "Although it's unclear whether she is even aware of that." He went to the door, beckoning for Benjamin to follow.

"What do you mean?" asked Benjamin, walking after him. "How can she not know?"

"The mind has amazing coping mechanisms," said Dr. Holst, as he closed the door. He continued down the hall, motioning for Benjamin to come along. "I recently read of a stroke victim who had completely disowned the left side of her body. She wouldn't bathe her left side, wouldn't brush the hair on the left side of her head. When given lipstick, she'd apply it only to the right side of her mouth. If a doctor pointed out to her that her left arm was clearly connected to her body, she would make all sorts of excuses for it. If pressed, she would get angry and tell the doctor that she didn't know whose arm it was, but it wasn't her problem." They turned down a corner, passing a couple of orderlies who regarded Benjamin curiously.

"But you're talking about brain damage," said Benjamin. "A physical problem with the brain."

"Yes," said Dr. Holst, "but the line between mental illness and brain injury is not as clear-cut as many believe. Particularly in certain types of brains."

"Where are we going?" asked Benjamin.

"You said you wanted the truth," said Dr. Holst. "I'm going to give it to you."

"So no more worries about me shutting down? Losing myself inside the delusion, because I can't handle the truth?"

"I'm very concerned about the possibility," said Dr. Holst. "But to be honest, I'm out of time. I've tried to work with you, but you keep fighting me. As I said, this program is under a great deal of pressure to produce results. Maybe my mistake was not in pushing you too hard, but in not pushing you hard enough. Maybe you need to be confronted with the truth."

They came to another door, which bore a placard labeled RECREATION ROOM.

"What's this?" Benjamin asked, as they paused in front of the door. "The truth is in the recreation room?"

"Part of it, yes," said Dr. Holst. "If you don't feel you're ready for this, we can return to my office."

"Ready for what?" asked Benjamin. "What's behind that door?"

"It's time to decide," said Dr. Holst. "Do you want to retreat into the illusion or do you want to know the truth?"

"I want to know the truth," said Benjamin.

Dr. Holst nodded. "Then follow me." He opened the door and walked inside. After a moment, Benjamin followed.

He found himself in a large room lit by natural lighting that filtered in from high-placed windows. To his left were a ping-pong table and a foosball table. To his right were a number of plush chairs and a bookshelf containing several dozen hardbacks and piles of magazines. Two boys and a girl sat together, talking quietly. They appeared to be between the ages of eight and twelve. Both boys seemed to be of Hispanic descent; the girl looked like a mulatto. They looked up when Benjamin entered the room. They exchanged anxious glances, and their conversation became muted.

Benjamin looked around the room. There was no one and nothing else of interest here.

"Why are we here?" he asked. "Are we going to play a therapeutic game of ping-pong?"

"I wanted you to meet some of our other patients," said Dr. Holst.

"Subjects, you mean," said Benjamin.

"I'd ask you to avoid that word in here," said Dr. Holst. "As far as those three children are concerned, they are patients."

"Because you don't want to upset them with the truth?"

"Upsetting *them* is the least of my worries. Come, let me introduce you."

Dr. Holst led Benjamin to the group. The three stopped talking and looked up as he approached.

"Benjamin, I'd like you to meet Miguel, Thomas and Marina. Children, this is Benjamin. He's a new patient here."

"Hello," said Benjamin.

The three exchanged confused glances, and one of the boys murmured something to the others that Benjamin didn't catch.

"Children, don't be rude," said Dr. Holst. "Say hello to Benjamin."

"Hello," the children said.

"Much better," said Dr. Holst, with a smile. "We'll leave you alone now. I was just showing Benjamin around." He took Benjamin's arm and escorted him away from the group.

"Do they know me?" Benjamin asked, as they made their way to the door.

"Why do you ask?" said Dr. Holst.

"I just... got the impression they recognized me."

Dr. Holst opened the door and they began walking back toward his office. "They've met you before," he said, "but you wouldn't remember them, of course."

"Is that all of them? All of your subjects?"

"Besides you, you mean?"

"Well, yes."

"Yes. Estefan, Miguel, Thomas, Marina and you. Why, did you expect more?"

Benjamin shrugged. They had reached Dr. Holst's office, and he followed Holst inside and they sat down.

"Why did you take me to meet those kids?" Benjamin asked.

"Why do you think?" asked Dr. Holst.

"I don't know!" cried Benjamin. "Just tell me what the fuck is going on!"

"Quantos años tienes?" asked Dr. Holst.

"I don't speak Spanish," Benjamin grumbled.

"Neither does Estefan," said Dr. Holst. "I'm lucky you speak English."

"What the hell are you talking about?"

"The mind has amazing coping mechanisms," Dr. Holst mused. "People can convince themselves of just about anything. How old are you, Benjamin?"

"I told you. I'm fifty-eight."

"You were born in 1942. It's currently 1950. How old are you? Quantos años tienes?"

"I'm done with this," said Benjamin, getting out of his chair. "I'm going back to my room."

Dr. Holst unbuttoned his right sleeve, rolled it up, and planted his elbow on the desk. "Arm-wrestle me," he said.

"You've lost your fucking mind."

"Arm-wrestle me," said Dr. Holst again. "Beat me and I'll let you go back to your room. Hell, I'll discharge you. You can be a free man, if you think you can handle it."

"I'm leaving," said Benjamin, walking to the door.

"The hell you are," said Dr. Holst. "You walk out that door and it'll take me thirty seconds to have security subdue you and drag you right back in here. Beat me at arm-wrestling, and I'll call off the dogs."

Benjamin exhaled angrily. He'd had enough of Dr. Holst's mind games. All he wanted to do is go home. But where was home? If it was really 1950, then the place he thought of as home wouldn't exist yet. He wondered what would happen if he showed up on his parents' doorstep. Would they be relieved to see him? Would he meet another of himself? There were no answers. Nothing made sense. He needed psychiatric help, but he couldn't trust Dr. Holst to help him.

Benjamin sat down, rolled up his sleeve, and leaned over the table. Even at fifty-eight, he was stronger than most men. Dr. Holst was a slightly built man in a sedentary occupation. Benjamin didn't think he'd have much trouble beating him. The question was whether Holst would live up to his promise when he did.

Dr. Holst smiled and clasped Benjamin's hand in his. Benjamin's hand practically disappeared in Holst's grip; Benjamin hadn't noticed before how massive the man's hands were. Holst began to exert pressure, and Benjamin leaned into it. A heartbeat later, Holst slammed the back of Benjamin's hand against his desk. Benjamin was still trying to figure out how this was possible when Holst encircled Benjamin's wrist with his thumb and forefinger and pulled Benjamin's hand over the desk toward him, palm up.

"You see this?" he said, squeezing Benjamin's hand like a vise. "This is your hand." He held out his own left hand. "Compare it to mine."

"Let go," growled Benjamin, struggling against Holst's impossibly strong grip.

"Look at my hand," Holst said. Benjamin looked away. "Look at it!" Holst cried.

"Let go of my arm!" screamed Benjamin. "Let it go!"

His voice sounded strange. Small and high-pitched. He heard the echo of Jessica's voice: *Let it go, Dad.*

Holst released him, and Benjamin fell back into his chair. He stared at the red mark on his wrist where Holst had held him, turning his hand over slowly as if seeing it for the first time. A small, nearly hairless hand, unscarred and unwrinkled.

He heard a child's laughter, and realized it was his own. The laughter turned to sobs. He blinked away the tears, wiping his face with his sleeve.

"No," he murmured, staring at his hands. "This isn't possible." He was struck again by the strangeness of his own voice. "My name is Benjamin Stone. I'm fifty-eight years old." But as he said it, his own voice mocked him.

"I'm afraid you aren't," said Holst. "I understand this is quite a shock."

Benjamin laughed again at the understated absurdity of Holst's comment, and again his voice betrayed him. The laughter turned to screams. At some point, he became aware that he was lying on carpet, with many hands clutching at him. A bee stung his arm, and everything went black.

CHAPTER TWENTY-SIX

Benjamin awoke in the same bed, with gray light still filtering through the window. Had he slept the night? He had no way of knowing how much time had passed. If he had dreamed, he wasn't aware of it. He felt groggy from the sedative.

He found himself staring again at his hands. They stubbornly remained small, soft, unscarred, and virtually hairless. That part hadn't been a dream. Either that, or he was still dreaming now; it was becoming almost impossible to tell. His life had become an endless series of disconnected delusions, some of which seemed to be anchored to an underlying reality. He found himself laughing, and was again arrested by the strangeness of the sound.

Had it always sounded like that? Had he always been in this strange body? No. It was impossible. He had fifty-eight years of memories as Benjamin Stone. He had lived through the Beatles, the Moon Landing, the Vietnam War, Reaganomics, the Persian Gulf War. He had worked for thirty years as a cop in Portland, investigated hundreds of crimes. He had gotten married, had a daughter, watched his wife succumb to cancer. All of that was real. It had to be.

And yet, here he was, in this body, fifty years in the past. His mind had tried to deny it, like the woman who didn't recognize her own left arm, but something Holst said had forced him to see the truth. No, it wasn't what Holst had said. It was Jessica telling him to let it go. He realized now that was when the walls he'd assembled around his psyche had begun to crumble. His own subconscious had been trying to tell him the truth, through his visions.

The only possible answer stared him in the face: he wasn't a "special case," as Dr. Holst had claimed. He was just another subject. A child who had developed the ability to see the future, and had been brought to this hospital to serve the interests of GLARE. That's what Holst had been trying to show him by taking him to meet the other subjects. They were all children. And not only that, but one was missing: Felipe. "Because I'm Felipe," he said aloud. The high pitch of his voice jarred him again, but the words themselves carried no meaning. He had no memory of being Felipe. He occupied Felipe's body, but he remained Benjamin Stone. He had distinct memories of his childhood—living in the old farm house in the middle of his father's apricot orchard, just outside of Sunnyview. Despite the incontrovertible physical evidence, he couldn't make himself believe that he was Felipe Sanz.

No, he was to Felipe Sanz what that poor German woman was to Estefan: a host for the subject's consciousness. Somehow, like that woman, he had been pulled back through time into the subject's body. And if Estefan was any indication, he'd spend the rest of his life this way. Would it drive him insane, as it had that woman? Had it already? Was there any hope for him to live anything like a normal life? Even if he were ever released from this institution, he was physically and legally an eight-year-old child. He'd be sent to live with Felipe's family, to grow up all over again, with a family that in all likelihood barely spoke English. Jesus Christ, he'd have to go through *puberty* again. The whole thing was absurd. And he hadn't even begun to consider what had happened to Felipe. Had Felipe awoken one morning to find himself in the body of 58-year-old Benjamin Stone? Was he even now wandering around modern Sunnyview, even more baffled and terrified than Benjamin was? It was like a time-traveling version of that silly movie where the mother and daughter changed places: too ridiculous for him to take seriously. No, he couldn't worry about what had happened to Felipe. He had to concentrate on the here and now. How long had he been in this hospital? The whole time he had thought he was in Sunnyview in the year 2000, had he really been here?

But that was the wrong way to think about it. He hadn't been in the year 2000 and the year 1950 simultaneously. He had lived in the year 2000, and then his consciousness had been dragged back to the past. The process hadn't been instantaneous; he'd gradually become more and more aware of the past intruding on the future. And in

1950, Felipe had gradually lost more and more of his identity to Benjamin. And now the transition was apparently complete. He, Benjamin Stone, was fully inhabiting Felipe Sanz's body. He was struck anew by the absurdity of Felipe awakening in the body of a 58-year-old man in the year 2000. No, it was too bizarre to contemplate. He had enough weirdness to deal with in 1950.

He got out of bed and made his way to the bathroom to urinate. He did his best to mentally prepare himself for this activity, but there was really no way to prepare oneself for suddenly waking up with prepubescent genitalia. At least, he found himself thinking, Felipe hadn't been in the throes of puberty at the time Benjamin took over his body. The hormonal surges on top of everything else would surely have driven Benjamin mad.

After finishing this business, he splashed some water on his face, trying to clear the fuzzy residue of the sedative from his mind. He dried his face and took several long, deep breaths. When he felt reasonably steady, he returned to his room and tried the door to the hall. It was locked from the outside. He considered banging on it, but wasn't sure there was any point. In an institution like this, the staff would be inured to the sound of maniacs pounding on doors, screaming to be let out.

He went to the window and spent some time trying to discern objects through the frosted glass, but it was hopeless. Somewhere beyond what he experienced was a real world populated by real people going about their daily lives, but Benjamin could only imagine that world, based on the hazy shapes that reached his eyes. Trapped in this room, there was no way to know what was real.

After some time, the nurse came to check on him. "Benjamin?" she said, much the same way she had the last time. He realized now that she hadn't simply been checking whether he was awake; she was checking what name he would respond to. He apparently responded appropriately, because she made a note on her clipboard and asked him to follow her down the hall. This time, she took him to an observation room where she took his blood pressure, checked his irises, and performed a number of other mundane tests that presumably were designed either to determine whether the sedative had left his system or whether he could respond to simple commands without collapsing in a hysterical episode. Evidently he checked out okay, because after making a few more notes, she led him back down the hall to Holst's office.

"Benjamin," said Holst, as Benjamin took a seat across from him once again. "How are you feeling?"

Benjamin wanted to laugh, but bit his lip. He wasn't sure he'd be able to keep laughter from morphing into hysterical sobs. He took a deep breath. "I'm fine," he said. "Considering." Considering that I'm a grown man who has been sucked fifty years back through time into the body of an eight-year-old.

"Any dreams last night?"

"Not that I'm aware of," said Benjamin. He wondered if he would ever dream again. What would he see if he did? Who would he be in the dreams?

"Do you recall our conversation yesterday?"

"Yes,"

"Good," said Holst. "That's progress."

"Is it," said Benjamin flatly. "You consider it progress that I'm stuck here permanently. "In Felipe's body. I am stuck here, right?"

Holst hesitated a moment, but evidently decided that the direct approach was warranted. "Yes. We're not certain yet if the phenomenon is permanent. A reconciliation between the two personalities may be possible." But Benjamin thought of Estefan Lopez, who was still not himself, fifty years later.

"What do you mean, a reconciliation?"

"You have to find a way to reconcile the Benjamin Stone personality with the Felipe Sanz personality. It isn't going to be easy, but I can help you, if you let me."

"I don't understand," said Benjamin. "I'm Benjamin Stone. Felipe's personality is gone. There's no 'reconciliation' going on. It's just me stuck in this strange body."

"I need you to understand something," said Holst. "You've made a breakthrough. You've seen through one delusion. But it's important that you not fall victim to another."

Benjamin stared at his hands, Holst's words barely penetrating. "What are you talking about?" he asked after a moment. "I finally understand what is happening to me. I've been pulled back through time. Just like Estefan. The person Estefan has become, I mean."

"No," said Holst.

"Don't try to bullshit me, Holst," asked Benjamin. "What is happening to me is exactly what happened to Estefan."

"You've seen someone whose mind has been taken over by an alternate personality," said Holst. "But you're misinterpreting the nature of the phenomenon. Those personalities… they're not people who exist outside of the respective subjects. They're constructs. Figments of the subjects' imagination."

Benjamin laughed. "Estefan is *imagining* that he's an elderly woman who can only speak German? That's quite an imagination."

"Yes," Holst said. "It is. An imagination orders of magnitudes more powerful than normal. It takes a very special sort of brain to imagine on such a scale. A child's brain that has been altered to have certain natural conceptual barriers removed."

"What are you saying?"

"I'm saying that Benjamin Stone is not a distinct person, separate from Felipe Sanz. He is a creation of Felipe's unconscious mind."

Benjamin could hardly believe what he was hearing. "So I'm not really Benjamin Stone?" he said incredulously. "I'm a figment of Felipe's imagination?"

"Benjamin Stone is a construct," said Holst, softly but firmly. "A device Felipe created to allow his brain to make sense of his perceptions. Understand that I'm not saying that Benjamin Stone isn't real. In a sense, he's as real as I am. And you may very well continue to think of yourself as Benjamin Stone for some time. Felipe's original personality will probably never fully return. But we are all ultimately the product of our memories, and many of your memories are false. The product of Felipe's imagination."

"My memories are real," Benjamin insisted. "I've been pulled back here, into this body, just like Estefan. Estefan projected his mind into the future, into someone else's body," said Benjamin. "That person somehow came back instead of him. The same thing happened to Felipe. To me." As he said it aloud, he realized how insane it sounded. Either he was making a huge leap toward sanity, or he was on the verge of losing himself completely.

"That isn't what happened," said Dr. Holst. "Felipe didn't project himself forward into Benjamin Stone's body. Felipe constructed a fictional reality and placed himself into it, in the form of Benjamin Stone."

"So after all this, you're denying what GLARE is doing? You're still going to insist there's no secret precognition program?"

"No," said Holst. "I'd have preferred to allow you some level of delusion, as it's more conducive to gathering information, and frankly I don't think the human brain is designed to handle the level of cognitive shock you're experiencing. But I'm out of time, and you insisted on the truth, so I'm giving it to you. GLARE exists, although it isn't known by that name. Just as William Glazier exists, more or less, in the form of David Stockton. The major outlines of your memories are accurate. We created a group of subjects with what you might call precognitive abilities, for intelligence purposes. But the details of your memories are fiction."

"Details like *who I am*?" cried Benjamin, his voice cracking.

Holst sighed. "The alternative is that you're a grown man who got time-warped back into the body of a child in 1950. You must hear how ridiculous that sounds."

"You work for a secret program that causes mutations in the brains of children to predict the future, and you're going to accuse *me* of being ridiculous?"

"This program is unorthodox, to be sure," said Dr. Holst. "It was the result of a fortuitous accident, and our methods lie on the fringes of modern science. We've learned that the human brain is capable of things we never imagined possible. But there are some hard limits to what can be done. Limits imposed by the laws of physics and brain chemistry. Two things that we know to be impossible are time travel and the transfer of consciousness from one person's body to another."

"Everything you're doing is premised on a kind of time travel!" Benjamin shouted.

Dr. Holst shook his head. "Felipe's mind didn't travel forward in time to the year 2000. He simply *imagined* the year 2000, and projected himself into the construct he imagined. We refer to this as projecting consciousness into the future, but that's really just rhetorical shorthand. It's more like someone drawing a map of a place he's never been to and then tracing his finger along a path on the map. By virtue of his unique brain chemistry, Felipe just happens to be an exceptionally good cartographer."

Holst's narrative made a strange sort of sense, but Benjamin found himself shaking his head. And not just because he found the idea repugnant: he couldn't quite square what Holst was saying with his own experience. "You're telling me that everything I think I've experienced over the past fifty years is simply the imagination of an eight-year-old boy?" he asked, dubiously. "If that were true, what would be the point of asking me about what I've seen, what I remember? I could imagine that Martians attack the Earth tomorrow. That doesn't mean it's going to happen."

"That's correct," said Dr. Holst. "Unrestrained imagination is generally too random to be of much use in projecting events. But recent work in the field of psychology has demonstrated that the unconscious mind tends to revert to certain well-established cultural patterns."

"Yeah, the collective unconscious. Archetypes and all that," said Benjamin, still unconvinced. "I read Jung in college. In 1962. *Twelve years from now.*"

Dr. Holst nodded, smiling. "Jung was one of the first—at least in Western culture—to see how unconscious patterns in thinking mirrored events of which the individual had no direct knowledge. He writes, for example, that racial memories of past events can be inherited by individual members of the race. But Jung also thinks that the unconscious can reflect future events."

"You're saying that people can remember things that haven't happen yet," said Benjamin.

"Events that are important to the race, or to the species as a whole, yes. Jung himself recounts a vision he had in 1913 in which he witnessed a monstrous flood covering Germany. He saw mighty yellow waves, the floating rubble of civilization, and the drowned bodies of uncounted thousands. Then the whole sea turned to blood. Jung was perplexed and nauseated, assuming this vision was personal. It was not until World War I broke out a year later that he realized its collective nature. That experience led him to conclude that each person's unconscious possesses not only a personal but also a collective dimension."

"You're contradicting yourself," said Benjamin. "If Jung saw World War I, then he was seeing the future. You just said that was impossible."

"No, he was *imagining* the future," said Dr. Holst. "It seems like a semantic point, but it's an important one. Jung had a vague foreboding regarding catastrophic events, and his unconscious mind gave form to that sentiment. But the details of the vision were of his own creation. He didn't actually 'see' the future, as if there were some sort of tunnel through time that allowed him to glimpse specific events. He tapped into a collective awareness of the event, millions of individual points of view, each affected by the event in some way. Jung was probably one of the rare individuals with a congenital brain anomaly that allowed him to sense these impressions more strongly than most. The sort of anomaly that GLARE has been able to replicate with some success in its subjects."

"What you're saying Jung experienced, though…." Benjamin said. "That's nothing like what I've experienced. You're comparing a single vision lasting maybe a few seconds to an entire lifetime of concrete experiences."

"The difference is one of degree, not of kind," said Dr. Holst. "Felipe's gift is exponentially more powerful than Jung's, but he can't see the future. He can only *imagine* the future, based on impressions of major events. He seems to experience the events from a single, discrete perspective, but this perspective is really a synthesis of millions of viewpoints. In other words, the person he imagines himself to be in the vision doesn't actually exist. He's a sort of fictional character, a stand-in that represents a manifestation of the dreamer's consciousness. We call them avatars, after the Hindu concept of deities who manifest themselves in a physical form in the material world. The appearance of the avatar is not reflective of the deity's actual character or appearance, but rather is determined by the necessity of circumstance. Similarly, if Felipe's consciousness senses some important event occurring in Sunnyview in the year 2000, he will construct a persona to experience that event first-hand. Maybe a retired police detective who comes to town to find his missing daughter."

Benjamin couldn't believe it. *Wouldn't* believe it.

"I am not a construct!" he yelled. "I lived for fifty years before coming back to Sunnyview. Felipe Sanz didn't somehow bring me into existence a few days ago!"

"It's hard to say when Benjamin Stone became a distinct entity," said Dr. Holst. "Felipe's visions started a few weeks ago, but at first they were very vague. It's been five days since he first mentioned the name Benjamin Stone. At first he would awaken somewhat disoriented, as if uncertain who he was at first. Two days ago was the first time the persona persisted into his waking state, but when pressed on the details of his memories, he reverted to the Felipe persona. Today is the first day that the Benjamin Stone persona persisted through a full sleep cycle. It remains to be seen whether the condition is permanent, as it was with Estefan."

"But my memories," Benjamin protested. "Everything that's happened to me over the past fifty-eight years...."

"Figments of Felipe's imagination, mostly," said Dr. Holst. "The major world events you remember are probably real, because those would be the sorts of things that would make the most impression on the collective consciousness. And you seem to have an understanding of certain cultural touchstones—your knowledge of Jung being the prime example. But it's very unlikely an actual Benjamin Stone will ever exist, per se. Even the name is a giveaway."

"My name?" Benjamin asked. "What do you mean?"

"Well, for starters, in the book of Exodus, Benjamin is the brother of Joseph. Joseph's dreams anger his brothers, which results in him being sold into slavery in Egypt. But Joseph rises to a position of power in Egypt, and years later his brothers come to him, begging for food. Joseph demands that they bring their youngest brother, Benjamin, to him. So Benjamin is literally summoned by Joseph, the dreamer. Later, Joseph arranges for a silver cup to be placed in Benjamin's sack, as a pretext to have Benjamin arrested and brought back to him. Benjamin is just a dupe, at the mercy of the guy who's really in charge. Joseph, the dreamer, who in this case is equivalent to Felipe. These sorts of cultural references come up in dreams often. You may recall that Jung called them archetypes."

Benjamin swallowed hard. "That doesn't mean anything. Benjamin is a common—"

"Secondly, the surname Stone. It's a bland, American-sounding name that carries the connotation of strength and solidity. A fixed point around which events whirl. And it's a particularly interesting choice when you contrast it against the name Glazier."

"Glazier?" asked Benjamin, surprised. "What are you talking about?"

"A glazier is a glassmaker," said Dr. Holst. "A person who transmutes sand into glass panes for windows, mirrors, lenses. Tools that allow one to see what he otherwise couldn't. Felipe's mind was making a pun. Glazier and Sanz. The glassmaker and the sand."

Benjamin's stomach churned as Holst's words triggered associations in his memory. Sand. Pane. Lens. It had to be a coincidence. What did Jung call it? Synchronicity.

"If you examine your memories carefully," Holst was saying, "I think you'll find other such references. Not just archetypes, but unlikely coincidences, and possibly events that seem inexplicable. The unconscious mind is playful. It likes to fold back on itself, making subtle jokes at its own expense."

Sandford. Payne. Lentz. How had he not noticed it before?

"Starting to see it, are you?" said Holst. "I've gotten fairly good at it. We have to strip out the noise of the individual's unconscious mind and determine the underlying events that prompted the vision. Benjamin's struggle to find his missing daughter probably reflects Felipe's distress at being separated from his family, so we can discount that thread of the vision entirely...."

"Wait," said Benjamin weakly. "You're telling me Jessica isn't dead?"

"There is no Jessica. Benjamin Stone doesn't exist. How could he have a daughter?"

Benjamin began to feel dizzy. "No, you're lying. Jessica is the only reason I found out about GLARE. How could GLARE be real if Jessica isn't real?"

"As I said, the broad outlines of your memories reflect reality to some extent. GLARE does exist, but we use a different acronym for it. I assume GLARE is an acronym?"

"The Glazier Lab for the Advanced Research of Electronics," said Benjamin.

Holst nodded. "Interesting."

"Why? What is the program really called?"

"Does it matter?" asked Holst. "It's confidential, but if you really want to know, I'll tell you. As a gesture of goodwill. I do want to help you. But if I'm going to have a chance to do that, you have to help me as well."

Benjamin shook his head, shutting his eyes tight. "No," he said. "It doesn't make any sense. I know things an eight-year-old boy couldn't possibly know. How would Felipe learn police procedure? How the hell did Estefan learn German, for Christ's sake?"

"The collective unconscious," said Holst. "Small impressions taken from millions of points of view. Felipe and Estefan tapped into a vast well of collective knowledge and used that knowledge to create fictional constructs with certain definitive characteristics."

"A composite character created from the unconscious memories of millions of people," Benjamin murmured. "Memories of events that haven't happened yet."

Holst shrugged. "I can only tell you what we know. Some of it is only conjecture. But with the limited experience we have, I can tell you that there's no evidence to indicate the avatars actually exist outside the mind of the subjects."

"But *why?*" Benjamin protested. "Why would they go to so much trouble?"

"Imagining a complex character with a complete history of memories is not difficult for someone like Felipe. And in fact, it's quite necessary."

"Necessary how?"

"Felipe's unconscious mind had a reason for projecting himself into Sunnyview in 2000. It wasn't random chance. Just as a person's dreams often reflect an unconscious attempt to work out some problem of his waking life, Felipe's projection into this time and place reflect an urge on the part of the collective unconscious to resolve some conflict. The people you met, the events you experienced, were all part of the collective unconsciousness's attempt to work out some problem. To have those experiences, you had to be a particular person. In this case, a retired police detective with a missing daughter."

Benjamin found himself holding his head in his hands. He wasn't sure how much more of this he could take. Even with all the inexplicable events he'd experienced over the past few days, he had on some level always believed that the nightmare would eventually end, that ultimately he would find some answers, and some peace. But now it was beginning to seem that the line between fantasy and reality would be blurred forever. He wanted to deny what Holst was telling him, but somehow he knew it was true. The idea that Felipe had transported his mind forward in time, into Benjamin's body, was a fantasy. Benjamin was nothing more than a facet of Felipe's personality, filled out with details assembled from millions of strangers, many of whom hadn't yet been born.

It was simply too much to process. He was Benjamin Stone, but there was no Benjamin Stone. He had experienced fifty-eight years of life, but he was only eight years old. GLARE both existed and didn't exist. He needed something to hold onto. An anchor. A rock. *A stone*, he thought, and realized he was laughing hysterically.

"I can help you, Benjamin," said Holst. "I can help you separate what is real from what isn't. You can adjust. There is no reason you can't have a normal life, once we—"

"Once you get what you need from me," said Benjamin.

"I promise you," said Holst, "I will do everything I can to help you, and to get you out of here as soon as possible. Mr. Stockton is a very driven man, but he can be reasoned with, and I do have some influence with him. But you have to give me something, Benjamin."

"Or what?" Benjamin snapped. "What can you possibly do to me that is worse than this?"

"I'm not going to lie to you," Holst said. "Dealing with your circumstances is going to be an adjustment. But I *can* help you."

But Benjamin wasn't talking about being trapped in Felipe's body. As bizarre as his physical circumstances were, they weren't nearly as troubling as the realization that his memories were a lie. Before this moment, Benjamin would have thought that losing his daughter was the worst thing he could imagine. But now he realized he was wrong: the idea that Jessica might never even have existed was far worse. Benjamin searched his memories, desperate for something to connect to Jessica, some reason to believe she was real. If what Holst was saying was true, then his memories of important historical events, events that affected large numbers of people, were the most accurate. But he couldn't connect Watergate, the Moon landing, or the Cuban Missile Crisis to Jessica. For that matter, he couldn't think of any major historical events that he could directly connect to *himself*. He'd watched the Moon landing on TV. He'd been too young to be drafted to fight in Vietnam. The assassination of Kennedy, the fall of the Berlin Wall, the Persian Gulf War... he had no direct experience with anything. Only news coverage and second-hand reports. He was no one. A faceless, nameless observer.

"...presents us with an unprecedented opportunity," Holst was saying. "We've never had a subject with full recall of their alternate personality. Usually we only get snippets of data, interpreted through a child's eyes. Or, as in the case of Estefan, the subject is so overwhelmed by the idea of having to reconcile his fictional persona with the subject's original personality, that he becomes impossible to communicate with. The information is there, but we can't get to it. In your case, though, you have fifty years of historical data in your mind, and the ability to communicate it. The value of that information in terms of saving American lives and promoting American interests is incalculable."

"I get it," said Benjamin bitterly. "I'm a tool to you," said Benjamin. "A repository of information."

"Even if that's all you were to us," said Holst, "the fact is that our interests are aligned. You need help separating fact from fiction, and I can give you that help if you give me the information we need. Please, Benjamin, you must try to understand that."

"What do you want from me?" Benjamin asked. "What would you do, even if I wanted to cooperate? If I *could* cooperate? Stop the entire future from happening? Would you stop the Vietnam War, or just make sure we win it? Would you avoid the mistake of supporting the Shah of Iran, or simply be more aggressive about it? How do I know that all of our government's mistakes aren't the result of acting on intelligence I gave you?"

Holst was busily jotting notes. "When you say 'Vietnam,' are you referring to French Indochina?"

Benjamin laughed. "These questions haven't even occurred to you, have they? You just gather your data, pass it along to the powers that be in Washington, and hope for the best."

Holst set down his pad. "Believe it or not, Benjamin—"

"Don't call me that," Benjamin said.

"You would prefer Felipe?"

"No. Just don't patronize me by calling me Benjamin. Call me Subject Seventeen or whatever the hell I am. That's all I am to you bastards anyway."

Holst took a breath, obviously trying to remain calm. "As I was about to say, no, you aren't the first person to have considered these philosophical questions. David and I have talked about them quite in depth. As well as many others. For example, if you were to tell me the details of this war in Indochina, and the U.S. government were able to alter the outcome of it, what would the effect be on other events you foresaw? Would they still happen, or might we change the timeline so much that your subsequent memories would become increasingly inaccurate? We really don't know the answers yet, but we have to consider the possibility that acting on one piece of information you provide will make the information less useful overall, and therefore only intervene when absolutely necessary. Admittedly, the flow of information is mostly one-way, by necessity. We are an information-gathering entity. We pass the information on to Washington and they take action as they see fit."

Benjamin shook his head. "And you have no qualms about this system?"

"Any qualms I may have are secondary to the goals of this program, which exists because of special dispensation from the federal government. David and I don't set the terms. And as I've mentioned, if we don't start producing results, we may very well get shut down. That would be very bad for American interests."

"How do you know?" asked Benjamin. "I've seen how things turn out, fifty years from now. America does alright."

"But GLARE exists in that vision of the future," said Holst.

"What's your point?"

"My point is, maybe America survives only because GLARE exists to help us avoid the worst mistakes of the next fifty years. Maybe America survives only because of *you*."

"That's circular logic," said Benjamin. "You sound paranoid."

"I have good reason," said Holst. "We are at war with the Soviet Union. I don't know who wins that war. From what I can gather from Estefan's remarks, and what you've just told me, the United States comes out on top. But from my perspective, that outcome is far from certain. In fact, our victory may be dependent on this very conversation. Maybe, if you tell me as much as you know about the history between the U.S. and our enemies over the next fifty years, we can ensure that victory occurs."

"But we *know* it occurs!" cried Benjamin. "If it didn't happen, I wouldn't have experienced it! Your whole program is set up to prevent tragedies from occurring. But now you're telling me you're going to use the intelligence I give you to make sure those tragedies occur!"

"As I said, all we can do is pass on the intelligence you provide, with recommendations for intervening. You mentioned something about Vietnam. Do the French lose Indochina? Can you tell me what happens in Korea? We're hearing reports that the North is planning to invade."

It was becoming clear that Holst wasn't going to give up. He was going to keep pressing Benjamin for information, and Benjamin was tempted to give it to him. How many people suffered under totalitarian rule in North Korea today because of the outcome of that war? And yet, Benjamin wasn't sure how much valuable intelligence he could impart, though, even if he wanted to.

Holst had told him it was June 14, 1950. Had the Korean War started yet? Evidently not. Benjamin vaguely recalled that the North had invaded sometime in the summer of 1950. He'd been only a child at the time, but of course he'd learned all about the conflict later in school. He could tell Holst that the North would invade sometime in the near future, that the U.N. had landed troops at Incheon for a counter-attack, and that the war ended in a draw in 1953, with the border near where it was at the beginning of the war. He couldn't imagine any of that information being of much use to General MacArthur. He also recalled that Truman had relieved MacArthur of his command late in the war because of disagreements over strategy. Had Truman been privy to information that wasn't available to MacArthur, thanks to GLARE (or whatever it was called)? Did the war end in a draw because Truman had known in advance that victory was impossible, or because Benjamin had refused to tell Holst what he knew? Did it make any difference?

And even if he could alter (or ensure?) the outcome of the Korean War, would it improve America's situation overall? Would the war in Vietnam still occur, and would the result be the same? Would the Cuban Missile Crisis still happen? What about Autumn Forge, the military operation that, according to Glazier, had nearly resulted in all-out war with the Soviet Union? Glazier had said they had learned about the threat from a girl named Marina Evans. If he could get Spiegel to tell him about Marina, it might give him a fixed reference point to work from.

"That girl," Benjamin said. "Marina. What does she see in her visions?"

"We haven't gotten any solid intelligence from her yet," said Holst. "She's spoken a few words of what we believe is Finnish. Why? What do you know about her?"

Benjamin didn't reply. Holst's comment cohered with Glazier's story about Marina warning of Soviet overreaction to NATO troop movements in Finland in 1983. That presumably meant that GLARE didn't need Benjamin to forestall that particular catastrophe. Anything that Benjamin said to Holst about it would therefore be redundant, and maybe even counterproductive. The best course of action, then, would be to say nothing.

Anything he said to Holst about events occurring before Autumn Forge might also derail attempts to prevent war with the Soviet Union. For that matter, how many other close calls had there been in the past fifty years? How many times had the U.S. and the Soviets almost wiped out the human race with nuclear weapons? How could he know whether anything he said might tip the scales of any of those crises toward total annihilation?

And what would happen if the government acted on intelligence he provided, and it prevented something that one of the other subjects experienced? Would their memories change, or would their visions change to match the new reality? Or was each imagined timeline a self-contained narrative? There was simply too much Benjamin didn't understand about how all this worked, and he got the impression Holst and Stockton didn't understand it much better than he did. They just passed the information on to some mysterious figure in Washington and hoped for the best.

Beyond such abstract philosophical concerns, there was another idea nagging at the back of his mind; something that Holst had said: that Felipe's unconscious had a reason for projecting himself into Sunnyview in 2000. Some specific problem he was trying to solve.

If that were true, it seemed unlikely that Felipe had chosen that particular place and time in order to change the outcome of the Korean War. No, whatever reason Felipe, God, or the "collective unconscious" had for devising the persona of Benjamin Stone, it had something to do with what was happening in Sunnyview in

2000. Felipe's consciousness had imagined that particular time and place in order to gather some specific bit of data. But what had Benjamin learned in Sunnyview that could be of use to GLARE? He'd experienced no major turning points in world history that he was aware of. Although, now that he thought about it, he realized he had met one person who had experienced something that might qualify: Sofia. But that raised another question.

"You said that my experiences—Benjamin Stone's experiences—are mostly imaginary, except for elements that connect with actual historical events. David Stockton is an important historical figure, so his presence bleeds through to the delusion, and I experience him as William Glazier."

"That's one way to put it, yes," said Holst.

"But what about Estefan? How is it that he existed in both places, the real world and the delusion?"

Holst nodded. "It's a good question," he said. "I would conjecture that subjects in this program act as additional 'anchors,' connecting the delusion to reality. Their visions, like yours, are grounded in reality, so they also 'bleed through,' to use your terminology. Because of their cognizance of important historical events, they become, in a sense, critical historical figures."

Benjamin wondered if the same was true of Chris Sandford. Was he "real" as well? Or had he simply been the unlucky figment of Felipe's imagination who had somehow seen the illusion for what it was?

"That's why you were interested in Sofia's visions," said Benjamin. "Because she's real too. Another touchstone to reality. So what she sees, the airplanes hitting the buildings... that actually happens. It's not just part of Felipe's imagination."

"Yes," said Holst. "A vision within a vision. It's a little like the conundrum of asking a genie for an infinite number of wishes. If it really is possible to encounter future subjects of this program in your visions, the possibilities are endless."

"So you think Sofia is real? That she *will be* real?"

"Well, it's certainly possible that Felipe imagined Sofia, but Felipe's unconscious mind would have had some reason for doing so. So we would have to ask what unconscious desire prompted the creation of the Sofia character. It's fairly clear, for example, the Jessica character was created to give Benjamin Stone a reason for coming to Sunnyview. That was Felipe's unconscious mind creating a bridge between itself and the desires of the collective unconscious. But what purpose does Sofia serve? Why would Felipe invent her? Her name may be a clue. *Sofia* is the Greek word for wisdom. It's possible that Felipe gave her that name because of her insight."

Benjamin gave the matter some thought, but came up with nothing. Sofia seemed to serve no purpose in the visions other than to communicate the content of her own visions to Benjamin—which would seem to indicate that what she had seen was real. But he hadn't gotten enough detail from her to provide any useful intelligence to GLARE. He didn't know where or when the event occurred, or who was responsible. And if his purpose had been to prevent that attack, why hadn't Felipe been projected to the scene of the attack himself, rather than projecting himself to Sunnyview in 2000 to experience the event second-hand? No, he was still missing something. Benjamin had been meant to meet Sofia, but not to prevent the attack she had witnessed. What tragedy, then, had he been meant to prevent?

The tragedy he had experienced in Sunnyview hadn't been world-shattering; it had been personal. The death of his daughter, who didn't exist. *That* was the really inexplicable element of the visions. The real question wasn't why Benjamin had come into contact with Sofia, but rather why Felipe had invented Jessica. Why had it been necessary for Benjamin to go through that pain? What was the point of it? Surely Felipe's unconsciousness could have devised some other way for him to have learned what he had learned.

But he realized, as he reflected on his memories of Jessica's death, that it wasn't true. The memories were false, but they still held power. They reflected an underlying truth that he would not otherwise have grasped. William Glazier hadn't killed his daughter, but he *would* have, in order to save GLARE. And although David Stockton undoubtedly differed from Glazier in some ways, Benjamin had no doubt that he was as cold-blooded as his imaginary counterpart. He had to be, to have devised this program.

The tragedy Felipe had foreseen wasn't a war or an assassination; it was GLARE itself. Experimentation on children for the purposes of promoting "American interests." That was what Felipe had wanted to stop. No, not Felipe. The collective unconsciousness. Humanity itself was screaming across time, "Stop!" Because reducing humanity to a herd of cattle to be manipulated by those who could see the future was anathema to the human spirit. The genius of humanity rebelled against this effort to control it. Spiegel had said it himself: Felipe was sand, and Stockton was the glassmaker. But Felipe had turned himself into a stone. Stone shatters glass.

He smiled as he realized the truth. What Felipe had been trying to show him through his visions. Benjamin's purpose wasn't to help GLARE. It was to put an end to it.

CHAPTER TWENTY-SEVEN

But how could Benjamin stop GLARE?

The obvious answer would be to kill David Stockton. If Stockton was the real-world analog of William Glazier, Benjamin had no qualms about it. Glazier had killed Jessica; Stockton had not. But Stockton would commit murder to protect GLARE if he had to. That was the sort of person he was. The sort who considered the rights of children to be secondary to "American interests." At least, that's what his knowledge of GLARE led him to believe. What if he was wrong?

"What is it really called?" he asked.

"This program?" said Holst, with a smile. "It's the Western Institute for Strategic Estimation."

"WISE," said Benjamin.

"Yes," said Holst. "We generally refer to it simply as 'the program.'"

"Did David Stockton start the program?"

"He and I did together," said Holst.

"You're partners."

"More or less."

"But he handles the political end of things."

"Yes. He works with the people in Washington. Delivers the reports and makes sure that the program receives...."

"Funding?"

"Money isn't really an issue for David Stockton. What we get from Washington is... assurances that our program will be allowed to continue."

"You mean they look the other way when you experiment on children."

Holst actually appeared uncomfortable for a moment. It had occurred to Benjamin that if the analogy of Glazier was Stockton, then the analog of Dominick Spiegel was Dr. Holst. Spiegel had developed misgivings about GLARE. Might Holst be the program's Achilles' heel? But Spiegel had ended up dead, and the program continued without him. Should Benjamin warn him? Would doing so make him realize the sort of man Stockton was? Or would it frighten him into silence? The causal conundrums were maddening. There was simply no way to know.

"I'm well aware of the more unsavory aspects of this program," said Holst at last. "I'm also convinced that it's necessary. I treat all the subjects as humanely as possible."

"I'm sure," said Benjamin. He wondered if Holst really did know everything that was going on. Did he know that the poisoning of Sunnyview's water had continued even after it was discovered that the dumping was causing birth defects? Spiegel's letter indicated that he had found out about the intentional exposure after the fact, but was Benjamin's recollection reflective of reality, or just an arbitrary element of his delusion? Again, there was no way to know how telling Holst about the continued dumping would affect the course of events. It might help stop WISE, or it might simply warn them of a potential security threat. As much as he wanted to trust Holst to eventually do the right thing, he couldn't leave the matter in Holst's hands.

"What would happen to me if I were to cooperate?" Benjamin asked.

Holst studied him for a moment. "As I said, I would do my best to help you adjust to your circumstances."

"But I would continue to be imprisoned here."

"You're not 'imprisoned,' per se," said Holst. "Legally, you are a minor. If you weren't here...."

He didn't need to complete the sentence. I would have to spend the next ten years living with Felipe's parents, Benjamin thought. Pretending to be a child. He shuddered at the idea.

"We'll make you as comfortable as we can," Holst went on. "You can apply for legal emancipation as early as sixteen, but until then, it's probably best that you remain in our care."

Benjamin couldn't help but laugh at the thought. It was a fantasy, of course. They would never let him go. Once he had provided some useful information, they would hold onto him forever. He had a lifetime of historical data in his head; they would never run out of questions to ask him. He wondered if Holst really was naïve enough to believe that Stockton would let him go. Again, it was better not to press the issue.

"North Korea invades," he said, and Holst quickly grabbed his notepad and pencil. "I'm not positive of the date, but I think it was in late June of this year. The United Nations will land troops at Incheon a few months later."

Holst was busily scribbling all this down. "What else?" he said eagerly. "Do we win? Do the Russians get involved? The Chinese?"

Benjamin shook his head. "I'll tell the rest to David Stockton," he said.

"Mr. Stockton doesn't meet with subjects," said Holst.

"Then he doesn't get to know how the Korean War ends."

"Why do you want to speak to Mr. Stockton?"

"If I'm going to help you," said Benjamin, "I want to know who I'm dealing with. You say that Stockton writes up the narrative that gets sent to Washington. I want to make sure I can trust him."

"We have protocols for this," said Holst. "Mr. Stockton has no contact with the subjects. It works better that way."

"You're not listening," said Benjamin. "I don't care about your protocols. You need me. You need the information in my head. And you're not getting it until I talk to Stockton."

Holst regarded him coldly. Benjamin could imagine what he was thinking: *We have ways of making you talk.* But if he were to threaten Benjamin now, he would destroy the nice guy image he'd been cultivating. And who knows, maybe Holst had moral compunctions about forcing subjects to talk. In any case, if he was telling the truth about the pressure they were getting from Washington, he didn't have time to forcibly extract information from Benjamin.

"I will mention it to Mr. Stockton," Holst said.

"You better do more than mention it," Benjamin replied. "Because I'm not saying another word until I talk to him."

Holst nodded and closed his notepad. "I'll have a nurse see you to your room."

Benjamin spent the next several hours sitting on his bed, wondering what he was going to do if David Stockton actually agreed to see him. Where would the meeting take place? Would he be able to get his hands on any kind of weapon? Over his—evidently imaginary—career as a cop, he'd seen people killed with all sorts of improvised weapons, from a pair of scissors to a softball trophy. But there would be very few weapons to be found anywhere in this hospital. The best option he'd spied while in Holst's office was a heavy steel stapler. Even with Felipe's arms, he could kill a man with something like that, if he had the element of surprise. Hell, he could kill Stockton with a pencil if he could get the drop on him. But if Stockton were at all suspicious of Benjamin's motives, it would be very difficult to surprise him. Even if Stockton weren't particularly strong, Benjamin would never be able to overpower him; surprise was his only chance. And if anyone else were in the room at the time, his odds were even worse.

He was still deliberating on this when the door to his room opened and a man entered. Benjamin didn't recognize him, but he knew immediately who the man was. Superficially, he bore little resemblance to the man Benjamin knew as William Glazier: this man was, in addition to being fifty years younger, taller and heavier than Glazier—much to Benjamin's chagrin. But something in the man's eyes and the way he walked tugged at the same visceral aversion that permeated Benjamin's memories of Glazier. He was not the man Benjamin knew, but he shared a soul with that man. He was the sort of man who weighed the lives of innocent children as negligible when compared to the importance of promoting "American interests." An evil man. A man who needed to die. Benjamin struggled to hide his revulsion as David Stockton entered the room, closing the door behind him. He noticed Stockton held a hardcover book in his left hand.

"Hello," said Stockton, stopping a few feet in front of Benjamin's bed. "Benjamin, is it?"

Stockton's tone was patronizing, as if he were talking to a child—which he was, of course. But Stockton seemed to lack Holst's understanding that Benjamin wasn't simply a child pretending to be to be an adult. Benjamin could use that to his advantage.

"I guess you're Mr. Stockton?" said Benjamin, affecting a slight air of anxiety, so as not to spoil Stockton's impression of him. Benjamin swung his legs over the side of the bed to face Stockton, but didn't get up.

"Yes," said Stockton. "I'm a very busy man, Benjamin. Dr. Holst said that you insisted on talking to me. Why?"

This was going to be tricky. Stockton appeared to be content to meet with Benjamin in his room, which meant there would be no opportunity to stab him in the eye with a pencil or brain him with a stapler. He would have to make do with whatever he could find in this room, which wasn't much. He could conceivably strangle Stockton with a bed sheet, but that would have been an unlikely scenario even if Benjamin had thought to remove the sheet from the bed in advance—which he hadn't.

"I want to know what you're going to do with what I tell you," said Benjamin. "I don't know you, and I don't really know Dr. Holst. I saw a movie once where an American spy was caught by Russians who spoke perfect English, and they pretended to be with the FBI."

Stockton smiled. This was a concern he could understand. "You want to make sure we're the good guys," he said.

Benjamin nodded.

"I had a suspicion you might have such concerns," said Stockton. "That's why I brought this." He held up the book. The cover read:

The WISE Men: How David Stockton's Band of Scientific Wizards Helped Beat the Nazis

Stockton handed the book to Benjamin. "It's a highly sanitized and somewhat cartoonish account of what this program did during the war, but it's quite entertaining and mostly accurate."

Benjamin took the book, opening it to a random page. It was a section describing, in gee-whiz 1950s language how RADAR worked. He paged through the book, browsing chapters about atomic bombs and theoretical energy beams. The book seemed woefully short on historic detail; anyone reading the book with an expectation that the content would answer the question posed by the title would be disappointed. The lack of causal connection between WISE's work and the defeat of the Nazis was in some places explained offhandedly by nods to "government secrets" or "still-classified operations." There appeared to be no mention of eugenics, and the chapter on "Event Forecasting" was laughably generic. Benjamin couldn't help but smile at the reference to "number-crunching machines the size of buildings" that could one day be used to predict events in the distant future. The concluding chapter of the book gave the impression that the program had been shuttered after VJ Day.

"Look at page 136," said Stockton, taking a seat on the bed to Benjamin's left.

Benjamin dutifully turned to the page, where he was greeted with a half-page black-and-white photo of the man sitting next to him. Behind him in the photograph was a bank of machinery with exposed wires and vacuum tubes. The caption read: *David Stockton, in his Sunnyview lab*.

"You could have just printed up this book," said Benjamin, closing the volume and inspecting its binding. "If you were Communist agents, I mean."

"I suppose so," said Stockton. "In the end, you have to look at the preponderance of evidence." He added, as if Benjamin might not understand the word, "That is, you have to think about what's more likely: that this whole hospital and everyone in it is part of some Communist conspiracy, or that we really are the good guys."

Benjamin nodded thoughtfully, suppressing a sneer at Stockton's condescending reassurances. He wondered if Stockton even saw the irony: the man behind an illegal government program trying to dissuade a subject of that program from giving credence to conspiracy theories. Somehow he doubted it. He supposed that once you've convinced yourself that you're experimenting on children in order to further the cause of "freedom," you're well beyond the point where you can view your actions with anything resembling objectivity.

"What we're doing here is very important," Stockton went on. "The information you have could make the difference between victory and defeat in the war against Communism. I know this is all probably very confusing to you, but it's vital that each of us do our part. You are in a unique position to—"

He stopped speaking then, because Benjamin had slammed the spine of the *The WISE Men* into his windpipe. Benjamin had considered backhanding him to ensure surprise, but decided that the risk of the book flying out of his hand was too great. So instead he held the book with his right, swinging it across his body and into

230

Stockton's throat. His aim had been good: Stockton doubled over, gasping for breath. He wouldn't be yelling for help anytime soon.

Benjamin got a solid grip on the book with both hands and brought it down as hard as he could on the base of Stockton's skull. The binding gave way, and the book erupted into a flurry of pages, scattering across the room. Stockton fell off the bed, landing on his knees. A low croaking sound emitted from his throat as he struggled to get air through his collapsed windpipe.

His weapon gone, Benjamin stood on the bed and considered his options. If he could slam Stockton's head into the metal bed frame hard enough, he could shatter the man's skull—but Benjamin lacked the strength to drag Stockton close enough to the foot of the bed to make that happen. The floor was linoleum—not hard enough to crack Stockton's skull, particularly if he was resisting, which of course he would be. Benjamin scanned the room in vain for anything hard or sharp. He was losing precious time. Every second he wasted gave Stockton time to recover, and while he doubted he'd made enough noise to attract any attention from the staff, there was always the chance someone would walk in to check on them.

Benjamin leapt off the bed, turning his foot sideways to connect with the nape of Stockton's neck. He doubted he weighed enough to break Stockton's spine, but he hoped to keep him incapacitated long enough to think of a better plan. Stockton instinctively reached up to the base of his skull where the book had struck him, so Benjamin's heel struck the back of his hand and Benjamin fell awkwardly to the ground. He lay on his back for a moment, dazed. Stockton was getting to his feet.

But Benjamin was younger and faster, and he managed to spring forward and wrap his arms around Stockton while he was still off balance, knocking him once again to the floor. He found himself sitting on top of Stockton's chest, and before Stockton could throw him off, he grabbed the man's hair close to his scalp. He pulled toward himself, then pushed, slamming Stockton's head against the linoleum. Then he did it again. At first, Stockton tried craning his neck forward, but this just made it easier for Benjamin to thrust it back to the floor. He slammed Stockton's head three more times before Stockton changed tacks, arching his back and trying to throw Benjamin off.

It was clear Benjamin wasn't going to be able to maintain his advantage. Out of the corner of his right eye, he caught sight of the cover of the book, which now lay by itself several feet away, detached from the pages. He pivoted on top of Stockton, so that his head was pointed toward the cover, bringing his knees to his chest. Then he thrust his legs outward, his right heel catching Stockton beneath the chin. He felt a crack in the man's jaw, followed by the thud of his skull again hitting the floor. Benjamin shot across the floor toward the book cover. He grabbed it and tore the front of the cover off at the spine. He bent the cover until, folding it at the corner to make a shallow triangle, then folded the larger section back on itself to make the triangle more acute. The whole process took about five seconds, and now he had a makeshift cardboard shiv. Not a particularly dangerous weapon—unless you had an incapacitated subject and a lot of motivation.

Stockton still lay on his back, gasping for breath and holding his broken jaw. Benjamin scrambled back to him and jumped on his chest, letting his right knee slide over Stockton's collarbone and press against his bruised throat. Stockton tried to call out, but could only wheeze and cough. Benjamin felt Stockton's weight shifting under him as the man prepared to throw him off. Benjamin would only get one shot at this. All he needed to do is hold Stockton's head still for a second.

Pressing most of his weight on Stockton's throat to pin his head against the floor, Benjamin gripped the shiv tightly and brought it down on Stockton's right eye. The point held, penetrating the eye socket an inch left of Stockton's nose. Stockton's wheezed as his arms grasped at Benjamin's legs. Stockton's body twisted underneath Benjamin as the man desperately tried to throw him off. But Benjamin shifted his weight to his arms and, gripping the shiv with both hands, thrust it deep in the eye socket. He felt tissue tear, and Stockton managed a strained scream. He had managed to get a firm hold on both of Benjamin's legs and hurled Benjamin against the bed. Benjamin landed with a crash.

Benjamin had to release his grip on the shiv rather than pull it out of Stockton's eye socket. The shiv had gone at least three inches into Stockton's skull, far enough to enrage him but not to kill him. Stockton grasped at the shiv, trying to pull it out. Benjamin scrambled back toward Stockton.

At that moment, the door opened and the nurse walked in. Seeing Stockton lying helpless on the floor with the shiv protruding from his eye and Benjamin pulling back his fist to pound it home, she dived at him, tackling him to the ground. She screamed for help as she put a knee on Benjamin's chest, pinning him to the ground. Moments later two orderlies ran into the room. One of them knelt to assist Stockton while the other helped subdue Benjamin. Once again, there was the flash of a syringe and the bee sting on his arm. Before he lost consciousness, he caught sight of David Stockton sitting up, the shiv lying on his lap. He held a bloody towel to his eye. Benjamin had failed. David Stockton would live.

CHAPTER TWENTY-EIGHT

Benjamin didn't see David Stockton again. When he awoke, it was dark. He lay in bed for several hours, wondering what would happen to him. He'd missed his chance to kill David Stockton, and he had revealed his intentions—but WISE still needed him. He doubted they would kill him. They certainly wouldn't let him go. Would they torture him for information? If so, would Holst be forced to oversee his interrogation? He wondered just how far Holst could be pushed before he turned on WISE, as Dominick Spiegel had. Some time after the sun rose, the door to his room opened and Holst walked in. He looked tired.

"Good morning, Benjamin," he said.

Benjamin didn't reply.

"David Stockton is going to lose his eye," said Holst. "The eyeball was ruptured, and the extraocular muscles were damaged. You also broke his jaw. But he is conscious and coherent. Any brain damage appears to have been minimal." He paused a moment. "You could have killed him."

"That was the idea," said Benjamin.

"Why?" said Holst, who seemed genuinely baffled. "Surely you see the importance of this program. You must see the threat we are facing."

"I see a threat," said Benjamin. "Probably not the same one that you obsess about, though. So what's the plan now? Extract my memories by other means?"

Holst sighed. "We don't have to go down this road, Benjamin. We both want the same thing: to find out what in your memories is real, and what is not. That is the path out of here for both of us."

Benjamin shook his head. "See, this is your problem, Holst. You think that the details of my memory are just filler. Noise that you have to filter out from the signal. But I think you're missing the point. Felipe didn't construct an entire world so that I could communicate to you a series of discrete facts—dates of battles and assassinations. Everything about the world he created, everything in my memories—real or not—has meaning. My experiences aren't raw materials for you to sift through; they're a complete history of Benjamin Stone. And those memories end in Sunnyview in the year 2000. Why?"

"You can't read too much into that," said Holst. "It may be merely coincidental that—"

"No," said Benjamin. "There are no coincidences. You said it yourself. The moments in time that the subjects pick aren't random. I was projected into Sunnyview at that particular time for a reason. And it sure as hell wasn't to warn you about the Korean War."

"Then perhaps the key is this other subject you met, Sofia. If we could determine—"

"No!" cried Benjamin again. "I didn't travel to Sunnyview so I could give you third-hand information about some future terrorist attack. I came there to find the truth about Jessica."

"You know the truth," Holst protested. "Jessica is not real. She's a figment of your imagination!"

"*Everything* is a figment of my imagination! This is what you're not getting. You want to pick out the 'true' aspects of my vision, but it's *all* true. My daughter's death is just as meaningful to me as the Korean War or the Kennedy assassination. More so, if I'm honest. And Jessica's murder showed me the kind of man William Glazier is—the kind of man David Stockton must be, to have masterminded a program like this."

"You're telling me that you decided to kill David Stockton for a crime you *know* he didn't commit?"

Benjamin laughed. "How many people do you think will be assassinated by the CIA because of the information this program has provided? People whose crimes are just as imaginary as Jessica's murder. What crime did I commit, Dr. Holst? What crime did Estefan, Miguel, Thomas or Marina commit? What crimes were committed by the hundreds of children in Sunnyview who have developed birth defects because of this program?"

"The exposure to those chemicals was an accident. We merely took advantage of—"

"Bullshit!" Benjamin snapped. "Glazier Semiconductor dumped tons of dangerous chemicals without having any idea what those chemicals might do to the people drinking the water. And even if they didn't realize what those chemicals would do then, they sure as hell know now."

Holst frowned. "The dumping has stopped," he said.

"Are you sure of that?" Benjamin asked. "Have they stopped, or did they just find a stealthier, more efficient way of introducing the chemicals to the water supply? You know how valuable your subjects are. Do you really think David Stockton willingly cut off the supply?"

Holst regarded Benjamin silently, ruminating on his words.

"You don't see it," said Benjamin. "Not yet. But I do, because I've seen who David Stockton really is. Are my memories fiction? Maybe, but I see the truth about this program more clearly than you do."

"I see," said Holst. "I suppose this means you aren't going to cooperate with us."

"Not willingly, no," said Benjamin. "Although you might get some information from me by force. Maybe I will tell you about the Luxembourg Cheese War or the time Martians invaded Delaware."

Holst sighed. "We don't torture, if that's what you're concerned about. As you imply, the threat of physical pain is not a good catalyst if one is seeking to separate truth from fiction. Besides, that isn't our area of specialty. We prefer to focus our efforts on the mind."

Benjamin suppressed a shudder. "Meaning what?" he said. "Hypnosis? Partial lobotomy? Some kind of truth serum?"

Holst shook his head. "None of those would produce the results we need. We require a subject who is able to give a clear and complete accounting of his memories. We can't make this project work with uncooperative subjects."

"And you can't force me to cooperate," said Benjamin.

"I don't have to force you," said Holst. "Every day I get a little close to getting the truth from you. Yesterday was by far our most productive session, but the price was revealing to you the truth about this program. I can see now that was a mistake. But each session, I learn a little more about how to get answers from you."

"Yes, but I'm on to you now," said Benjamin. "You can't make me forget what I've learned."

"That's where you're wrong, Benjamin. It's no trouble at all for me to send you back into a hallucinatory state. I've just got to administer the right mixture of drugs. If I increase the dosage a bit, I think I can elevate the vividness of the hallucination to the level that your experiences in this hospital disappear from your memory completely. When you wake up tomorrow, you'll once again be unaware that you're Felipe, and I'll get another chance to probe you for information. And if I fail, I'll bump your dosage up a little more and try again the next day. It's only a matter of time before I convince you to cooperate."

"It won't work," said Benjamin, trying to sound certain. "If you send me deeper into the delusion, it will just strengthen my hatred for David Stockton and this program. And you said yourself, you're out of time. You don't have an unlimited amount of time to get answers from me."

"Not unlimited, no," said Holst. "But we appear to have bought ourselves some time. One of our other subjects, Marina Evans— who you met the other day—has been jabbering in Finnish all morning. We're recording it all, and a translator is on his way. We played some of what she said over the phone to him, and she seems to be talking about troop movements in Eastern Europe. We don't know yet what time period she's projected to, but it seems to be a critical moment in the struggle against the Soviets."

A sense of unease crept into Benjamin's gut. He knew the year: 1983. Marina Evans had projected herself to somewhere in Finland, where she had come into possession of information about Autumn Forge, the military operation Glazier had told him about. Presumably she would witness some part of the escalation that would result ultimately in all-out war between the United States and the Soviet Union. David Stockton would write up her account and send it to Washington, where it would sit in a filing cabinet for the next 33 years, waiting for events to catch up to the prediction.

No, that wasn't right, he realized. No one would ever look in that filing cabinet. No one in the government would remember it existed, and there were no fancy computer systems to make bells go off when the words Autumn Forge came up. Even if WISE correctly predicted the exact dates Autumn Forge occurred, and even if the CIA or whoever they were working with took them seriously, there was no way any government agency was going to have any kind of system in place to alert anyone of the danger 33 years after the warning was made. The only way anyone would know the danger posed by Autumn Forge was if WISE was still in operation. David Stockton—or someone else working for WISE—must have made a call to Washington some time in 1983. So not only had Benjamin failed to kill Stockton; he'd failed to stop WISE. Thanks to Marina Evans, the program would go on for another fifty years. A profound feeling of defeat washed over him.

"Marina," he said. "Is she…?"

"She's still Marina, as far as I can tell. She slips in and out of this Finnish persona. She's not as far gone as…."

"As me," said Benjamin. "Completely delusional."

"I was going to say 'as Estefan,' but yes."

So at least Marina hadn't lost herself completely. Maybe someday she'd even get out of here, and live something like a normal life.

"Of course, the information Marina can give us at this point is nothing compared to what's in your head. We could try pushing her harder, but she may very well end up like Estefan. I doubt very much we'll ever have another subject like you: one who retains full memories of the next fifty years, and remains in possession of his wits. That's why I can't give up on you. You're simply too valuable."

"That's why you'll risk giving me an overdose of dangerous drugs? Because I'm so valuable?"

"I have nothing to lose. If you don't talk, you're worth nothing to this program. I'm doing what I can to help you, Benjamin, but I can't change that underlying fact. If you give me something—anything—I can work with you. I don't want to put you back under. But if you don't, I have no choice."

"Of course you have a choice," said Benjamin. "You're choosing to work for this program, choosing to ignore what it really is. Look into the dumping. Ask David Stockton if he's still working on creating more subjects for you. See what he says."

"I'll do some poking around," said Holst. "If you tell me everything you know about the war in Korea. How long it lasts, who wins, whether the Chinese get involved."

"Not a chance," said Benjamin. "I've told you everything I'm going to tell you."

Then I can't help you."

"I'm not asking you to help me," said Benjamin. "But at some point you're going to have to come to grips with what you're doing here." Benjamin wondered again if he should warn Holst about Stockton's retaliation. Would Holst believe that Stockton was going to have him killed? If he did, would that make him realize the kind of man Stockton was, and spur him to try to stop WISE? Or would it scare him into silence? Perhaps if he told Holst the details of Spiegel's accident, he could avoid being at that intersection at that particular time—but of course he didn't have that information. That was the one absolute flaw in his memories, the thing that couldn't possibly have happened the way it had appeared to happen. He couldn't warn Holst about the accident if he wanted to. And if there really were no coincidences, then that blind spot existed for a reason. Perhaps he wasn't meant to warn Holst.

"Well," said Holst uncertainly, "I suppose we're done here."

"Yes, we are," replied Benjamin.

Holst looked like he wanted to say something, but then he turned and left the room. It was the last time Benjamin ever saw him.

A few minutes later, the two orderlies entered his room, followed by the nurse. The orderlies held Benjamin down while the nurse gave him a series of injections. Benjamin didn't resist.

CHAPTER TWENTY-NINE

The car fishtailed, sliding perpendicular to its vector of motion. Agent Hill tried to correct, but the Lincoln's mass fought against him. The car's right tires left the ground and the vehicle rolled. The next thing Benjamin knew, he was lying crumpled against the roof of the car.

Taking a moment to get his bearings, he realized that Hill and Kassel were still in their seats, hanging upside down from their seatbelts. Both front airbags had deployed. The rear windshield had spider-webbed into a thousand pieces, and it only took a couple of kicks for Benjamin to detach it from the frame. He crawled onto the street and stood up. He was shaking with fear and adrenaline, but other than a few scuffs and bruises, he was unhurt.

Several other cars had stopped, and a ring of onlookers had formed. Benjamin was vaguely aware of people asking him if he was hurt, but he ignored them. He was straining to see beyond the ranks of onlookers to get a glimpse of Jessica. Was she an illusion? Maybe. But she had appeared to him for a reason, and he wasn't going to let her get away this time.

"My daughter," he mumbled. "Jessica."

The people let him pass. In the distance he heard sirens. Hopefully Hill and Kassel weren't seriously injured, but Benjamin couldn't worry about them right now. He needed to find Jessica.

Benjamin strode past the gawkers and stopped traffic to the section of road where Jessica had appeared, but she was nowhere to be found. Once again, the apparition had vanished. Benjamin looked around frantically, but there was no sign of her.

He stopped. Something was wrong. He'd been here before—experienced these events before. After this, he would go to find

Felipe, but Felipe could only speak in echoes. He would try to leave town, but the highway looped back on itself. Then he would find Jessica.

But how was this possible? How could he remember what hadn't yet happened?

This is a dream, he thought. No, a vision. A vision I've had before.

He had a vague memory of being in another place, another time—a dark, sterile place. A man had been talking to him, pleading with him to do something, but Benjamin wouldn't do it.

He realized suddenly that the street had become unnaturally quiet. Snapping out of his reverie, he looked around to find that the cars and pedestrians on the street had vanished. The street was completely empty.

No, not completely. A woman was walking down the street toward him. Her hair and clothes were damp. Jessica.

"Hi, Dad," she said, stopping a few feet from him.

"Jessica," he said. "How…?"

She smiled at him, and he remembered her words. *This isn't a mystery you can solve.*

"You're not real," he said.

"I'm as real as you are," she said, and he laughed bitterly.

"I suppose that's true," he said. "I'm sorry, Jessica. I tried to stop them. To stop this."

"Don't be sorry, Dad," she said. "You *did* stop them."

"No," he said, shaking his head. His experience in the hospital was coming back to him in flashes. He remembered driving the shiv into David Stockton's eye. "I tried to kill him, but I failed."

"You planted a seed," said Jessica. "Adam Holst will look into the dumping, and realize that Stockton has been lying to him. He will write that letter, and fifty years later someone will find it. That will be the beginning of the end for WISE."

"Fifty years!" Benjamin cried. "They're going to get away with this for *fifty years*?"

"You were never going to be able to stop them," Jessica said. "The best we could do is contain them. We tried before, with other subjects, but the lure of self-preservation in the others was too strong. You were the only one strong enough to see it through."

"I don't understand," Benjamin said. "See what through? What do I have to do?"

"Nothing," Jessica said. And he remembered what she had told him before, in the orchard: *You need to let go of the past. Just live. Just be.*

"You wanted me to stay here," he said. "In the delusion."

"It's what you have to do," Jessica replied. "You can't go back, ever. They will extract your memories. Everything you know. They will try to shape the future, to improve it. But they will make things worse. Much, much worse."

Benjamin shuddered to think how bad things could get. Would WISE somehow cause the nuclear war between the U.S. and Soviets they were trying so hard to prevent?

"How do you know all this?" he asked. "Who are you?"

"I'm Jessica. Your daughter. I've been chosen to explain these things to you, now that you're ready to understand them."

Benjamin set aside for a moment the fact that he didn't *have* a daughter. "Chosen by who?"

"I'm not sure I can answer that," she said. "It may be what you think of as the collective unconscious. Or possibly some higher power. God, maybe."

"How can you not know?" Benjamin cried.

"These kinds of questions aren't going to get you anywhere. You need to accept that I've been told things about the future that you aren't aware of. Events that make it very important that you never return to the year 1950."

Benjamin shook his head. This was all too confusing. It was too much to take in. "Why did you try to keep me from going back to 1950—back to the hospital—if you... I mean, if whoever is behind all this needed me to convince Holst to try to stop Stockton?"

"Because I'm your daughter," Jessica said, as if she were surprised at Benjamin's confusion. "I didn't want you to go back to that place."

"You're not my daughter!" Benjamin cried. "You're a construct! Your whole purpose was to get me to try to stop WISE!"

"Well, then I guess it worked," said Jessica, with a smile.

Benjamin could only laugh at that. She was right, after all. She had done what she needed to do, and so had Benjamin. After all, he was just a construct too. Felipe—or God, or the collective unconsciousness—had seen what needed to happen, and had created the people necessary to bring it about. What needed to happen had now happened—or was going to happen—and so the constructs were no longer needed.

"What happens now?" he asked. "To you, I mean."

"You don't need me anymore," Jessica said. "I should go."

"Go where? If you leave, won't you just pass out of existence?"

"I'll live on in your memories," Jessica said. "That's all I am anyway. It's all anybody is."

"No," said Benjamin. "Please, don't go. I can't lose you again."

"There's no place for me here, Dad. You know that. It's okay. You mourned me once; you don't need to do it again. I'll just be gone."

"No!" Benjamin cried, stepping forward to embrace Jessica. He felt her damp hair against his cheek, the warmth of her body against his chest. "Jessica, what will I do?"

She hugged him back for a moment, and he felt the dampness of her clothes soaking through his shirt. Then she pulled away, and he released her. "Whatever you want," she said, with a smile.

"But I don't understand. I don't even know who I am. Am I Benjamin, or am I Felipe?"

"That's up to you," said Jessica. "You have plenty of time to figure it out. Goodbye, Dad." She looked into his eyes for a moment and then turned away. He watched as she receded down the street. Benjamin wanted to call after her, to stop her, but he knew that it was pointless. Whatever force or being had created Jessica had now decided that she was no longer needed. And that raised another question: was Benjamin still needed?

He stood on the curb, considering this, while he watched Jessica vanish in the distance. He was now completely alone in this strange town, this imagined version of Sunnyview, with its Starbucks, its Blockbuster, and its sushi restaurants. Impossible questions bombarded him: What was this place? Why did the illusion persist, even after he'd seen through it? Who is creating this place? Felipe? The collective unconsciousness of humanity, past, present and future? God? Or am I creating it, even now, by continuing to believe in it? If someone other than me is creating this place, where do they end and I begin? Who the hell am I?

But as he walked, Jessica's words kept coming back to him: *Let it go. This isn't a mystery you can solve.* He was beginning to realize the truth of her words. He would never fully understand what this place was, how it came to be, or how "real" it was. He would never know for certain what had happened to GLARE/WISE. He might never know who he was. But like Jessica said, he had time to figure it out.

Another realization struck him as well: Somehow he felt less alone in this ghost town than he had when it was bustling with khaki-clad engineers and soccer moms. It felt almost like home. He began walking toward downtown, without any real purpose in mind. If he didn't look too closely at the updated storefronts, he could imagine that he was back in the Sunnyview of his childhood again. The main thing that was missing was the sounds: shopkeepers sweeping in front of their stores, dogs barking, children yelling and laughing in the distance, the occasional roar of a passing Chevy or Buick. He closed his eyes for a moment and he could almost hear it.

No, he *did* hear it. He opened his eyes and stopped short on the sidewalk. Down the street, a 1940s model Ford was sputtering toward him. On the next block, a young couple was window-shopping at a jewelry store. He heard a yell in the distance behind him, and turned to see a policeman chasing a teenage boy down an alley.

Benjamin smiled. He looked up at the buildings and saw hand-painted signs marking an appliance store, a plumbing supply company, and a drug store. Further down the street was the feed store and Schulman's Hardware. Somehow he'd managed to tap into the creative power that had built this illusion, and bent it to his will. This was his town, the town that existed in his memory. It was perfect, down to the smallest detail. It was exactly like the Sunnyview of his youth.

Well, not *exactly*. As he closed his eyes, spreading his consciousness to each corner of his creation, he acknowledged one small difference, a flaw he had allowed to creep in. He had left the course of Sand Hill Creek as it existed in the year 2000, allowing Fremont and Olive to intersect near the edge of town. In this reality, there would be no Sand Hill Children's Hospital. GLARE/WISE would not exist, and no children would ever be subjected to dangerous experiments for the sake of "American interests." This would be Sunnyview as it should be, not as it was.

He opened his eyes again, and took in the aroma from Clark's Bakery down the street. Yes, this was a place where he wouldn't mind killing some time.

"Good morning," said an elderly woman in horn-rimmed glasses, as she passed him carrying a bag of groceries.

"Good morning," said Benjamin with a smile.

"Beautiful day," she said.

"It certainly is," Benjamin replied, and began walking toward Fenneman's corner store. He had a hankering for an ice cream sundae.

A *real* ice cream sundae.

AFTERWORD

I originally envisioned *City of Sand* as "*Chinatown* as told by Philip Dick." I've long been fascinated by stories about memory and identity, and I'm a fan of the hardboiled noir genre and *Chinatown* in particular. Those who have read Dick's *Time Out of Joint* will recognize the town-that-isn't-what-it-seems trope, and those who have seen *Chinatown* will recognize the device of the murder that connects to an Evil Conspiracy. The use of the city's water supply as a plot device is, of course, also a nod to *Chinatown*.

Much of the inspiration for the setting of this book comes from my own experience. I lived for twenty years in a small farming town in the California Central Valley, commuting several times a week to work in the San Francisco Bay Area. In a small way, I experienced on a near-daily basis the culture shock that Benjamin Stone experiences as he tries to reconcile modern-day Sunnyview with the town of his youth.

Before the tech bubble burst, I worked for several years as a software developer in the East Bay Area, making the astoundingly bad decision in January of 2000 to leave an established Fortune 500 company to go to work for a small startup. The promise of riding the Internet wave to success and riches was soon revealed to be a collective delusion, and I spent most of the next three years unemployed. I went back to work full-time in 2003, and in 2008 I started a two-year contract working at Google headquarters in Mountain View. Google was a bizarrely idyllic, almost utopian, place to work at that time, like being on a college campus with arcade games and ping-pong tables in the halls, pick-up volleyball games between the buildings, and free food in fourteen different cafés. Google ultimately pulled the plug on my project, but the time wasn't wasted: I got really good at Joust and finished my first novel, *Mercury Falls*.

The idea for *City of Sand* didn't really come into focus, though, until I ran across an article about the staggering amount of water pollution in the Silicon Valley area. Santa Clara County, it seems, has the most Superfund sites in the country. You might think that honor would be reserved for some industrial wasteland in New Jersey or strip-mining capital in Appalachia, but it turns out that beneath the heart of the new economy flows some of the most polluted water in the United States. This issue first received wide attention in 1981, when it was learned that the groundwater in south San Jose was contaminated with chemicals such as trichloroethane and Freon, toxic substances that were later suspected to be the cause of birth defects in many children.

The source of this pollution was primarily two tech giants: Fairchild Semiconductor and IBM. Information technology is popularly thought of as a clean industry, but the process of making semiconductors and other electronic components produces a lot of toxic byproducts. When these companies started out in the 1950s, there were very few if any environmental controls to prevent them from simply dumping these byproducts into the ground. Sandy soil and a shallow water table contributed to the fast spread of the chemicals into the local water supply. Even today, it's very difficult to determine the extent of the damage this pollution caused, partly because those who were most affected were poor immigrants who tended to move around a lot, making precise data collection and analysis difficult. It was a bit unsettling to find all this out after having worked in the area for several years, and this sense of something very wrong going on literally beneath the surface was a big inspiration for the paranoia of *City of Sand*.

The character of William Glazier/David Stockton was inspired by legendary technological pioneer William Shockley. During World War II, Shockley was involved in radar research for Bell Labs in New Jersey. This research, as well as Bell Labs' other work on counterintelligence technology, was the inspiration for GLARE/WISE. (There's no indication Bell Labs worked on anything more exotic than scrambling radio communications, but Benjamin's accounts of MKUltra, Operation Paperclip, and CIA conducting experiments on unsuspecting civilians are horrifyingly accurate.) William Shockley, like Glazier/Stockton, was a proponent of eugenics and seemed to be a believer in a rather brutal ends-justify-the-means ethos—as well as an interest in prognostication. The excerpt in chapter eight from Glazier's report in on probable casualties from an invasion of the Japanese mainland was copied verbatim from an actual report written by William Shockley. That report provided justification for dropping atomic bombs on Hiroshima and Nagasaki.

Shortly after the end of the war in 1945, Bell Labs formed a solid state physics group assigned to find a solid-state alternative to fragile glass vacuum tube amplifiers. The ultimate result of this work was the development of the transistor in 1947. Virtually all modern electronics are based on this discovery. In 1956, Shockley moved to Mountain View, California to start Shockley Semiconductor, the first company to specialize in manufacturing semiconductors.

After winning the Nobel Prize in 1956 for his contribution to the invention of the transistor, Shockley became increasingly authoritarian, erratic and paranoid. In one well-known anecdote, he claimed that a secretary's cut thumb was the result of a malicious act and demanded lie detector tests to find the responsible party. In late 1957, eight of Shockley's key employees (the "traitorous eight) quit in protest over his management style and went to on to form Fairchild Semiconductor, a loss from which Shockley Semiconductor never recovered. Over the course of 20 years, these eight men started 65 new enterprises, shaping the future of what became known as Silicon Valley.

I should clarify that although Shockley was a controversial figure who held some distasteful views, I have no reason to believe he was a villain on the level of Glazier/Stockton. Glazier/Stockton is a fictional character who, while he shares many traits with Shockley, is really more representative of the American security-industrial complex than any particular person. And whatever one might think of Shockley, it's thanks to him and a few other brilliant individuals that I was able to write this book on a portable machine filled with semiconductors.

Rob Kroese, 2/6/2015

ABOUT THE AUTHOR

Robert Kroese's sense of irony was honed growing up in Grand Rapids, Michigan - home of the Amway Corporation and the Gerald R. Ford Museum, and the first city in the United States to fluoridate its water supply. In second grade, he wrote his first novel, the saga of Captain Bill and his spaceship *Thee Eagle*. This turned out to be the high point of his academic career. After barely graduating from Calvin College in 1992 with a philosophy degree, he was fired from a variety of jobs before moving to California, where he stumbled into software development. As this job required neither punctuality nor a sense of direction, he excelled at it. In 2009, he called upon his extensive knowledge of useless information and love of explosions to write his first novel, *Mercury Falls*. Since then, he has written seven more novels.

I love to hear from readers! Email me at rob@robertkroese.com or connect with me on the Internet:

Website: sfauthor.net
Facebook: facebook.com/robertkroeseauthor
Twitter: twitter.com/robkroese

If you enjoyed *City of Sand*, I would also greatly appreciate a review on your favorite book retailing website. Thanks!

MORE BOOKS BY ROBERT KROESE YOU MIGHT ENJOY

Schrödinger's Gat
The Foreworld Saga: The Outcast
"Mercury Begins" (short story)
Mercury Falls
Mercury Rises
Mercury Rests
Mercury Revolts
Disenchanted
"The Chicolini Incident" (short story)
Starship Grifters
The Force is Middling in This One

MORE BOOKS FROM WESTMARCH PUBLISHING

Westmarch is an author-run publishing cooperative. We publish fiction in a variety of genres, including science fiction, fantasy and mystery. Check us out at Westmarchpub.com!

Imaginarium: A Collection of Westmarch Fiction by Denise Grover Swank, Robert Kroese, et al.

Half a Prayer by Rick Gualtieri

Mercury Revolts by Robert Kroese

Ansible 15715, Ansible 15716, Ansible 15717, Dante's Heart, The Running of the Tyrannosaurs by Stant Litore

The Bellbottom Incident by Neve Maslakovic

Stolen Spring by Cynthia L. Moyer

The Big Keep by Melissa F. Olson

An Officer and a Gentleman and *The League of the Sphinx: The Purple Scarab* by Richard Ellis Preston Jr.